7/10

THE OFFICIAL MOVIE NOVELIZATION

INTERNATIONAL

THE OFFICIAL MOVIE NOVELIZATION

INTERNATIONAL

NOVELIZATION BY R. S. BELCHER

BASED ON THE SCREENPLAY WRITTEN BY
ART MARCUM & MATT HOLLOWAY

DIRECTED BY F. GARY GRAY

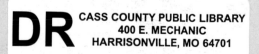

DR CASS COUNTY PUBLIC LIBRARY
400 E. MECHANIC
HARRISONVILLE, MO 64701

TITAN BOOKS

0 0022 0584075 0

MEN IN BLACK INTERNATIONAL: THE OFFICIAL MOVIE NOVELIZATION
Print edition ISBN: 9781789091083
E-book edition ISBN: 9781789091090

Published by Titan Books
A division of Titan Publishing Group Ltd
144 Southwark Street, London SE1 0UP

First edition: June 2019
10 9 8 7 6 5 4 3 2 1

This is a work of fiction. Names, characters, places, and incidents
either are the product of the author's imagination or are used
fictitiously, and any resemblance to actual persons, living or dead,
business establishments, events, or locales is entirely coincidental.
The publisher does not have any control over and does not assume
responsibility for author or third-party websites or their content.

Men in Black International TM & © 2019 Columbia Pictures Industries, Inc.
All rights reserved.

No part of this publication may be reproduced, stored in a retrieval
system, or transmitted, in any form or by any means without prior written
permission of the publisher, nor be otherwise circulated in any form of
binding or cover other than that in which it is published and without
a similar condition being imposed on the subsequent purchaser.

A CIP catalogue record for this title is available from the British Library.

Printed and bound in the United States.

To my children, the greatest wonders in the universe I've ever seen:

Stephanie Joy, thank you for my Goofy, and for always making me happy.

For Jonathan, for always being strong and true, but especially for having a good heart.

And for Emily, my very own Agent Em, for never giving up.

I love you all to the moon and back.

1

The brilliant full moon was not alone in the sky above the City of Lights. It had been a hot summer in Paris, and lightning capered across the cloudless heavens. The electrical storm seemed to have come out of nowhere. It was gathering, strengthening, above the city's most iconic structure: the Eiffel Tower.

The black car roared through the streets of Paris, resembling more a space fighter from some science fiction movie than the typical vehicle found on the road. The car's massive rocket engines spewed flames behind it as it swerved onto the Avenue Gustave Eiffel, spun in a 180-degree turn to a stop before the vehicle barriers that protected the tower grounds. There was a low hum as the rocket engines shifted, folded, and disappeared into the body of the car.

Two men climbed out of the now-normal-looking car. The younger of the two was handsome, bright-eyed, and clean-shaven. The older man carried himself with a coiled power and quiet authority. His mere presence implied he was competent, and hinted at him being a bit dangerous. His eyes, however, held a sadness and a weariness that sometimes comes from living too long, seeing too much. Both men were dressed in black suits and ties.

"God do I hate Paris," the older man said, shutting his door.

"Not to worry," the younger man replied, gazing up at the brooding clouds gathering around the apex of the Eiffel Tower, "it probably won't be around much longer."

The two young lovers on the tower's lower observation deck were oblivious to the massing clouds and the fire in the night sky. They only had eyes for each other. The young man took a deep breath and then knelt before his girlfriend. The lights of Paris, like glittering jewels, were their backdrop.

She gasped, her hand coming to her mouth, when she saw the beseeching look in his eyes, and the ring he was holding up to her.

"Lisa, will you marr—" He paused as he looked past his prospective bride-to-be. "Who the hell are you guys?"

Two men stood on the deck with the couple. Both were dressed in black suits and ties. They were both carrying black gunmetal cases.

"We're with Tower security," the younger man said.

"You're not supposed to be here," the other added. He nodded toward Lisa and the still-kneeling Lars, and then toward the bank of deck elevators.

Lars glanced at Lisa. She was practically vibrating with emotion and growing frustration. This was their perfect moment, the greatest moment of either of their lives, and these two rent-a-cops were spoiling it. The sky flashed with lightning, and the young couple jumped at how close the discharge was to them.

"Did she say yes?" the older man asked Lars.

"I haven't asked yet!" Lars snapped.

"He hasn't asked yet!" Lisa shouted in unison with Lars.

"That's a real shame," the younger man in black said, pointing to a corner of the deck, "because that big blinking light back there—" They saw a black door with a red light flashing frantically above it. The door had a sign on it that said in many different languages: STAFF ONLY. "—means there's been a breach in portal two."

Taking Lisa's hand, Lars struggled back to his feet.

The younger security guard glanced at his watch and continued, "Which means that in just a few minutes, the Hive—the most vile creatures in the known universe— are going to devour every last one of us from the inside out. It's disgusting, really, the way they burrow their way through any orifice they can find..." He gave a tight but genuine smile, as if commiserating on their shared fate. Lars and Lisa both paled at the nonchalant announcement of impending doom.

"H, that's quite enough." The older man gave his companion a disapproving stare and shook his head curtly. "Or," he went on to the couple, in a reassuring tone, "it could be that a rather large Parisian rat just chewed through one of our cables. We're hoping for the latter."

"I don't understand," Lisa said. She noticed that the younger man—had his companion called him "H"?—was wearing sunglasses. It ought to have looked ridiculous at night, but she was afraid. The reassuring older man was putting his own sunglasses on, as if it was a perfectly natural thing to do in the dark. Now she saw that the younger one had a small, silver, tubular device in his hand.

"Of course you don't." The man who had been addressed as "H" nodded to the silver wand. "All will be explained if you look right… here."

Both Lars and Lisa followed his instructions without even thinking about what they were doing. There was a high-pitched whine and a flash of brilliant light from the tip of the device, and the couple fell into a trance-like stupor. "The Tower is closed for repairs," the younger man told them. He paused for a second and addressed Lars, "Ask her again, on the way down."

The couple blinked and looked around. The younger man led them to the elevators, and they followed him in a daze, allowing him to guide them into an elevator car. He reached inside the car, pushed the down button, and withdrew his hand. Lars and Lisa stared out rather blankly as the doors shut and the elevator descended.

His partner glanced at his watch. "Shall we get to work now, H?"

Before H could answer, a massive surge of red lightning cascaded down from the star-filled sky, striking the antenna at the apex of the tower. The energy blew the black door to the portals off its hinges and sent it flying into H. He was knocked backward by the force of the blast, crashed through the metal lattice of the trellis doors to the elevator and tumbled down the yawning elevator shaft.

H flailed about for something, anything, to slow or stop his fall. His fingers grazed the tips of the metal girders separating the elevator car shafts from one another, but he hurtled by too quickly. He smashed onto the roof of the descending elevator and nearly rolled off the side of the elevator, but managed to hang on. Swinging over the side of the car, he found himself witness to another touching scene through the glass. Lars was kneeling before Lisa again, ring in hand.

"Lisa, will you—"

H knocked on the window. The two lovers stared at the handsome, well-dressed stranger clinging to the side of their elevator car.

"Who the hell are you?" shouted Lars. H held up the small silver wand, and there was another flash. The young couple was again dazed by the device's light.

"Ask her again," H called, "down on the ground!" He launched himself off the side of the elevator car before Lars and Lisa recovered, grabbing and swinging himself up onto the network of beams between the elevator shafts. Without missing a beat, H jumped again to grab a bar on the bottom of another elevator car that was rushing upward. He watched Lars and Lisa's car shrink as it headed to the ground level.

On the lower observation deck, H's partner, High T,

checked his watch again. Lightning flashed as he peered down the exposed shaft, searching for some sign of H. There was a *ding* announcing another elevator's arrival. The door opened, and H walked out, brushing off his immaculate suit and striding toward his partner as if he were late for a lunch date, not the end of the world.

"Ah, there you are," High T sounded as nonchalant as his partner looked. They fell into step beside one another, as if they were synchronized. The two men picked up their metal cases and strode through the damaged doorway.

They climbed a grimy metal spiral staircase. It led them to a large room covered in dust and cobwebs that was reminiscent of a train station combined with a power station. The style of the architecture summoned a nostalgia for a future that had never been, as if the whole place had been designed by H. G. Wells. Rusted steel grating covered the floor and the catwalks above. Exposed pipes of all sizes ran all over the depot, bending and disappearing into the floors and ceiling. Some were bare and utilitarian, others were ornately decorated with Victorian-style relief. They passed a wooden kiosk with an iron-barred window. It looked like a ticket counter. Scraps of crumbling timetables and announcements clung feebly to the sides of the kiosk.

Wooden benches ran along the walls. They passed numerous rolling carts covered in cobwebs. One capsized vendor's cart bore a striking resemblance to the skeleton of an overgrown wheelbarrow. A distant wall peeked out past wrought-iron staircases and ladders leading up to the catwalks above. The wall held banks of old-style meters and gauges, their dark, filthy glass faces cracked and shattered, their needles buried.

H and High T walked to a spot on the platform that gave them a view of three large archways the size of subway tunnels. Each of the arches was illuminated with blue light and was numbered with roman numerals, I through III, above it, and each was shuttered closed by a thick metal slab of a door with a circular lock at the center that also glowed with the same blue light.

A console stood on a catwalk above the three doors, resting on a pedestal; it was made up of three equidistant circular control panels filled with antiquated gauges and levers. The whole apparatus was sculpted from polished brass.

H looked up through the ceiling's circular skylight, wrapped elegantly in glass and steel. The moon, swollen and bright with cold light, drifted closer to filling up the skylight's central aperture. The portals could only be accessed—would only open—when the full moon was centered in the skylight. Both men set down their metal cases in unison, knelt, and opened them. Inside were the shiny, silver-finished components of their Series-7 De-Atomizers: big guns designed with one purpose: to kill a single alien race, the Hive. The two men began assembling their weapons quickly and efficiently.

At first they worked in silence, but H didn't seem comfortable with that. After a while he stopped and watched as High T slid the barrel into the weapon's central housing and locked it into place with a twist and a metallic click. H grunted and checked his watch: 11:06.

"So, what's our play here?" H asked as he attached the weapon's stock.

High T locked the last piece of the gun into place. "We've been in this situation before," he replied.

"We've never faced the Hive before." H knew the Hive's reputation well, knew it was likely they were about to die.

"They've never faced us." High T knew his partner well enough to see he was worried, even though H hid it well. He went on, "Always remember—the universe has a way of leading you to where you're supposed to be at the moment you're supposed to be there."

"The universe gets it wrong sometimes," H said.

The moon's light began to filter through the central aperture and fall slowly on a circle of alien symbols and lunar pictograms on the depot's floor, fashioned much like a compass rose. The symbols surrounding the circle flared in the bright lunar light. There was a loud noise, a rumbling as if the tumblers of some massive lock had just turned within the archway doors. The grinding of the tumblers grew louder.

"C'mon," High T said, standing up, futuristic rifle in hand. "I want it to be you someday. To take my place. To run MiB."

H stood as well. "Sounds like a lot of paperwork."

"You'll survive."

The two agents, two friends, nodded to one another, again in unison. They slipped their sunglasses on and pumped the actuation chambers of their Series-7 De-

Atomizers like they were shotguns. The guns whirred to life as they powered up. High T and H leveled the De-Atomizers at the second portal as the chamber filled with moonlight.

The loud tumbler sound increased as the second portal's heavy door creaked open, a cloud of long-undisturbed dust swirling around the base of the opening door. White light, pure and blinding, spilled out from the other side of the portal, filling the long-abandoned depot. Dark, undulating tendrils shot out from the light, thrashing about. H and High T opened fire, the Series-7s roaring like the wrath of an angry lightning god, blasting away the Hive's grasping tendrils as fast as they slithered through the portal. The agents heard the howls of the injured Hive creature as even more tendrils exploded outward from the portal's maw. The bolts of destruction from the guns flashed out, hitting the invaders again and again, but the tendrils seemed legion. High T and H stood shoulder to shoulder, not giving an inch as they held the line against the monsters coming to devour the Earth and her people.

A tendril got through. It wrapped itself around High T's lower leg and yanked him off his feet. His De-Atomizer clattered to the floor as he was dragged toward the portal. H dived to the ground, his Series-7 still strapped to him, and grasped his mentor's hand, pulling with all his might. The Hive was stronger. Both agents were dragged across the floor toward whatever it was that waited to devour them on the other side of the light.

H flailed out with his other hand and grabbed the edge of an exposed girder, anchoring them only feet from the mouth of the portal and the writhing bloom of Hive tendrils. H found a foothold to further brace them against the relentless pull.

"Let me go!" High T shouted over the rushing wind of the open portal and the alien shrieks that came from beyond. "That's an order!"

"Not a chance!" H shouted. He brought his Series-7 up in a blur of motion. He thumbed the De-Atomizer to maximum discharge. Angry, red warning lights on the weapon reminded him that this was a really, really bad idea. The Hive creature pulled again, and H fired into the heart of the portal at point-blank range.

Brilliant, white light enveloped the Hive creature and the two men who stood against it. The light poured outward, illuminating the top of the Eiffel Tower, and filling the sky all across Paris. For a frozen moment, the whole universe seemed lost in the blinding light of an Earth-born star.

2

BROOKLYN, NEW YORK, TWENTY YEARS EARLIER

The stars in the plaster sky were pink, blue, green, and yellow. They were plastic and had five points and glowed softly on the ceiling of the dark bedroom. Silhouetted against the counterfeit sky were mobiles of slowly rotating solar systems and drifting astronauts tethered to papier-mâché space shuttles.

Tucked under the covers, ten-year-old Molly Wright had fallen asleep in her bed reading *A Brief History of Time*, by Stephen Hawking. Mom didn't like her to stay up after bedtime so she'd been using Dad's flashlight. She had been trying to understand Professor Hawking's arguments about Einstein's theories and black holes until she had drifted off. Molly's favorite math teacher, Mrs. Edwards, had given her the book, telling her, *"Your memory is already very good, Molly, and that's why you've won all those spelling bees and awards. But there's more to math and science than just memorizing equations. There's mystery in the universe, too, and endless possibility. And there's a lot that even the smartest people, like Professor Hawking, haven't figured out yet. Pay attention to details. That's really important to understanding pretty much everything. The details matter, Molly."*

Her eyes popped open when a bright light streamed through her window accompanied by a strange whooshing sound, almost like the sound a jet might make as it flew by. As she came back to consciousness, she realized it must be a car pulling up in the driveway. Molly heard the doors slam and a moment later a brisk knock at the front door downstairs. She sat up, trying to catch each word.

"That was... fast," Mom said to whoever was at the front door.

"Yeah," Dad said, sounding puzzled, "I haven't even called you yet."

"Yes, sir," a stern voice she'd never heard before replied. "You say you saw something?"

Molly climbed out of her bed, and clambered over to the open window. Below, she could see Mom and Dad talking to two men in black suits. She couldn't make out their faces against the bright headlights of their black Ford LTD.

"I'll say," Mom said, sounding more than a little panicked. "It looked like a... like a cat, but it wasn't a cat, it was—"

"More like a big frog," Dad blurted out, interrupting, "with hair. I've never seen anything like it."

"The creature you saw," the stranger with the stern

voice said, "is an unlicensed Tarantian, from Andromeda Two. Very rare, very dangerous."

"Tarantian." Molly rolled the strange word around in her mouth as she said it quietly. The word sounded like a secret, and now she knew it.

"He's cute now," the man in the black suit continued while his partner silently scanned the yard, "but when these things hit puberty, they turn into real monsters."

There was a strange sound like someone huffing in frustration combined with a cat purring. Slowly, Molly looked to her left, and jumped back from the window in surprise. The little creature that had been next to her jumped back, too, as if it was just as shocked to see her there.

The creature that had been standing on the sill next to her was small, about the size of a dog, but broad-shouldered. Its skin was covered in a fine down of gray fur. A wild mane of turquoise, green, and purple hair sprouted up above ping-pong-ball eyes that bulged out of a face that reminded Molly of a cross between a bulldog and a shovel. The tiny alien put a finger to its lips for Molly to stay silent. Its big bug eyes pleaded with the girl. She had to agree with the stern-voiced man: although the little guy was really ugly, he was also very cute.

Molly noticed the little Tarantian was trembling in fear. She also noticed, to her amazement, that she wasn't.

"Is there anyone else in the house?" the stranger in black asked.

"Just our daughter," Mom answered. "She's sleeping."

"Shhh," Molly whispered to the little extraterrestrial. "Don't be scared. It's okay."

There was a brilliant flash of light from outside the window. Molly and the Tarantian hopped back up on the sill and looked out the window.

One of the black-suited men was holding a slender silver wand in his hand, and Mom and Dad were staring at it, as if in a daze. He put the device away as he spoke to Mom and Dad. "A raccoon, that's your problem, folks. Make sure those trash can lids are on tight—and," he added, "*we* were never here."

Molly watched the black-suited men walk back to their idling car. She noticed they had brought backup with them, two more Men in Black—a slender, young black man and an older, gruff-looking white man with a very craggy face—leaned against the hood of their own black LTD and nodded to the other two agents as they pulled out of the driveway and sped away.

Molly turned away from the window to the little Tarantian and knelt down to meet his big, dark eyes. "We gotta get you out of here," she whispered. "Come on."

She opened her bedroom door quietly and padded down the hallway, motioning for the Tarantian to follow her. Reluctantly at first, the alien accompanied her toward the back of the house. Near the door to Mom and Dad's bedroom, Molly struggled to raise a window. The little Tarantian lent a hand and the window slid up easily. *Wow, he's strong*, Molly thought.

Molly gestured toward the open window. Beyond it, the city skyline at night glimmered like a million stars.

"Go on," she said. "It's okay." The alien regarded the window and then Molly once again. "I'm Molly," she said tapping her chest.

"Mol-ly," he said. She smiled and nodded.

The Tarantian leapt onto the open window's sill. He paused before he departed, turning back to the little girl, gratitude in his saucer-like eyes. "*Kabla nakshulin*," he said with great formality, then launched himself from the window to the roof of a neighbor's house, like a bouncy ball. He ran a few feet on his short, stubby legs and jumped skyward. Molly lost sight of him once he cleared another neighbor's house and seemed to vanish into the brilliance of the swollen moon. Molly waved goodbye, her eyes filled with wonder and starlight.

"Young lady, what are you doing up?" Molly spun to see Mom standing in the hall.

"That creature, the one you saw, I let it go," she reported.

"Creature? You mean the raccoon?"

"You don't have to lie." Molly shook her head. "I saw the policemen, the guys in the black suits?"

Her mom looked genuinely puzzled for a moment and then seemed to dismiss Molly's behavior. "Honey, parents never lie. Now go back to bed. You'll forget about it by morning."

"No, actually," Molly said, "I won't." She stomped past her mother back toward her bedroom. She paused and glanced back at her confused mother. "Well... *kabla nakshulin*. It means 'goodnight' in Tarantian."

Back in her room, Molly jumped back into bed,

trying to match the small alien's fantastic leaps. She fell a bit short. She picked up *A Brief History of Time* again and began to read with a renewed eagerness to understand the universe, to understand the way it all worked. She glanced out the window at the sky full of twinkling mysteries, and turned the page.

3

SOME YEARS LATER

The walls of Molly's Manhattan apartment were covered in college diplomas and yellowed old tabloid newspaper articles. Surrounding her framed degree in astrophysics (she'd minored in quantum mechanics and anthropology), were crumbling newsprint containing stories with lurid titles like WHO ARE THE MEN IN BLACK?, ALIEN BAT-BOY DISCOVERED IN JERRY SPRINGER AUDIENCE, and MYSTERY UFO OVER WHITE HOUSE.

Molly had grown into a confident young woman. Her dark eyes and hair lent her a natural beauty she was dimly aware of, but her focus was on other things. She sat before a bank of monitors, wearing a coat over her rumpled white blouse and thin black tie, ready to be out of the door at a moment's notice. Her hands danced over the keyboard, her eyes flickered from screen to screen. "You're not getting away from me this time," she muttered.

She had been saying that for most of her life. As a child, and then a teen, she had sought out and studied every scrap of information about extraterrestrials, planets, galaxies, and the seemingly mythological "Men in Black" that she could find, from scholarly works and scientific papers, to supermarket tabloids and the dingiest corners of the Internet.

She had excelled at college, driven by her obsession to find out the truth about aliens and the MiBs. Once she'd graduated, she had flirted with the notion of joining the FBI, CIA, or NASA, but decided that such agencies were either fronts for the MiBs, or deliberately kept in the dark about their existence. She'd even considered teaching to pay the bills, but soon realized such a career would put too much of a demand on her time and take her away from her search. She had been supporting herself through the gig economy, taking contract IT jobs, research assignments, and proofing mathematic and engineering formulas for grad students, and even professors. It paid her rent, and gave her the freedom to continue the search she had so long been pursuing—the search she was confident was going to end today.

A monitor beeped and Molly spun in her chair to read the data that flashed on the screen: ALERT: HUBBLE TELESCOPE: PERSEID METEOR SHOWER— TRAJECTORY UPDATE. ENTER PASSWORD.

Molly smiled and began entering a password. "Okay, let's see where you are now."

In response to the password, a new message box appeared: WELCOME BACK PROFESSOR ARMITRAGE. Next to the greeting was a photograph of a middle-aged man, apparently the real Professor Armitrage.

Molly tapped in a series of commands and a display appeared that was labeled as NEAR EARTH OBJECTS. It was tracking the speed, path, and trajectories of numerous meteors. The tracking system beeped again as one of the objects in space suddenly performed a radical change.

"I didn't know meteors could change speed and direction. How about you, Lilly?" Molly's long-dead houseplant gave no response except to drop a withered leaf. Molly shrugged, "Yeah, well, you've always been a skeptic. Lighten up, man!"

The object Molly was tracking vanished from the screen. She quickly made a note of the exact coordinates. "Not a meteor after all, is it? Definitely an unauthorized landing." She jumped to her feet and began to riffle through stacks of tabloid newspapers, scanning the headlines quickly. She wore a black skirt and combat boots. Molly stopped at a copy of the *World News Daily*, nodding at the headline: "Real Housewife of Queens—'I want back my Alien Ex!'" The photograph with the story showed a woman holding three babies, all of the children had a look about them—like they just *might* be from another world. A smaller headline for the same story declared: "Alien Ex Jimmy says, 'I'm coming back, baby!'"

Molly grinned as the realization hit her. "This is it. It's really happening!"

She quickly downloaded the Hubble data on the last known coordinates of the missing "meteor" to her phone. She gave Lilly the last of her water as the data ported over. The plant thanked her by dropping another desiccated leaf. Data in hand, Molly grabbed her wrinkled black suit jacket off the back of her chair and her black backpack as she dashed outside to meet her destiny.

Out by the curb she flagged down a taxi, still looking at the data on her phone screen. She spoke to the cabbie—who looked like a reject from the *Jersey Shore* cast—from the curb. "I need to get to Brooklyn," she said to him.

The driver snorted in frustration. "Gonna need an address, lady."

"Forty-five degrees inclination," Molly read off the data, "sixty-two degrees declination." The driver looked like she had just hit him over the head with a very heavy math book, and then he scowled. Molly did a quick equation in her head. "Okay, down under the Manhattan Bridge."

The cabbie nodded, and Molly leapt in. He hit the button on the meter and the cab sped away from the curb.

4

Molly directed the driver to a quiet, deserted street that ran parallel to the Manhattan Bridge. She climbed out of the cab and handed the cabbie a twenty. "Keep it running," she told him.

She walked down the street, checking and rechecking the coordinates on her phone. Most of the houses she passed were boarded up and seemed empty; a few were covered in graffiti. One or two of them still looked like they might have occupants. At the end of the street was a large underpass. Just before the bridge, a series of heavy, orange construction barriers squatted across the road. Past the barriers was a tall, chain-link fence that closed off the end of the road.

Molly walked between the barriers and into the shadow of the underpass, up to the fence. She could hear the rumble of the traffic on the bridge and the cooing of the pigeons flocking together on the structures above her. The metal signs bolted to the Con-Ed fence announced, in series, HIGH VOLTAGE, DO NOT ENTER, and CLOSED FOR MAINTENANCE.

Through the fence Molly could see sections of the street had been jackhammered in numerous places and open trenches were everywhere. She saw a dump truck and a back hoe parked near a pair of blue plastic portable toilets. She couldn't spot any of the Con-Ed maintenance people, nor any other people at all. More importantly, there was no sign of any illegal alien space ship.

She checked the coordinates on her phone again and confirmed she was in the right place. She looked around and sighed. Nothing. The frustration and disappointment washed over her. After a moment, Molly spun and walked back toward the taxi. The pigeons, startled by her sudden movement, erupted into flight all around her. She ducked and turned away to avoid the madly fluttering birds, and stopped. Two of the birds were flying straight at the electrified fence—she gasped in horror, and waited for the sparks, but the birds flew on, unscathed, through the fence as if it wasn't there, and vanished from sight.

She paused and walked back to the fence, near the warning signs that threatened swift and certain death if the chain-link was touched. She took a deep breath, preparing herself for the worst, and slowly reached out her hand toward the fence, closer, closer… and then she found that she wasn't even touching the fence; her hand had passed right through it as if it wasn't there, just as the pigeons had done. She couldn't see her hand or wrist on the other side of the "fence," but she could still feel them. Molly pulled her hand back and it magically reappeared. Stunned, Molly wiggled the fingers of her hand and then leaned in closer to the fence with her face. She closed her eyes as her head, neck, and part of her shoulders all vanished as they touched the chain-link. She opened her eyes and after a second of taking the scene in, a look of revelation and relief spread across her features. "I knew it."

The street was not torn up. There was no construction site, no work trucks. Instead, right in front of her was an alien space ship; it had crashed in the middle of the street. And *they* were there. The ones Molly had been searching for, chasing, and missing for most of her life—the Men in Black.

There were several black Lexus sedans parked in front of the ship and a cadre of MiB agents, their backs to Molly, confronting the alien pilot, weapons trained on him. Molly psyched herself up for a second to do what she was thinking of doing next. Then she stepped through the illusory fence entirely and quickly took cover behind an abandoned junker of a car that was parked at the curb nearby.

The alien, a scraggly-looking humanoid who bore a distinct resemblance to the three babies in the tabloid story she'd been reading some minutes ago, had his hands up and was shuffling nervously. "Whoa, hey, this is Earth? My bad, guys!"

"Yeah, yeah, Jimmy," the lead MiB agent replied in a distinct Brooklyn accent. "Tell it to O back at HQ." The lead agent approached Jimmy and escorted him into the back seat of one of the Lexuses as he called out to the other agents, "Get a containment unit in here. I'll escort our Zamporan friend back."

Molly smiled and whispered, "Yes, you will."

She slipped back through the fence camouflage field as the MiBs secured Jimmy and his ship. She hurried back to the cab waiting near the entrance to the street, taking off her coat as she did so, and tossing it into the back seat of the cab. Underneath the coat, she was wearing a rumpled black trouser suit, white shirt and tie—the makeshift MiB uniform she had assembled for just such a moment as this. She climbed back into the taxi. Two MiB Lexus sedans drove past as she closed the door.

"Don't lose them," she instructed the cabbie.

A short while later, in a more salubrious part of town, Molly paid off the cab. She was dressed in her best MiB disguise, and almost pulling it off—except for the scuffed boots and backpack. She had been dressing up like this since she was ten, stealing Dad's suit jacket and ties.

Down the block and across the street, the sedans belonging to the mysterious Men in Black were parked in front of a formidable edifice of concrete. Carved into the face of the building was "Brooklyn Battery Tunnel Triborough Bridge & Tunnel Authority." The Battery Tunnel was the largest underground tunnel in North America. The Brooklyn building was one of four ventilation stations designed to provide a fresh air system to the tunnel. It was genius for the Men in Black to use the building and its vast underground networks as a base of operations. It was sure to give them unobserved access to so much of the Five Boroughs.

"Here we go," Molly said. To her, this building was a holy shrine. She ditched the backpack behind a bush and stepped off the curb, so close to the goal she had been seeking all her life. She needed to act and sound like she belonged here. She strode across the street like she owned it, and put on a pair of sunglasses as she entered the building. Her heels clicked on the marble floor as she walked toward the bank of elevators. An old security guard, a bald black man, was sitting in a chair in front of a wall-sized fan that was slowly rotating. There was an equally massive vent on the opposite wall from the fan and the guard. He was reading a tabloid newspaper, but looked up as Molly approached.

"They bring in that Zamporan yet?" Molly asked as casually as one might discuss last night's ball game. "Guy tried to sneak in behind a Perseid meteor shower. Amateur hour, am I right?" She walked past the guard, who did nothing to stop her.

"Right as rain," the guard said. "Came in a couple of minutes ahead of you." He went back to reading his paper. Molly couldn't help but smile a little as she pushed the button for the elevator.

I am Jane freakin' Bond, she thought. She tried to stop herself pushing the button again, but she couldn't resist. There was a *ding*, and the elevator doors opened. Molly walked inside, turned, and watched the old security guard poring over his newspaper until the doors closed and she began to descend.

Without looking up from his tabloid, the guard keyed the walkie-talkie on his belt. "Code Black," he said, licked his finger, and turned the page.

The back wall of the elevator was transparent. As Molly descended, the solid concrete of the Battery Building disappeared to reveal a huge complex below her. What she saw was a dream come true. The MiB New York headquarters was a sprawling cathedral of chrome, white marble, and light. The facility was several stories in height and Molly could see the offices and terraces that were part of the curved and illuminated walls overlooking the central floor. Hundreds of black-suited agents and support staff hurried about below her amid massive silver columns. The apparent seal of the MiB organization—three oval, intersecting orbital rings, each with two dark, equidistant dots that appeared to be electrons—was set into the marble floor at the heart of all the activity. Work desks were set in long, seemingly infinite rows along one side of the main floor. All the monitors, including the massive view screens that hung everywhere, were oval-shaped. They reminded Molly of giant electric eyes.

Most wonderful of all, on the opposite side of the floor from the desks, among the sea of black suits, there were beings of every imaginable shape, size, and color—a rainbow of aliens! There were so many, all so different. The aliens streamed across the MiB headquarters in lines, almost as if they were in the departures hall of an airport. Most of the aliens carried bags, trunks, packs, and other containers. She even saw a basket of weird alien fruit and some New York City souvenirs being examined by the Men in Black standing behind oval-shaped, illuminated counters. These MiBs were checking the visitors' travel documents and interviewing some of them. Many of the aliens sat on padded circular benches looking bored and frustrated, while others gazed around the Earth terminal with the same sense of wonder with which Molly was watching them.

She saw a mass of yellow grapes about the shape and size of a large Christmas tree shambling through the line. She suddenly realized that the "grapes" were in fact eyeballs, and they were boggling around the terminal in every conceivable direction, including at her. A tentacle of yellow eyeballs waved to her as she descended. Molly found herself waving back.

Another alien in the line was only a few feet tall, and the space around it shivered and warped constantly, like it wasn't fully connected to this reality. As it moved up in the queue, the alien's distorted after-images remained behind it for a few seconds. Each reflection moved and behaved like an independent entity until they faded away.

Then, suddenly, Molly's elevator *dropped*. The descent became a fall as the car plummeted into the subterranean darkness.

5

The elevator doors opened and Molly found herself staring into a sparse, white room. Light seemed to radiate from the bare walls. There was an illuminated pedestal with a black leather and chrome swivel chair mounted at its center. The chair faced her. The wall opposite the elevator door contained only a large mirror, most likely for two-way observation, Molly surmised.

Confidently, she strode over to the pedestal and sat down in the swivel chair as the elevator door closed behind her with a soft hiss. She spun the chair around, facing the mirror, and crossed her arms and legs. "For the record," she told the mirror, and whoever was behind it, "you didn't catch me. I caught you."

There was a small part of her that was afraid, but the rest of her that had been looking for this, waiting for this, her whole life told the fear to shut up.

* * *

It was late morning the next day when the grande dame of MiB arrived, though none of her subordinates had ever had the nerve to call her that to her face. Agent O, Chief of Operations for MiB's North American station, strode into the observation room behind the mirror with her usual commanding air of detached calm. O was a slender woman with short, gray hair, dressed in an impeccable black dress with a high white collar and cuffs—and, like so many of the people in MiB, there was a lot more to Agent O than met the eye. She had been the first female MiB agent in America, and very few of her fellow agents knew that she had also created the portable neuralyzer. She had run the New York station with distinction since the passing of Agent Zed, and she was keenly interested in how this young woman had compromised their organization. She took a place at the observation window next to a gray-haired veteran agent, who was observing Molly's reactions and responses through the glass. The young woman looked tired after the long night of questioning; a lie-detector device was attached to her forearm, but the MiB agent questioning her didn't look satisfied with her answer.

"Who is she working for?" O asked, removing her wire-rimmed glasses.

"Nobody," the gray-haired agent said. "She claims to have been working alone."

O examined the young woman's face as she continued to spar with her interrogators.

"So, a civilian with zero training just waltzes in off the street?"

The senior agent handed her the interrogation transcript. "Hell of a story," he said.

"Mmhmm…" O scanned the report, flipping through the pages. "Mmhmm… Mmm…" She handed the papers back to the senior agent and flipped the switch on the observation console that turned on the intercom in the interrogation room. "Neuralyze her."

In the interrogation room, the lead interrogator drew his neuralyzer out of his jacket pocket. Molly's face changed when she saw the silver wand. It was clear she knew what it did, and that the prospect made her frantic. "No, no, *don't*. I know what that thing is," she said, getting to her feet.

O gave her subordinate a questioning look.

"She had… an experience once," the veteran agent started to explain, but Molly was talking again, this time looking directly into the mirror, as if she could see them.

"You erased my parents' memories, but you didn't get mine. My whole life, everyone told me I was crazy. 'Molly off her trolley.' They said I needed therapy—" Molly nodded grudgingly "—which I did, but not for this."

Behind the mirror, Agent O's arms were crossed; her face was stone. The steel cuffs attached to the swivel chair's arms restrained her, but she struggled against them nonetheless, still keeping her eyes on the mirror, still pleading with her own image and the shadows behind the glass. "You start to think you *are* crazy, but I never stopped looking. It took me twenty years, but I found you."

The agent with the neuralyzer popped it open and

began to adjust the control dials. Molly glanced from the wand to the mirror.

Behind the mirror, O frowned as she leafed through the agent's notes again, stopping at the point that had been troubling her. She re-read a part that had stuck with her. "She really hacked the Hubble Telescope to look at Andromeda Two, and we didn't catch her?"

"In the old days, we'd have hired her," the senior agent commented, a little wistfully. O looked at him and then at Molly. Then she strode into the interrogation room.

"So," O said to Molly, "you found us and proved you're not crazy. Now what?"

"I want in," Molly replied, without missing a beat.

"We don't hire; we recruit."

"Then recruit me."

"Give me one good reason."

"Because I'm smart, I'm motivated and—"

"You're going to have to do better than that," Agent O told her. The neuralyzer in the lead interrogator's hand was whining now, at full power, ready to discharge. Molly looked O straight in the eyes, and the older woman saw the steel and determination fixed there.

"Because I have absolutely no life whatsoever," Molly blurted out. O cocked her head a bit at that. "No dog, no cat, no Netflix, *definitely* no chill. Nothing I can't happily walk away from. I'm perfect for this job, and you know it."

O looked at Molly as if she were weighing her soul against a feather. Finally, she said, "Well, that's all rather... sad." Molly glanced quickly at the two agents who had been trying to steal her memories. They nodded sadly in agreement.

"No love?" O asked Molly. "Relationships?"

"They just distract us from what's important," Molly said.

"And what's important?"

"The *truth*," Molly responded. "I want to know how it all works."

O nodded for the lead interrogator to put away his neuralyzer. The other one clicked a release on Molly's chair, and the arm cuffs retracted. Molly rubbed her wrists as she stood.

"You really think a black suit is the answer to all your problems?" O asked.

"No, but..." Molly sized up O, "it looks damn good on you."

O let a smile slip for the first time.

The tailor, a tall, middle-aged man with a widow's peak and a measuring tape draped over his shoulder, helped Molly out of the makeshift MiB suit she had bought at Ross, so that she was just in the vest top she'd been wearing underneath.

Different styles of suits for male and female agents hung from transparent bars along either side of the room. Illuminated transparent shelves were fitted discretely into alcoves at the far end of the room. She stole a glance at the tailor and his assistant in the mirror. He was dressed in a stylish black vest and white shirt;

the young blonde woman with a severely short hairstyle wore a black sleeveless dress with a white, long-sleeved blouse underneath it.

The tailor ran a scanner over Molly, temporarily bathing her in a grid-like hologram. An unspoken instruction passed between him and the woman. The assistant noted something in the electronic tablet she held, and moved away to pull a suit from the rack.

O's words to her echoed in Molly's memory as the tailor helped her into the chosen suit.

"*You are a rumor, recognizable only as déjà vu and dismissed just as quickly.*

"*You will have no identifying marks of any kind. You will not stand out in any way. You are no longer part of 'the system.'*"

She was hustled to another section of the room. There the assistant picked up one of several closed, black-lacquered boxes. The tailor opened the box to reveal a row of identical, triangular-shaped MiB wristwatches. The tailor studied them and then Molly for a moment, and nodded sagely. He plucked one of the watches out of the box and strapped it carefully to Molly's wrist. She admired it, holding up her wrist. Cool.

Another wooden box came off another shelf. The tailor opened it and Molly smiled. With a reverence she didn't realize she possessed, but apparently did, she lifted the MiB sunglasses to her face and slipped them on.

Her final stop was the armory. Molly felt like a kid in a candy store. So many ray guns, blasters, De-Atomizers, Tasers, lasers, phasers, masers, sonic bowel disruptors, melters, maulers, fusion projectors, photonic shotguns, and space-time staplers were displayed along the walls, mounted on transparent screens, or resting on shelves.

When the armorer opened a small black box with rows of a tiny pistol neatly arrayed, her voice dripped with disdain. "C'mon on, guys, are you kidding me?" The armorer frowned, then shrugged and retrieved another box from the alcove. She opened it to reveal a large, silver-finished, futuristic pistol, something Robo-Cop and Dirty Harry might fight over. A Series-4 De-Atomizer.

A wide smile came to Molly's face. "That works."

Molly and O entered O's elevated, elongated oval-shaped office, which overlooked the agents' work desks and the arrival and departure terminals for the aliens. O explained that the agency had now completely deleted all traces of Molly Wright from the Internet. All that remained of her old life, her old name, was the letter M on an MiB computer screen.

"We're above the system, over it. Beyond it. We're 'them.' We're 'they.' But we are still, I'm afraid, called the Men in Black," O concluded. The two women looked at one another a bit awkwardly for a moment.

"The *Men* in Black?" Molly sounded incredulous.

"Don't," O said. "I've had the conversation. They can't let it go. It's a process."

O sat behind her desk, plucked a manila envelope from it, and handed it to Em. "Your first assignment."

Em seized the envelope as if it held the secrets of the

universe. "Okay, but when do I get my…" She held up her hand, made a neuralyzer gesture with her thumb.

"It's called a neuralyzer," O explained, "and you don't get one, you *earn* one." Off Em's crestfallen face, she added, "You've been accepted for a probationary period. Impress me… and we'll see."

Trying to contain her disappointment, Em opened the envelope and slid a sheet of paper out. When she saw what was written on it, she looked up at O with a hurt and almost accusatory glance.

"You're a fan of the truth, aren't you, Agent M?"

Em looked back at the paper. The transfer paperwork had a letterhead that said, "MiB London."

"We may have a problem in London," O began.

6

The private gambling club's empty rooms and hallways were lined with rich mahogany paneling and empty, high-backed leather chairs. Most of the club's exclusive membership had made their way home hours ago, when the club closed down for the night. Only a single circle of light remained above a table of players, a ring of onlookers around them. There was a scream from the table that echoed through the rooms. A second later, a cheer went up from the audience watching the game.

Two burly, tattooed bodyguards dragged a convulsing player, clutching his wrist, eyes bulging, away from the table, still in his chair. Only six players remained at the table, now. Agent H, sporting a three o'clock shadow and wearing a brown corduroy jacket and green T-shirt, was one of the remaining players. In the years since he and High T had saved the world in Paris, something had changed in H. Something indefinable about his demeanor. Some of the light had gone out of his eyes.

H proffered his empty tumbler to a uniformed waiter who was so unobtrusive that he almost blended into the woodwork. The waiter poured a viscous purple liquid into H's glass from an ornate decanter of smoked crystal. The liquid sloshed and moved about in H's tumbler of its own volition. The agent tossed back the moving drink and winced as the kick hit him. "Oh, that's smooth," he said to the waiter, gesturing with his glass again. "Keep 'em coming."

At the center of the table was a cage. Inside it was a three-headed, viper-like creature. H knew it was a Fmekian Trench Viper, a nasty species of animal with one of the most lethal venoms in the universe. The viper was coiled, its heads scanning and hissing only a few feet away from the players. Covering the floor of the viper's cage were poker tiles, each marked like a terrestrial playing card. If a player wanted to make their hand, they'd have to risk the viper's bite.

The other players around the table with H didn't look like the club's regular clientele, at least not during operating hours. H knew them to be local human scumbags—arms dealers, drug dealers, human traffickers—and worse. The man running the game, however, was not a local, far from it. His name was Anatoli, at least on this planet, and he wore a custom suit easily as expensive as H's own. His face, neck, and hands were a looping road map of scars and tattoos. His eyes were as hooded and reptilian as the three-headed viper's in the cage. Anatoli was a Cerulian crime lord. He'd fled to Earth years ago and had made a meteoric and bloody rise to the heights of the European underworld. It was his club, his game, and his rules, and H was here for him.

H had gotten a lead on one of Anatoli's people quite by chance in Berlin, while there on some other business for MiB. He knew how long the organization had been trying to shut the crime boss down, and had managed to worm his way into the role of middleman in a deal involving a cargo container of Cerulian narcotics. While the drugs provided their user with a hallucinogenic euphoria, they were also addictive and tended to drive humans insane.

The deal went down and that led to a few other fake criminal ventures, that eventually got H an invitation to Anatoli's club in London and his personal after-hours game.

"Can I just say how much I like this place," H said, scanning the room with an eye for any hidden traps and exit routes. He'd spotted the bodyguards' Pizimian blasters tucked in their shoulder holsters when they dragged away the now-departed Player Seven. Pizimian hardware in circulation on Anatoli's thugs meant the truce between the Pizim and the Necdorph had collapsed. The MiB office would want to know about that. "Formal but not too stuffy, classic but modern," H continued. He eyed Anatoli's companion, who stood by his side as he played. The woman wore a gossamer gown with a gauzy hood that obscured her features, save her beautiful eyes. When she caught his gaze on her, her eyes widened slightly, and H was pretty sure she was smiling, perhaps blushing, beneath the hood.

"How much are we talking membership-wise, per year?" H looked to the player to his left and added some money to the pot, piled up on top of the cage. "I'll raise you…"

The player, an East End gangster, pulled up the sleeve of his leather coat and slid his hand inside the cage slowly. He lifted the tile he needed to complete his straight flush. The viper was still, three sets of dead eyes unblinking.

"It's invitation only. No vacancies," Anatoli said, in a thick accent reminiscent of Eastern Europe, his eyes on the gangster's hand. He was bringing the tile out of the cage, slowly, carefully. He licked the sweat from his upper lip and began to smile. That was when the viper struck. The player dropped the tile, gasping, and jerked his arm out of the cage, clutching at his wounded wrist as his eyes began to swell and puff, like over-inflated balloons. Before Anatoli's bodyguards could reach the East Ender, he gurgled and fell from his chair to the floor, dead. Anatoli's and H's eyes never left one another, even as the man died.

"I think a spot just opened up," H said as the bodyguards dragged the body and the chair away.

"Your turn," Anatoli replied, not missing a beat.

H looked at his tiles: 10, jack, queen, king, all spades. He spied the Ace of Spades tucked near the coiled body of the Fmekian viper. He slid his arm into the cage easily, fluidly, with no hesitation, no apparent fear. He continued talking to Anatoli as he edged closer to the tile, "And is there a gym here? Sauna? Can you get a bite to eat, or is it mostly just the lethal high-stakes gambling?" H smoothly, fearlessly, slid a hand into the cage, plucked the tile off the floor, and pulled it out, missing the viper's strike by a millisecond.

Gasps and cheers went up around the table. H held up the tile, showing it to a glowering Anatoli, and then placed it in sequence with the other tiles. "Huh, look at that," he said. "Straight to the ace." H raked in the pile of cash off the roof of the cage while the agitated viper hissed and thrashed.

The surviving players dropped their tiles back into the viper's cage for the next hand and anted up. H raised his empty glass, and the waiter refilled it with the moving purple ooze. "Now, let's talk business," he said to Anatoli, gesturing with his full glass of motile liquor. "I can move this stuff." He was a little buzzed and that was bad. It was dangerous, and prohibited on any mission, but especially reckless on an undercover operation with no backup. MiB had special chemicals that agents could take prior to going out into the field that neutralized most forms of intoxicants, at least temporarily. H had eschewed them. Again, he was pushing out past the edge, and he found himself feeling practically nothing at all. "Who do I need to talk to to to get a whole lot more of it? 'Cause... I'm in." The hooded woman batted her eyes at H and then gave him a wink. Again, there was the hint of a smile under the obscuring hood. H didn't hide his flirtations with Anatoli's companion. Another dare, another risk. "I could get used to this place."

"I wouldn't," Anatoli said dryly as he took his turn, thrusting his arm into the cage. The Fmekian viper's heads all swayed and hissed, but the snake didn't strike. The alien crime boss took the tile he wanted and began to move his arm out of the cage as if he had all the time in the world. He placed the tile on the table and turned his reptilian gaze on H. "You see, I have a very strict no Men in Black policy."

Silence fell over the room. Everyone's gaze fell on H, who, seemingly oblivious to the attention, was counting his winnings.

"I don't blame you," H said. "Who'd want those assholes coming in here, spoiling the vibe? All it takes is one bad apple."

Anatoli was impressed by this undercover cop. Not a single tell that he had been compromised. Was he that good, or just that drunk? If he didn't know better, he'd swear his intel was bad, but it wasn't. The information that his new potential business partner was MiB had come at the most fortuitous time to avoid getting busted. Just imagining having all he had worked and fought for taken away from him by a bunch of cosmic do-gooders who knew nothing of how life really worked made his poisonous blood boil. H's identity was worth the small fortune he had paid for it on the black market. Though they would never meet, the Cerulian mobster was in debt to whoever had been leaking MiB classified data. Anatoli nodded to his men.

One of the bodyguards slipped a garrote around H's neck from behind, attempting to choke him. H jammed his feet against the edge of the table and used it for leverage to flip himself up and over the goon. He drove a powerful kick into the man's back, sending him flying forward. The bodyguard crashed onto the table. Plumes of money flew up around the room. The guard's face smashed against the cage, knocking it open. The Fmekian viper's three heads all struck, biting the guard. The dying guard's eyes inflated and swelled as he rolled off the table with a groan, and collapsed on the floor.

The angry viper slithered from its cage onto the table. Players and onlookers shouted, screamed, and fled from the room as the second bodyguard charged at H. H kicked a chair into the guard, sending him tumbling to the floor. Another goon came at H. Swiftly, the agent grabbed the Fmekian viper off the table and hurled it at him. H knelt and recovered the dead guard's blaster from his holster, rising to take aim at Anatoli, who was still seated, the hooded lady still at his side.

"I am MiB, you Cerulian scum," H said, "and FYI, I think your club sucks. It's pretentious. Now you're gonna give me everything—suppliers, sellers—your whole network." H winced in pain, suddenly.

"Your luck ran out," Anatoli said, glancing down. One of the viper's mouths was attached to H's leg. "You're already dead."

H's eyes had already begun to swell up as the venom took effect. It felt like freezing acid was being pumped into his veins, his heart. Despite the pain, he sneered at the Cerulian crime boss as he tore the viper loose and tossed it skyward. It landed in the crook of the ceiling's rafter beams and hissed down at him.

"Am I?" he slurred. He fumbled with numb fingers

for his jacket's interior pocket. "Antidote, asshole." But where the vial of antidote should have been in H's coat pocket was only a wet spot; he pulled the shattered vial out as Anatoli began to chuckle. H tossed the bottle away and desperately licked his fingers—nothing! He wrestled with his jacket, trying to suck any of the precious fluid out of the cloth of his pocket.

"Bad luck, mate," Anatoli said. "Only one person here has the antidote, don't they, sweetheart?"

H's vision was blurring, but he saw Anatoli's companion produce a slender vial from her purse. She held it up as she regarded the struggling H with those beautiful eyes.

Before Anatoli could continue gloating, the Fmekian viper dropped on him from above, striking with all three heads to his face and neck. Anatoli fell from his chair and gasped on the ground, his eyes now growing, expanding. He looked at H with sheer hatred and then snapped his fingers at his companion, gesturing for the vial. H fell to his knees, his lips turning blue. It was getting hard to think, to see, to breathe. The hooded woman looked to H and then to Anatoli and back again.

"Please," H said, fighting to focus on those beautiful eyes. "Whatever you want..."

Anatoli tried to scoff, but he was losing control of his muscles.

"Ha!" he gasped. "You think someone as gorgeous as her would be interested in someone like you?"

Both men looked to the alien woman for salvation. She wrapped her fingers tighter around the small vial and pulled it close to her chest. She looked at H. Her voice from within the hood was thick with an eastern European accent, like Anatoli's. It was also honeyed with desire.

"Did you say, 'whatever I want'?"

Those were the last words Anatoli ever heard.

The late Anatoli's suite was on the top floor of a very exclusive London hotel. H awoke, the sunlight peeling his eyeballs a layer at a time. His stomach ached, and his head swam. He couldn't be sure if it was the self-propelled purple port or the viper's venom that was making him feel like Tarantian poo. He rolled over slightly and saw that his bedmate, Anatoli's former girlfriend, was still sleeping. Her long, tentacled arm was draped over his chest. He tried gingerly to dislodge it, but it was stuck to his skin. Carefully, he lifted it off, with the suction cups making a *pop-pop-pop* sound as the vacuum seal was broken. The cups left tiny red rings in a diagonal trail across his chest. The alien woman—H hadn't caught her name—stirred but didn't wake up. He climbed silently out of bed, his striped socks hitting the floor, and dressed quickly. Standing before the vanity's mirror in the bedroom, H searched the drawers until he found some lipstick. He quickly scrawled a note on the surface of the mirror and then removed his neuralyzer from his jacket pocket.

Again, he was breaking a rule. Neuralyzation of one's own self was strictly prohibited by the MiB Field Agent's

Guide. It was dangerous and irresponsible. Technically, his memories were the property of MiB and he was deleting company files by doing this. He adjusted the small dials and then flashed himself squarely in the face with the memory-erasing beam. H blinked a few times and realized he had no recollection of anything after Anatoli's demise. There was a note scrawled on the mirror:

> DO NOT LOOK BEHIND YOU.
> JUST LEAVE. TRUST ME! H.

H took out his hankie and wiped away the message. He paused for a moment, staring at the bright red lipstick on his handkerchief, smiled, and almost turned around to see what he'd cautioned himself against—but then he remembered his own advice and quickly and quietly departed.

7

Em waited on the subway platform. It could have been any platform in New York City, but this one was part of the MiB Battery Tunnel complex. A few other MiBs and various alien support staff stood on the platform, looking at their phones or reading the paper, like anyone else waiting for a train. *Other MiBs...* She was one of them now, off on her first assignment, her first great adventure. It all felt so unreal.

Reality came wheezing and clattering to a stop at the platform. An old, dilapidated subway car, festooned with graffiti, shuddered to a stop with a groan and a hiss. *Not the Hogwarts Express*, Em thought, *but I'll take it.*

The car doors opened, and a group of four short aliens swaggered out. Their slender bodies reminded Em a bit of a worm's. They each had a pair of long, drooping antennae on top of their vaguely-frog-like heads; two long, slender, stick-like arms; and another pair of smaller arms folded close to their torso. The worms were pulling rolling luggage with them, and several of them were wearing Hawaiian shirts that were louder than an Iron Maiden concert. They were all chattering in Brooklyn accents. They immediately pulled vape pens from their shirt pockets as they cleared the doors of the car and started puffing. Others pulled out flasks and gulped from them nosily.

"Move it or lose it!" one of the worms shouted to one lagging behind as they sauntered by. They all laughed as they headed toward the command center in a cloud of what Em's nose suspected was Kushberry vape juice.

Em hefted her backpack and entered the car with the other agents. It was a typical old, nasty subway car inside. Em and the other passengers found their way to the seats with the least amount of questionable fluids on them. "Departing New York station in thirty seconds," an automated voice droned over the car's speaker. Em was impressed with how well a machine could mimic a bored city employee.

The doors hissed closed, sounding like a two-packs-a-day asthmatic, but then bumped open again to allow access to the car for a pair of aliens who seemed to be composed primarily of teeth. Em wasn't sure if one of the toothy duo smiled at her or bared its fangs. The doors closed again with a groan, and the whole car instantly began to undergo some kind of transformation, shifting, morphing. It reminded Em of how the MiBs' car had changed outside her house that night, so long ago. The stained plastic benches flowed and changed, becoming seats with heavy restraining harnesses like something in the cockpit of a race car or a fighter jet. "Departing New York in ten seconds," the mechanical Transit Authority employee announced. Em saw the other passengers clicking themselves into the harnesses and securing and tightening the belts. Em followed suit, and just in time.

The transformed car blasted away from the station at an unimaginable speed. It felt to Em like her brain had just sloshed to the back of her skull. She had to be pulling multiple G's of acceleration, but the hum and roar of the car didn't sound like any kind of conventional rocket engine. *Maglev?* Em wondered. *Magnetic levitation?*

She looked over at an agent reading the *Wall Street Journal*, his face pancaked, cheeks fluttering like a deflating whoopee cushion. Another agent held his coffee mug out in front of him and tipped it. The coffee sloshed through the air and landed in his open mouth—a ten from all the judges. There was movement on the ceiling. A small, furry alien, clearly a regular commuter, was clutching one of the ride straps on the bar above her. The alien was being pulled completely horizontal by the acceleration of the train, flapping like a flag. It was reading from a small tablet, indifferent to its condition. *Been there, done that.* Em felt a sense of civic pride swell up in her. No real New Yorker was fazed by anything on the subway.

The blasé automated voice said over the speaker, "Next stop, London Station." Em glanced out the car's window to see a blue whale drifting through the dark waters of the deep Atlantic, a cloud of small fish clustered around it. Then the maglev capsule shot past them and continued on toward the UK.

Beneath the waters of the venerable River Thames, which bisected the city of London, there was a glint and blur of something moving at unimaginable speed. Blink, and you would miss it.

"Arriving London Station," the automatized voice in the subway car reported. "Next stop, Amsterdam Annex." The voice paused for a second, then began again. "*Schtock-prith London Smitmonak. Vernox mip Amsterdam…*"

She disembarked the train and looked around the station platform. MiB agents streamed past her without a second glance in her direction. There were rows of polished, silver ascending and descending escalators with a sign at their base that simply declared, "London."

Em walked past a magazine kiosk near the base of the escalators. It was staffed by a man she wasn't sure was an alien or not. His pale skin and dark eyes were a striking contrast to his mop of curly blonde hair that had been meticulously braided into a halo-like crown that radiated away from his head in all directions. Beside the gum, phone cards, lighters, and candy, the magazines prominently displayed in the kiosk had titles like *Alien Charisma*, *Astronaut Gourmet*, and *The Galaxy Chronicles*.

Em was still feeling a bit like silly putty from the train ride as she ascended the escalator that took her from MiB London Station's maglev platform to the command center. London Station's architecture was similar to New York's immaculate, well-lit white walls and chrome. The vast, multilevel, man-made cavern of columns, braces, corridors, and walkways had a similar motif, but was laid out differently. The elevated office that she assumed belonged to O's London counterpart was a sphere, not an oval, and felt like an eye at the center of everything, overlooking all the chaotic activity taking place at different locations on the main floor.

Like the New York station, there was a customs terminal here, too, bustling with aliens from a thousand different worlds and hundreds of galaxies. Em watched in wonder at the lines of aliens arriving and departing her world. She saw two cactus-like beings say farewell to one another with a hug and an exchange of water in a ritual bone bowl. One headed to departures, the other remained and waved goodbye. An alien with an inordinate number of digits was holding up the line at the fingerprint recognition station, while a few counters over, Em saw an agent check and recheck the photo on a humanoid alien's ID. He shook his head, and Em could tell the picture wasn't matching the alien's mug. The alien gestured for the agent to wait a moment. A thing that looked like a cross between a snake and a crab erupted from the alien's chest, hissing and snarling at the agent. Unperturbed, the agent checked the photo on the ID again against the alien hanging from the humanoid's chest. He nodded in approval and waved the pair through his line.

Em skirted the line and took the route designated in numerous languages for "AGENTS" only. She paused to observe a large wall-sized monitor mounted near

a junction of corridors. The monitor was labeled as
CURRENT HIGH-PROFILE SURVEILLANCE, and showed
dozens of famous people Em saw all the time on TV and
in the news.

"It's never who you think it is," a man's voice came
from behind her. She turned to regard a distinguished
older man dressed in a well-cut black suit, with a vest and
a gold watch fob. He looked refined and authoritative,
with just a hint of a dangerous edge.

"Oh no," Em turned back to the screen. She pointed
at one of the surveillance images, a shot from within the
Oval Office. "That one makes total sense."

"So, you're the one who found us."

"I am," Em replied.

"I'm T," the man said. "High T. I run this circus.
Welcome, Em. O told us to expect great things."

"Then great things you shall get."

High T smiled. He pointed to a corridor past the
terminal complex. "Take two rights and a left." High
T continued on, and Em watched him go, feeling a
little cast adrift despite the directions. She looked down
and saw an adorable fluffy alien at her feet. Forgetting
herself, and where she was, she reached down to pat
it. Even as she did so, the alien shattered… into several
even tinier versions of itself. The little creatures scurried
off, running amok through the MiB customs agents, who
raced around trying to round up the little troublemakers.
Her face a mask of innocence, Em walked away as
quickly as she could.

Two rights and a left later, Em found herself in a

vast office cubicle farm. What looked like hundreds of humans and aliens sat at desks in front of computers, wearing headsets. Em began to get a very strange yet familiar feeling in her stomach. Em saw there was a vacant desk with a placard that had "M" written on it.

"Looks like we're going to be neighbors," an alien called cheerfully from the cubicle beside hers. "I'm Guy."

Guy was blue. He had two sets of eyes, two pairs of black-rimmed, hipster-style glasses, and six small, pointed-leaf-like ears. He was portly and dressed in a bowling shirt. Em couldn't tell if the sparse growth that covered his upper lip, chin, and one of his necks was hair or fine little tentacles.

"One sec." Guy clicked off the mute button on his headset. "Alien Services Center, how can I make your stay on Earth better today?" Guy's phone voice was smooth like butter. "Your human skin has torn? Hate it when that happens. There is the most *wonderful* tailor, just off Savile Row…"

Em sat down in her cubicle, half-listening to her new blue bestie give directions to his customer. On her desk was a plastic-wrapped headset, a thick manual entitled *Alien Code of Conduct, Earth Edition*, and a small, gift-wrapped box with an envelope. Em opened the envelope and read the typed note inside:

A journey of a thousand light-years begins with a single step—High T.

She opened the box. Inside was a pocket compass adorned with the MiB logo. It reminded her of the stress ball shaped like a customer's head she got as a

MEN IN BLACK INTERNATIONAL

gift on her first day at her old customer services job in Manhattan. In fact, she thought, looking around the cubicles, a lot about this place reminded her of her old customer services job in Manhattan.

Em's phone chirped with a call. She slumped in her seat. Her brand-new life suddenly felt very old indeed.

"What the fu—"

8

MARRAKECH, MOROCCO

The bright moon bathed the ancient city at the cusp of the desert in ghostly light. The sky was clear and gave a magnificent view of the stars from horizon to horizon. The city quarter that contained the medina, the famous, sprawling open-air marketplaces of Marrakech, was mostly deserted at this hour, the booths and stalls closed and locked. Even the cafes that dotted the fringes of the market district were closing. No one noticed, in the midnight hour, the strange particles that drifted down from space and seemed to capture the moon's brilliance, like stardust falling. The particles began to coalesce, picking up speed as they whirled about one another, forming a pearlescent cyclone that descended toward the slumbering city's rooftops.

It was after midnight and Kaden was still at work. It wasn't fair—he'd had plans for tonight that were gone now because his manager had insisted he stay late. The young waiter was handsome, lean, and tall. His black hair was styled in short dreadlocks and he was dressed in Moroccan-style street clothes. He dragged a mop across the wet tile floor of the banqueting room in the cafe he worked in. He listened to dance music on the local radio station on a cheap little portable radio that was up on a shelf. He let the music's driving beat distract him and danced a few moves as he mopped.

The music was suddenly lost in a wash of hissing and popping static. The television on the wall had snapped on by itself; the picture on the screen of a televised soccer match was warped and distorted. Kaden looked around, startled and confused as the overhead fans that had been rotating lazily jumped to life and began spinning faster than they ever had, shaking violently and starting to come loose from the ceiling. As quickly as it had begun, the chaotic flurry of activity stopped. The power shut off and plunged the whole cafe into darkness.

"It's the fuse!" the manager called out in French. "Go! Fix it!"

Kaden rolled his eyes. "If you paid for your own electricity, this wouldn't happen. Cheapskate."

"I heard that!" the manager bellowed. "*Allez!*"

The waiter sighed, leaned his mop against a wall, and headed up to the roof and the fuse box.

Kaden used his phone's light to navigate the dark stairs that led him up to the cafe's roof. Once he reached the top he noticed that it wasn't just their power that was out. The buildings all around him for a block were also dark. He might as well check the fuse box anyway; the manager would only ask about it if he didn't.

He navigated the cluttered rooftop, avoiding tangles of wires and cables and a forest of television antennas on his way to the small, antiquated fuse box mounted on a crumbling retaining wall. Kaden opened the box and held his phone closer to peer inside. There was a tangle of old wires, many wrapped with black electrical tape. Some of the sockets for fuses were covered with peeling masking tape that someone had long ago scribbled DO NOT USE on, in both French and Arabic. He sighed, shook his head in disgust, and began to fiddle with the loose wires, hoping he wouldn't get shocked.

There was a spark and a crack from the box. Kaden jumped back as the building lights came back on, including the few lights on the roof. Kaden didn't see, but behind him, on the other side of the roof, something that was not human stood, something from another world. It was faceless, amorphous. It looked as if it might be observing him.

The lights went out again, plunging the roof back into darkness. Kaden cursed under his breath and tried to recall which wires he had jiggled to make the power come back. The lights stuttered and came on once again. There were now two identical faceless creatures behind Kaden, closer than they had been a moment ago. The fuse box snapped and a flash of blue electricity arced between the wires. The roof plunged into darkness yet again.

Kaden fumbled in his pocket and removed a small coin, a ten-santimat piece. He found an empty fuse socket and wedged the coin into it, jerking his hand back as the box once again tried to bite him with electricity.

He nursed his stinging fingers as the lights came on and stayed on this time. Kaden smiled and turned to return to the cafe and his chores.

The two faceless creatures were directly behind him.

Kaden screamed as the things from another world reached out to grab him. After a moment, his scream faded away. Kaden's lifeless body crashed down from the roof to hit the floor of an abandoned alleyway beside the cafe. His form was covered in a viscous goo, and his features were melting away.

A moment passed and then two men—identical twins in appearance, who bore a striking resemblance to the late Kaden—walked past the liquefying body. The twins wore clothing that closely resembled Kaden's attire. They didn't give their victim even a passing glance as they disappeared into the night.

First came the dawn, then came the merchants, and finally the customers. The open-air markets of Marrakech were legendary for their color, vibrancy, and chaotic noise. The alien twins made their way down a narrow street, pausing now and then to examine both the usual and unusual things they passed—they were new to this planet—finally arriving at a small curio shop just down the street from the Souk Semmarine, one of the city's greatest, and most famous, marketplaces. Outside the shop, numerous items had been displayed to entice wealthy tourists to inquire within.

A delivery man had just dropped off a pile of overnight

packages near the door. Both aliens seemed confused by the purpose and function of the knick-knacks arrayed outside the shop. One of the twins paused and regarded the dead glass eyes of a stuffed ocelot. "We need to see the Queen," he demanded of the long-dead animal. There was no response from the ocelot.

The other twin looked at his brother like he was an idiot and gestured toward the door to the shop's interior. The first twin nodded and picked up the ocelot to carry with him inside. The second twin stopped him, took the stuffed animal away, and set it back down on its stand outside before they both entered the shop.

The tinkling of tiny brass bells on the door and the dimming of the overhead lights heralded the arrival of the twins into the cool, shady interior of the cluttered and cramped curio shop. The store's lighting flickered at the twins' arrival. The shopkeeper was a cadaverous scarecrow of a man with bushy eyebrows that gave him an owl-like appearance. He looked up from the old book he was reading to regard the twins.

The lights kept dimming and surging as the pair wandered about the shop, touching random items, their expressions filled with amusement at what humans seemed to value.

The shopkeeper glanced up at the shuddering lights and then back to the twins. "Help you guys with something?"

"*Oui*," one of them said, casually plucking up a statue in the shape of a hand as he walked toward the glass counter.

The owner winced a little at the cavalier way the

twin picked up the sculpture and pointed to the statue. "Be careful. You break it, you buy it." The sculpture of the hand flowed and melted in the first twin's hand. It became a vaguely hand-like blade with nasty, serrated edges and a wicked, curved point. The shopkeeper's eyes widened. "Or… I can sell it to you for half price?"

"*Non*," the other twin said, now approaching the counter as well. The shopkeeper took a few steps back, his eyes locked on the blade in his brother's hand.

"Keep it, keep it," he said, trying to keep the panic out of his voice. "On me."

"We need to see the Queen." The first twin placed the blade on the counter.

The shopkeeper relaxed a bit and nodded. With his foot, he pushed a concealed button on the floor, and the wall of shelves behind him folded up and slid away to reveal a thick and regal-looking curtain.

"This way," the shopkeeper told them.

Beyond the curtain was another room full of antiques, ancient and very valuable. Some of the items in the room, the twins recognized as being artifacts from hundreds of different worlds and many different ages. The shopkeeper held the curtain open for the twins and then followed them into the secret room, the shelf wall sliding back into place behind them.

At the center of the room on a pedestal was an ornate chess set. The exquisite stone and minerals used in making the board and the design of the pieces was not of Earth. The dark green and white squares of the board were elevated to different, seemingly random, heights. One end of the board had tall black columns that seemed to represent a "palace" of sorts. As they approached the pedestal, the twins saw the tiny pieces fold and change from their static appearance, and begin to move. The "pieces" were very small alien beings, each wearing armored suits and costumes that represented the parts they played on the board.

"Hey," the shopkeeper called down to the miniature royal court arrayed on the chessboard, "you have customers."

A four-inch-tall "pawn" wearing a conical helmet adorned with red hexagons on a black field, and brandishing a kite shield and an alien blaster weapon in his two tiny arms, looked up at the looming twin giants. The pawn's skin was dark green and scaly, and his features were similar to a tadpole's, with big, amber eyes, no nose, and a tiny slit of a mouth. The pawn moved forward two squares and addressed the twins in a voice much louder than his minuscule size belied. "State your business with the Queen."

"We need someone to die."

One of the twins activated a holographic dossier. The 3-D visage of a lumpy blue humanoid alien appeared in the air over the chessboard. The data stream to the side of the display identified the alien as "Vungus," a member of the Jababian species.

The pawn examined the data and then glanced back toward the black columns. The Queen, the same species as the pawn, though a little taller, appeared among the pillars on the board. She wore a glowing gown of crimson and a high hat-like helmet that served as a crown. She regarded the alien twins looking down on her kingdom and then scanned the information from the hologram that was slowly rotating above the board. She pointedly cleared her throat. The pawn approached his sovereign. The Queen gave a curt shake of her tiny, regal head. The pawn bowed and turned back to the twins.

"As clearly stated in Section 6a of the Treaty of Andromeda Two, we do not kill Jababians or participate in the murdering of." The twins glared at the pawn and his queen as they shut off the hologram. The pawn continued, either oblivious or unconcerned with the pair's obvious displeasure, "Not that we *couldn't* do it. I mean, Jababians are hard to kill, sure, but not impossible. There's a deadly little toxin called Zephos…"

The twins' glares of anger softened, and smiles spread across their faces as they looked down upon the pawn, the Queen, and her tiny court.

9

H parked his Jaguar beside a nondescript three-story corner building that resembled a giant wedge at the edge of a block of offices. He was back in uniform after a quick stop at his apartment but hadn't managed to get in a shave yet. He looked rumpled, and he felt that way, too. The aftereffects of the night's excesses were still hounding him. He was fuzzy-headed, nauseous, and his tongue was thick in his mouth. It felt like the purple goo he had been drinking that night was trying to make a break for it. He was thankful for the gap in his memory, however, especially after he kept finding odd red sucker-mark hickies on himself while he was showering. He tried not to think about it as he walked into the cluttered little typewriter repair shop that made up the ground floor of the building.

Typewriters from every era and in every state of disrepair filled every shelf, table, and nook of the shop.

"I'm in the market for a useless old broken-down

machine," H said, greeting the old man who was studiously at work on an antique Corona. The proprietor wore a visor and a magnifying monocle. He didn't appear to be fazed in the slightest.

"You're *not* going to get a rise out of me, H." The old man didn't even bother to turn his attention away from his work. "It's the Imperial with the red tab. Do try to keep up."

H smiled and searched the room until he found the heavy, antique typewriter. He punched the H key, and the machine made a loud clack. A slim black door near the back of the shop, labeled STAFF ONLY, swung open. "Thanks, Charlie," H said as he walked through the door.

Charlie continued with his repairs.

The door clicked shut behind H.

The main floor of MiB London was its usual, bustling dance of chaos and order. Em and her cube-buddy, Guy, were on their break, waiting in the queue at the tea trolley, which was parked today near the wall of framed photographs commemorating great moments in MiB history. Guy nodded to one prominent black-and-white photo of a group of aliens, all dressed in Earth clothes of the late-1800s era. The alien arrivals all carried bags and trunks and stood proudly, posing for the picture in front of a large room with three great arches, each labeled with a roman numeral.

"If you look closely," Guy said, "you can see my great-mum and dad." Em leaned in closer and saw a young alien couple that bore a strong resemblance to Guy. "The old portal depot, site of the first great alien migration. I actually still have that old suitcase."

Em had stopped listening. A handsome blonde agent had just entered the main floor. He strode confidently across the room. Everyone seemed to know him and paused to greet him. He handled the attention with charm and gravitas. Clearly, he was used to this kind of greeting. His every chiseled feature, his deep blue eyes, and his confident smile were on display as he seemed to Em to be moving in slow motion. Then she realized that he really was moving in slow motion, and everyone else behind him and around him continued to move at a normal pace.

"What's up with that guy?" Em asked. Guy snapped his head around to one of their coworkers, an alien woman named Nerlene. Nerlene's eyes were focused on the slow-moving agent, her hand against her big, pulsating, exposed brain, which to a casual observer looked a lot like a purple beehive hairdo.

"Nerlene," Guy chided, "let him go."

"Sorry," Nerlene said. "He's just so... yummy!" She closed her eyes and removed her hand from the side of her brain. The agent slipped back into normal time, just as he passed Em, Guy, and Nerlene.

"Hey, Nerlene," the agent said, smiling his perfect smile, as he passed. Nerlene wordlessly mouthed "Hi" to his back as he headed toward the property room.

"Who is he?" Em asked.

"H?" Guy said. "Only the best agent in the building. He saved the world once, with nothing but his wits and his Series-7 De-Atomizer."

"Saved the world? From what?" Em asked.

"The Hive." Guy seemed a little uncomfortable even saying the name, as if it might summon the fearsome species.

Em watched H ascending in one of the elevators. An idea was already taking shape in her mind as her eyes followed H inside the promised land of High T's office. She looked back to Guy. "Can you cover my calls for a sec?"

Guy's whole face beamed like a sunrise.

"Are you kidding me? I'd love to! I love the phone!"

Em smiled and began to run off.

"Wait!" called Guy. "Where are you going?"

"To do some homework," she said, disappearing into the crowd.

On the holographic display in High T's office was an unpleasantly graphic scene. The 3-D display showed the body of the dead waiter in the alley in Marrakech. A half-dozen senior MiB agents had gathered in High T's office, clustered around the data display he had pulled up for them to review.

"...a terrible incident in Marrakech," High T was saying. "The North Africa office is investigating." H strode into the office, and High T didn't miss a beat. "And in other business, H has decided to grace us with his presence after all." A murmur of chuckles greeted H from his fellow agents, except for Senior Agent Cee, a serious-faced, dark-haired martinet of a man, whose accusing gaze followed H as he quickly availed himself of some coffee to ward off his hangover. Cee was a senior agent, like H, and fancied himself an assistant to High T. He made no pretenses about wanting High T's job when the station chief finally retired.

"Sir," H said, sipping the coffee as eagerly as he had gulped down the antidote to the viper's venom. "Apologies. I was working late."

"That's funny," Cee said, the contempt dripping in his voice, "so was I. Cleaning up your mess."

H took another sip of his coffee. "It got a lot messier this morning, believe me."

Cee wasn't ready to let it go, not yet. "A totally unsanctioned op requiring two containment units—" he glared at H "—a full neuralyzer squad, and we still haven't found the snake."

"Found the dead Cerulian mob boss, though, didn't you?" H met Cee's eyes. "A huge success, I agree. You're welcome."

"And the names of his suppliers?" Cee asked. "Anything we can use?"

H paused for the span of a breath and then regrouped.

"I prefer to look at this on a macro level." He stepped toward Cee. "You always get bogged down in the details."

Cee snorted. "So, no."

"Did win about twelve hundred quid, though." H glanced over at High T. "Straight to the ace." Another murmur of chuckles drifted about the room.

High T struggled to hide the thin smile that came to his lips. "Which you will, of course, log into evidence."

"Literally just came from logging it," H said.

Cee's expression of despair was lost on both of them. They shared a bond he could never break through. Nothing could.

"One last item." High T addressed the crowd of agents. He tapped a console on his desk, and the holographic display reappeared. This time, the image of a lumpy, tentacular alien hovered in the center of the office. "A member of the Jababian royal family has a layover on his way to Centaurus-A. Vungus the Ugly. Inherited the title. Believe it or not, Vungus here is the looker of the brood." Classified data marked with the MiB seal streamed down like a waterfall on either side of the looming file photo as High T continued. "Jababian society doesn't allow for certain... indiscretions," he said. "In short: he wants to be shown a good time.

"We could say no, but Jababian mining vessels would ground us into galactic dust."

Cee shook his head in disgust. "We used to protect Earth from the scum of the universe. Now, we protect the scum." He looked at H. "Sounds like your cup of tea, H."

"I know Vungus," H replied. "Not really a tea guy. Vodka, tequila, cough syrup. You know, this one time in Bangkok, we woke up handcuffed to a horse—"

"H, shut up," High T said.

"Sorry, sir."

"You're going," High T went on. "In fact, he specifically asked for you."

"Always happy to show Vungus a good time," H said.

"Not *too* good," High T added.

"I'll have him home and tucked in by midnight."

10

The MiB virtual-reality archives were sited in a sparsely furnished room, which consisted of rows of curved, white-and-black VR chairs, suspended off the floor by wires. Em climbed into one of the hanging chairs and slipped a full-immersion VR headset on. One of the many things she had learned about the Men in Black was that they supplemented their operating budget by carefully patenting and introducing alien technology to Earth. Everything from Swedish Fish to 8-track tape players, Hot Pockets to ShamWow cloths were all originally not of this Earth.

Em had recently discovered that an addition to that list was virtual reality. VR was actually the psychic borderland between the species of her own universe and the Ithxxix, a species that only existed in human reality as a thought, an idea. VR had been created to provide an interface, so the tangible species could interact with the Ithxxix and thus they could learn from one another.

It made Em a little sad that her own species had turned such fantastic technology, a technology that bridged the divide between the imaginary and the real, into a way to play better video games.

She spoke out loud, addressing the archive computer. "Search Criteria: Agent H."

A virtual archives room appeared before Em's eyes, endless file cabinets in endless rows. The incident file Em was looking for flew down one of the infinite hallways. The folder hovered before her eyes, and Virtual Em reached out and opened it. Images and text flashed before her eyes from the file: she saw the Eiffel Tower; the old, abandoned portal depot that Guy had shown her in the photograph; and a note: "Belligerent Species: *HIVE*."

"Species review," Em said. "The Hive." Her field of vision was filled by a single, squirming, living tendril, a Hive strand.

"Perhaps the greatest threat to life in the galaxy as we know it," Agent O's voice said in her ears. The first tendril was joined by a second, and they rapidly entwined. *"Trillions of individual carbon-based strands, all connected by a single Hive consciousness."* Another tendril lashed itself to the two, then quickly a fourth, and then, with blinding speed, Em saw a mass of countless swarming, writhing tentacles, filling her field of vision like a horrific living curtain—creating a terrible Hive monster, like the one in Paris.

Em's point of view shifted through the Hive mass to a pastoral, blue-green alien world, a blissful Eden. Em followed the point of view down to a forest clearing.

The lime sky was lit by two distant pinpoints of twin suns. Water burbled from a small fall, and nearby a creature that looked a bit like a terrestrial buffalo grazed peacefully beside a stream that meandered away from the fall. The buffalo started, raising its head, sensing danger. It was suddenly lifted violently into the air by the tendrils of a Hive monster.

"*The Hive are a hyper-aggressive, invasive species,*" Agent O's voice continued as smaller Hive tendrils slid into the buffalo's ears and nose, as the beast groaned and struggled, "*taking over their victims from within. Subsuming them.*"

Em grimaced as the view zoomed out to allow her to see other creatures and even fauna being enveloped and devoured by other Hive monsters. A caption floated in the corner of her perception that said, "Reenactment of Hive Invasion of Pladimer Eight." Her view quickly zoomed out, further and further away from the planet's rapidly covered surface, now a slithering mass, all life choked out.

"*And so they spread,*" the narrator said. "*As much a plague as an army.*"

Em was horrified by the view of the planet that only moments before had been an oasis of life in the cold depths of space. It was now a brown, desiccated husk.

"*They will not stop until all biodiversity in the galaxy is eradicated. Until the many become one.*"

The scene shifted, and Em now had a front row seat for the battle of the Eiffel Tower. High T and Agent H, side by side, blasting slithering Hive tentacles in the old, now abandoned, portal depot. *"We would have succumbed to the Hive threat ourselves, on the night of June 6, 2015,"* Agent O's narration said in her ear, a hint of pride in her voice, *"had it not been for the heroic actions of Agents T and H. Armed with only their wits and their Series-7 De-Atomizers…"*

As the narration went on, Em found herself face to face with an image of Agent H in his prime. There he stood, the hero who had defeated the terrible Hive.

H was snoring deeply, face down on his desk, when Em found him. She wondered exactly how one woke up a hero, especially when the hero in question had a trickle of drool running down from the corner of his mouth.

"Um… hello? Hello?" Nothing except slightly louder snoring. Em took her officially sanctioned MiB tablet and dropped it on H's desk loudly. H snorted and bolted upright.

"Yep, yep." He wiped away the drool. "Totally awake!" He noticed Em standing there. "Just catching up on my daily meditation."

"I keep meaning to try it," Em said. "I read that it dramatically improves mitochondrial energy production."

"Yup, totally." H nodded vigorously. "My mitochondrial energy is through the roof." Em was pretty sure he had no idea what she was talking about. "And it builds up an appetite. Time for lunch. Hungry?"

"It's 9:30," Em said.

H's face beamed.

"Perfect. Tuesday is taco day." H stood and shouted across the bustling sea of agent desks. "Dave, Taco Tuesday! Let's get a lunch order going!"

"It's Wednesday," Em told him.

"Dave, scrap that!" H shouted out to a very confused Dave. H looked back to Em. "Who are you again?"

"Agent Em. I saw you were on the Vungus meet tonight and wanted to offer my assistance."

"Ah," H said. "You were in the briefing?"

"I asked around." Em picked up her tablet. "I'm somewhat of a Jababian wonk. I've compiled a dossier…"

"I love a good dossier," H said, "but I kind of work alone. Everyone knows that. Ask anybody. Ask Dave." H pushed a button on his phone's intercom and leaned toward it. "Hey, Dave—"

Em put her hand out to stop him. "I'll take your word for it."

H let go of the intercom button and looked at her hand on his arm for a second. Em let go and handed H the tablet with her report pulled up. H skimmed the screen, nodding.

"Did you know," she went on, "that Jababians are the wealthiest aliens in their solar system? Per capita."

H chuckled, still reading. "And yet there's not a tab in the universe they won't try and dodge."

"They are also clair-cognizant empaths," Em added. "Which means they can basically read your mind."

"And your cards." H set aside the half-read dossier.

"Yes," Em said, "but they have a tell." H sat up a little in his chair at this. "The subdermal spots on the underside of their arms change color, so you know when they're cheating." It was clear to Em that H hadn't known this. She figured that scored her a few points with the veteran agent. Instead, H handed her tablet back to her.

"Vungus and I once stayed up three days straight, playing poker and drinking White Russians in a flop house in Ho Chi Minh City," he said. "You spend *that* kind of time with somebody, in *that* humidity, there's nothing you don't know. But thank you."

"Okay," Em said, "message understood." She was disappointed and angry. It felt like another door had been slammed in her face, but she stayed cool. "I'll leave you to your meditation."

She moved away, but then the anger jabbed her, and she walked back to H's desk and spoke close to his ear. "You know what your tell is?" she asked. "You snore when you're meditating." And then she marched off.

H watched the probationary agent walk away. He couldn't help but smile. She had nerve, she had style, and no doubt with that Jababian-subdermal-spot thing, she was definitely on the ball. "Actually, on second thoughts," H said to her retreating back, "maybe I could use some backup."

Her back was still turned to him, so H couldn't see it, but an excited smile spread across her face.

11

East London was a curious mixture of loud nightspots, bustling commuters, and silent cobbled yards. H's black Jaguar pulled over and parked on a street made glossy by the lamplight. H and Em climbed out, and H led her down a quiet alley. The only thing in sight was an ancient black cab.

"I was thinking for the op," Em began, "I'll take the perimeter and you can make the approach to Vungus."

"Yeah, sounds good. But here's the thing." H turned to address her. "At this particular club, people just want to do their thing. The humans want to look like aliens; the aliens want to look like humans. It's probably best not to broadcast one's chosen profession. So we may want to loosen up a bit."

H undid his tie. Em, a little uncertain, followed suit, but clearly he wasn't satisfied with the result.

"May I?" he asked.

Em nodded, still a little confused. H adjusted her

collar so it popped up, and turned back her shirtsleeve cuffs. Finally, he tousled her hair with a stylist's flourish. She peered at her reflection in the window glass of the parked cab as she unbuttoned her collar button. She hated to admit it, but she looked good—not MiB-sanctioned, but good.

H nodded in approval at his handiwork. "Great. How'm I?"

Em squinted at him.

"It's a fine line," she said, "between cocky-casual and the saddest man on Earth."

H frowned.

Em buttoned up two of his shirt buttons, stepped back, and took him in. H opened the cab door for Em.

"I thought we were there already?" she said.

"We are." H climbed in and indicated that she should follow him.

The cabbie behind the wheel was chatting rapidly into his phone in a language Em didn't recognize.

"Step on it, would you, Freddie?" H said.

"You got it, H." Freddie didn't miss a beat. The driver stomped the accelerator with his inhuman-looking foot—and Em realized at that moment that the cabbie's human look only appeared above the waist; below, he wasn't hiding his alien shape. The entire back seat of the cab began to descend below the street, an elevator plunging them into the darkness below London. Then the silence gave way to a heavy, throbbing bass. As the seat lowered further, the darkness was punctuated by strobe lights, flashing in time to the relentless beat. In the stuttering light, Em looked over to H, who seemed as cool as ever.

"Entrance for special guests," H explained as their seat stopped and deposited them on a circular dais at one end of a churning, rollicking nightclub. Em's senses were assaulted by the colors, the fashions, and the outrageousness of the clubbers' costumes. There were people in nothing but blacklight body paints, others wearing rubber suits with built-in twelve-inch heels, hair made of multi-colored yarn, or plastic tubing, or feathers. A woman walked by in a fin-de-siècle-style evening gown, covered in chips of silvery glass. She wore round, mirrored sunglasses and a lace parasol. She had fangs and horns—Em wasn't sure if they were implants, or if she was an alien. A man in a green, foam "Gumby" suit swung glowing, hypnotic, LED poi sticks on a platform in the center of the dance floor, jumping and swaying to the music. A blue-skinned woman with braided octopus-like head tentacles danced with abandon in a crowd. Another woman sported ram horns, and a gold-skinned club kid with a vaguely conical head and wide, black visor-like eyes threw shapes.

It was all… like nothing Em had ever experienced in her whole life, even with her fascination with alien life. It was one thing to study every esoteric scrap of data she could get on alien life from supposed "crackpot" books and websites, it was another to actually see them doing Jell-O shots. It had never occurred to her that all those years she was studying and searching for MiB, she could have been missing out on all kinds of experiences she might have really enjoyed, like a club full of music and dancing, and aliens. H, of course, seemed as comfortable and accepted here as he was back at MiB command.

"Busy tonight," H said, surveying the floor like a king looking over his kingdom. "Good-looking crowd." They moved through the dance floor, and everyone parted for H.

"Hey. H!" a Kelortian wearing a huge sultan's turban shouted from across the room. The extraterrestrial, who looked like a classic "Grey" alien, was puffing on a high-tech, hovering hookah.

H waved to the alien. "Yordav! Hey! They let you out! Let's do lunch—I'll email."

H and Em made their way through the crowd to the bar. The bartender, who looked human to Em until he frosted a mug for a beer by simply touching it, slid a tumbler of Glenfiddich scotch, neat, to H as he leaned against the bar. "H, how's it going?" the icy bartender said, his breath white mist.

"Ah, good," H said, sipping the scotch. He glanced to Em, gesturing to the drink. Em shook her head. H turned back to the bartender, "Same old, same old, saving the world, still thinking of redoing my kitchen, like we discussed. Opening it up into one, big entertaining space, maybe."

The bartender nodded vigorously. "You will add *so* much value!"

Em spotted a couple rushing toward them. The woman was pretty and had black hair that fell to her shoulders. She was dressed in a print dress covered in stylized red-lipstick-covered mouths. She appeared to be human to Em. Her partner looked as if he had fallen through a wormhole from the seventies. He wore a club shirt, made of a strange blue and gold metallic fabric that was half unbuttoned, and painfully tight bell-bottom trousers. He was an alien—Em guessed he was probably a Yuliglian due to the brow ridges just above his eyes and along his jaw line. His short hair was disco-permed and he wore a gold chain around his neck, nestled in the hirsute wilderness of his abundant chest hair. The couple were holding hands as they cautiously approached the bar. They saw Em and looked concerned, even frightened. Then they saw H; and both seemed to sag a bit in relief.

H smiled at the arrivals. "Coco, Bjorg."

"Oh, thank God," Bjorg said, a little breathless. "We heard MiB was here."

"We were worried it might be an inspection," Coco added.

H waved dismissively. "Nah, it's just me," he said, ignoring Em completely. "I fancied some nineties classics and an overpriced cocktail. How are the kids?"

"Don't ask," Bjorg said, he and Coco both chuckled. "Jasper just turned six, and he won't stop shedding."

"Six already?" H shook his head. "Where do the years go?"

"H, why didn't you call ahead?" Coco asked. Bjorg snapped his fingers as if he were the one who had asked the question and pointed a hairy index finger at H.

"Vungus. Of course," Bjorg said. He pointed up to the second level at a shadowy VIP section cordoned off with velvet ropes and protected by bodyguards. "He's in his usual spot upstairs." Someone called out to H, and the agent excused himself and headed back into the crowd. Em, Coco, and Bjorg followed him as the music thrummed and lights flashed.

Em watched as H made his meandering way toward the spiral staircase and the upper level. He half-walked, half-danced as he went, stopping to accept fist-bumps and high-fives, hugs, and kisses on the cheek. Em heard one of H's admirers say, "Hey, it's Mr. Series-7!"

For an illegal, off-the-books alien club, everyone seemed to know H and love him here, even though he was MiB. Em didn't know how to feel about any of that. Suddenly, she was back in elementary school, being marginalized by the other kids.

"You must be H's new partner," Coco shouted into Em's ear over the music.

Before Em could respond, Bjorg blurted in her other ear, "He's a legend, but, you know, humble with it. Not at all show-offy, all 'Look at me, I saved the world!'"

"Did he tell you he saved the world?" Coco asked in Em's other ear. H was reaching the velvet rope that blocked off the stairs to the upper level.

"I did hear something, yes," Em replied. They caught up with H and Bjorg unhooked the rope to allow the two agents to ascend the stairs.

"H, if you need anything…" Bjorg said, as H and Em began to climb the stairs.

"Anything at all," Coco added.

The rest of their words were drowned by cheers as the DJ started a new set.

12

Em and H reached the top of the stairwell and the border of the shadowy VIP section. The club bouncers—both of them Rogians, each with four large, heavily-muscled arms—stood aside for H and lifted the velvet rope to allow the two agents through. A pair of burly Jababian bodyguards blocked H and Em for a tense moment and then let them pass. In the shadowy lounge, a gawky, lumpy figure struggled to rise from a booth, a champagne glass in hand: Vungus the Ugly.

"The Vungus among us!" H bellowed.

The figure stepped into the light. He was a Jababian, an exceptionally hard-to-look-at Jababian. He had blue skin and his features had a turtle like quality to them. His wide, squat nose was wedged between his slightly bulging eyes. The mop of curly, brown hair on top of his head may have been a toupee, Em suspected. Vungus the Ugly's clothes barely contained his 300-pound girth—skintight slacks and a gray shirt with a tan sports coat.

The clothes were all expensive, but Vungus made them seem cheap. He completed his Eurotrash look with a thick gold chain around his frog-like neck.

"H-Bomb!" Vungus called in a thick accent. Vungus and H rushed to each other, and for a second, Em thought they might hug, but instead, the two engaged in a complex ritual of bro-hand-and-tentacle-shakes and chest bumps. There may have been some flatulence, too, but Em wasn't sure if that was a biological mishap or language. It all went on seemingly forever. Em checked her watch and sighed.

"V-Dog!" H exclaimed. "You've lost weight. And did you do something with your hair?"

Em could tell Vungus was clearly eating it up like… whatever Jababians ate up. From the looks of Vungus, that could be a wide spectrum of stuff.

"I barely recognize you," H went on, laying it on thick. He turned and gestured to Em. "This is Em. Em, Vungus. Vungus, Em."

"Hell-o Emmm," Vungus said, almost leering at her. Didn't matter if it was the Bronx, or Manhattan, or an alien speakeasy, she had seen that look a hundred different times in a hundred different bars. Em played it all business, giving the slightest of bows to the slumming, intergalactic royal.

"Hello, Your Eminence," Em said, with her best fake-professional smile. "I've heard a lot about you."

"Highly redacted," H added.

Vungus began to make horrible sounds, grunts, groans, and phlegmy wheezes. He stopped, and both

Vungus and H looked at Em. After an awkward pause, H translated, "He says was your mum a Vangorian infidel? Because she must have stolen the Cillenial Vortex ammonites from the Cygnus A stellar stream nebulae and put them in your eyes."

"I'm sorry," Em said, "what?"

"Just a rough translation," H explained. "Probably works better on Jababia, but you know that, since you speak fluent Jababian."

Em attempted to hide her ignorance. "Of course," she said. "I'm trying to find the words to express how incredibly eye-catching Vungus is himself."

H leaned close to Vungus, but Em could still hear clearly what he said. "Em knows everything there is to know about Jababia."

"Well, not everything," Em interjected.

"It's like a fetish," H added.

"Definitely *not* a fetish," Em said.

"An unquenchable thirst," H continued. "It's Jababia this, Jababia that. Jababia, Jababia, Jababia."

"I am parched," Em said, glancing rather desperately toward the bar. She could feel the hole H was digging beneath her feet getting deeper and deeper every time he opened his mouth. Vungus laughed; it sounded like a clogged toilet attempting to flush. Em laughed as well, trying to fake being in on the joke.

H ignored the awkward silence that fell. "I knew you two would hit it off." He gestured out to the dance floor below them. "Have a dance. Em loves to dance." Em felt a little like that time when she was ten and had tried to simulate space flight by riding the Tilt-a-Hurl thirty-seven consecutive times. "I'll get us some drinks." H was already bounding toward a waitress. "You're still a vodka and cranberry guy, right?"

"You know it," Vungus said, sliding back into his booth. He turned his attention back to Em, patting the seat in the booth next to him with a tentacle. "Sit, Em. Sit next to Vungus." His mouth spread, wider than seemed possible, to show her rows of jagged, misshapen, and stained teeth. "I don't bite."

The realization fell on her harder than a mountain could. She was a cauldron of emotions, but bubbling at the top was anger. She kept her cool and raised a single index finger to Vungus.

"Just give me one sec," she said. She rushed to H, who was with the waitress now.

"It's alright; I'll get this," he told Em. "I'll put it on the company card. Little tip: expense everything."

"Oh, thanks!" Em said bitterly as the waitress walked away. "Just one question: Are you pimping me out to an alien?"

"First of all, that is sexist and demeaning." H tried hard to summon some indignation from somewhere and failed. "We're both here because we are charming and fun, and we're making sure V has the night of his life." He looked over Em's shoulder to Vungus, who was alone in the booth. "Coming, buddy!" he shouted. Vungus gave him a thumbs-up. H started back to the table, but Em blocked his way.

"If you want me to be Vungus-bait, tell me the truth

next time. I hate lies," she said.

"Like pretending to be an expert in something you're not?" he retaliated. Em's anger guttered as she realized she was busted. "In case you haven't noticed," H continued, "we're in the lying business."

"Good luck with that," Em said.

H wrestled with words, and Em could see he was trying to explain something real and important to him. He wasn't very good at it.

"Jababians are *prickly*." H smiled and waved to Vungus. "We want them happy. So they don't, you know, destroy our planet and everything on it. *That's* the mission, but if you're not down with the mission—"

"Oh no," Em said, stopping H right there. "I'm down with the mission." She snatched H's champagne glass, put on a fake smile, and awkwardly danced back over to Vungus. H followed her, pulling out his own MiB-sanctioned smile. Neither agent noticed the twins enter the club below. Twins who moved fluidly as one, and bore an uncanny resemblance to a dead waiter in Marrakech.

13

"And so the Cephilax says," H said, finishing his joke with a flourish, "'Not if he touched it first!'" Everyone laughed uproariously. Even the stoic bodyguards hovering over their charge in the VIP booth chuckled, with all the musicality of a bodily function.

"Okay," Em says, wiping a tear of laughter from her eye, "my turn!" She had heard this one at the office and once someone had explained it to her she hadn't been able to stop laughing. She was sure H and Vungus would get it. "You ever hear the one about the hungry Manitabian?" A shocked hush fell on the party. Vungus's face fell; his shoulder-humps slumped. Em looked around, confused.

"Vungus's mother was eaten by a Manitabian," H explained. "It was a horrible tragedy."

Em's heart sank. She turned to Vungus. "I... am sorry for your loss," she said.

"She was a precious flower, taken too soon." H

handed Vungus a glass, and raised his own in a toast. "Here's to her. Namaste." The two clinked glasses and drained their drinks. After a solemn moment, H picked up the champagne and worked at the cork. "So, how long you in town, buddy?"

The bottle opened with a pop, and the lights in the club flickered. At first Em thought it might be part of the light show, but the puzzled expressions on everyone's faces convinced her it wasn't. H was pouring the champagne into glasses, seemingly oblivious to the phenomenon.

"Vungus go home tomorrow," the Jababian said.

"Tomorrow?" H remarked. "You did a three-year hyper-sleep all the way from the Horse Head Nebula for one night out? We better make it a good one." He handed Vungus some champagne and took a deep gulp from his own glass as well.

"Came to talk, H." All the humor and playfulness had vanished from Vungus's voice and demeanor. "We need to speak."

The music shifted and flowed as a new song began— "Break Ya Neck" by Busta Rhymes—and the dancers on the floor forgot their anxiety about the flickering lights.

"Come on!" H cajoled Vungus. "You're here for one night. I can't go without seeing the V-man bust a move. You're a hip-hop guy, right?"

Em watched H drag Vungus out onto the dance floor, wondering if she should stop them. They were supposed to be here to show Vungus a good time, after all—but surely two agents of MiB should also be keeping an eye out for trouble if their guest was so important. Her gaze fell on the dancers. There were two identical twins down there who looked like they'd never seen a dance floor before. The twins had spotted H and Vungus, and for a moment she was worried that they were paying too much attention—but just as she was about to stand up, they turned away. And after all, H and Vungus, together, were the kind to command a lot of attention.

She let her gaze stray away from her charges again. She'd been wrong about the twins' discomfort on the dance floor. After a moment they began to move like the other dancers... Were they *mimicking* the moves of the dancers around them? As she watched, they began to combine the moves of different dancers, and then create moves she'd never seen before. Several other dancers stopped to circle them and clap as their moves became more intricate, more complex, and faster, much faster.

The twins were beginning to glow with an aura of some strange energy. The dance-floor fog swirled around their legs, reflecting the eerie light they were shedding. And H didn't seem to have noticed any of this—his attention seemed to be fully on an attractive girl he'd spotted. Vungus didn't look happy about that. Em stood up. If H couldn't spot the danger they were in, then she'd been right to come here with him. She began to dance her way awkwardly across the floor toward H and Vungus.

H was summoning his inner John Travolta, lost in the rapture of the thunderous waves of music, throwing his best moves. He wore a grimace of pleasure as he danced, commonly referred to as "white man's overbite." It was often credited with being a foolproof form of birth control and with frightening small children. He noticed that Vungus was dancing rather hesitantly, as if going through the motions. Something was troubling him.

Vungus caught H's glance and danced closer. "H, Vungus need to tell you something," he said.

"If it's about that night in Beirut," H shouted over the music, "I deleted the photos. Pinky swear."

He was aware of Em struggling to get closer to H and Vungus, kinda-dancing her way through the ever-shifting maze of the dance floor. She looked almost as if she was trying not to draw attention or spoil the party—weird attitude for a club, he thought.

"H," Em called. "Twelve o'clock."

"Already?" H shouted, still dancing—showing her how it was done. "The night is still young!" H spun toward Vungus, who was no longer even bothering to dance. "Not feeling it? Shall I get them to play something with a bit more of a housey vibe?"

Vungus reached out with one of his tentacles and wrapped it around H's forearm. "It's *serious*. You're the only one Vungus trust—"

Vungus stopped suddenly, looking down at his tentacle. Sparkles of pale light emanated from it where it touched H. This was part of the Jababian clair-cognizant empathy, how they "read" people's intentions and true motives. H didn't really mind Vungus doing it—for a Jababian, it was as much a form of communication as talking or sharing a glance.

But Vungus gasped and quickly released H as if he had just touched a hot stove.

"*What happened to you?*" Vungus asked. He sounded almost afraid.

Billie Ellish's remix of "MyBoi-TroyBoi" began to play across the club. The dance-floor lights dropped to a deep blue.

H blinked. "What do you mean?" On some level that H couldn't reach or even articulate, he understood, but on the surface, which is where he swam these days, he didn't comprehend, and didn't want to.

Em had watched this unfold with barely concealed impatience, aware that the twins were on the move, no longer hiding their interest in Vungus. Now she caught movement from her targets. One of the dancing twins opened his seemingly empty palm, holding it out the way you might if you were blowing someone a kiss. The other twin made a gesture, or a dance move—she couldn't be sure—as if he were winding up the way an anime super hero might to release a planet-destroying energy blast. Em tried to reach Vungus, but H was in her way. The second twin completed his gesture, and Vungus slapped at his neck, as if swatting a bug.

Vungus's eyes became unfocused and he stumbled into H's chest, staring at his old friend as if he didn't know him.

"Hey buddy, you don't look so good," H said.

"Vungus feel not well," he mumbled.

Em tried to spot the twins, but they had gone.

"Those vodka cranberries pack a punch," H said, trying to joke, but Em saw the concern in his eyes and something else she couldn't define. "We should get him home." H looked to Vungus's bodyguards. "Get his car."

As Em and H got Vungus to his feet, pulling him between them toward the exit, Em glanced over to the other agent. "Did you see that? Those guys, they…"

The music rose again, and drowned out her words.

Vungus's armored SUV, provided by MiB, screeched up to the curb outside the club, one of Vungus's bodyguards behind the wheel. H and Em slid the groaning Jababian into the back seat, aided by his other guard.

"Sleep it off, buddy," H said to Vungus through the open door. "Remember to hydrate." He slammed the door and the car screeched away down the dark street.

Em and H walked down the street in the wake of the Jababians' car, headed toward H's Jag.

"He doesn't look too good," Em said. "I mean, he didn't look good before, but…" She let her voice trail off for a moment. "I think something happened in there, H. Shouldn't we call this in?" The streetlight above them started to flicker.

"We're fine," H told her. "Trust me, as soon as you call it in the paperwork becomes a nightmare. I've seen Vungus way worse off—"

Suddenly there was a clap of thunder from the direction the departing car had taken. Vungus's car flew through the air, flipping as it tumbled, and slammed into the building, embedding itself upside down in the wall.

"What the...?" H murmured.

It wasn't that the car had crashed into the wall of the building, but more like it had phased through the brick and steel, before becoming solid again. The agents sprinted toward Vungus's car.

Just past the alleyway where H's Jag was waiting for them, the street looked like it had been through a miniature earthquake. Debris from crumbling streets and buildings and overturned and crushed cars were everywhere. Several car alarms whined, and thick dust swirled in the debris. The dust began to settle and clear around Vungus's upside-down car. They stopped running as they approached it, their Series-4 De-Atomizers drawn.

Walking out of the cloud on the other side of the car were the twins from the club. They made for the car—there was no question, now, what their target was.

"MiB! Freeze!" H shouted.

The twins paused and looked at each other quizzically.

"On the ground!" Em commanded, steel in her voice. "Palms down, now!"

At the same instant, H barked out, "Hands up, now!"

The twins were confused. The agents gave each other a similar look and then tried again.

"Hands up!" Em said.

"Palms down!" H shouted. He kept his eyes on the twins, and so did Em. "Which one are we going for?" he said to her. "I mean, either way is fine, but down the line we should probably come up with a system. You want 'palms down'?"

Em gave a thoughtful nod.

"Thank you," she said. "I appreciate the gesture."

"Palms down!" both agents said in unison. The twins complied, lying down on the cracked pavement, palms down. The agents cautiously approached the twins.

Neither H nor Em spotted the twins' hands glowing dimly as they touched the ground. The street near their fingers began to liquefy and ripple. The twins, in unison, slammed their hands down on the pavement, and kipped up to an upright position. A massive wave of liquefied concrete rushed toward H and Em. The agents spun to run from the tsunami barreling down on them. The wave crashed into them, feeling very solid, and sending cars parked on the curbs flying, and hydrants cracking and erupting up and down the street. H and Em crashed to the ground, some twenty feet away, near H's Jag, their guns clattering into the darkness.

The twins continued their advance toward Vungus's car. H and Em struggled back to their feet, covered in bruises, cuts, and dust.

"We should probably have gone with 'hands up,'" H said, sprinting to his Jag.

He reached the car door handle. He lifted it to the open position and then tugged out. A squat, ugly, chromed MiB pistol with a short, wide barrel pulled free, the door handle acting as the gun's grip. H thumbed the switch near the trigger, and the gun thrummed to life. He braced himself and opened fire on the twins as Em reached the Jag. "Petrol cap!" he shouted at her.

Em tugged on the cap and a cylindrical, long-barreled pistol slid free of the Jag, the grip and trigger unfolding as it was freed. Em flipped the gun's power switch, and blue energy flared to life along the silver barrel. She stood, joining H in opening up on the twins.

The twins tumbled and flipped, avoiding the agents' fire with an unearthly grace. Beams and bolts of energy from the MiB guns exploded all around them. One of the twins backflipped, raising a column of molten stone into the air where his feet had been a second ago. The other slid into the base of the pillar, sending it flying like a giant missile of lava toward the agents. They dived for cover behind the Jag an instant before the column struck the windscreen. Red-hot fragments of rock sprayed everywhere. The Jag crumpled and groaned, its windscreen shattered as it was knocked backward by the force of the projectile. The agents crashed to the ground as they were slammed back with the car.

H, teeth gritted, got to his feet again, recovering his weapon. "Well, now I'm pissed off," he said. Em scrambled back up, grabbed her own gun, and returned fire. One of the twins pushed his hand into the metal of the wrecked car's door. It rippled and flowed around him, reshaping, until he tore the transmuted door free, now formed into a shield. The bullets from H's and Em's guns ricocheted off the door shield, which seemed to have become something much stronger than steel in the transformation.

"We need more firepower," H shouted to Em over the whoosh and roar of the guns. "Side-view mirror!"

As H continued to lay down fire, pinning the twins for a moment behind their shield, Em examined the door mirror. She twisted it so the mirror was facing skyward and was rewarded with an electronic hum. A panel slid up over the door's window that held four large, powerful-looking MiB handguns.

"That," Em said, smiling. "I like that."

She pulled one of the pistols free of its case and fired on the twins' car-door shield. The shield shattered with a powerful explosion, exposing the twins. H took the shot the opening gave him, blasting a huge hole in one of the twins' chests. Super-heated particles of gas spewed out of his back like a tiny nebula. He took another blast in the shoulder, which evaporated in a spray of plasma-vaporizing matter. The wounded twin looked across in time to see a round from Em's gun hit his brother, whose face and neck exploded into particles as the spray of ionized energy tore into him.

For a moment, time seemed to hold its breath; then it seemed to flip into reverse. The exploding particles fell back into the twins, slipped back into place like a cracked vase being fitted back together. H and Em, still firing their weapons, looked on in disbelief as the twins reformed and repaired themselves before their eyes. The twins, now obviously in contempt of the agents' weapons, shredded the remainder of their shield and strode again toward their target, Vungus's car.

H kept firing, but now he knew each hit was nothing more than a distraction to the twins.

"Driver's side bumper!" he shouted to Em.

Em dashed over and tugged and pulled to no avail on the left rear bumper. She tugged with all her might and fell onto her backside. H glanced over long enough to see.

"The *English* driver's side!" he said.

Em grabbed the Jag's right rear bumper and twisted. A compartment broke open around the bumper, and Em withdrew a large, chrome MiB rifle. H smacked the car's rear panel as he tossed aside the ineffective snub-nosed pistol. The panel slid away to reveal a big MiB auto-blaster. H knelt by the rear tire. With a click and a twist of the hubcap, he withdrew a circular drum magazine. He slapped it onto the auto-blaster.

Both agents stood, side by side, and opened fire again on the twins. The blasts from the larger weapons tore into the aliens, pinning them down and ripping their bodies apart almost faster than they could reform them. The twins began trading particles between themselves, reforming arms, legs, and heads as they were blasted apart again and again.

One of the twins, looking angry now, knelt and touched the cracked and crumbling pavement. A seething, molten blade the size of a large tree erupted from the ground. He gestured, and the blade snapped free and flew toward his brother, who caught it and hurled it straight at the agents. Em and H dived for cover, but H's beleaguered Jag was nearly sliced in two by the red-hot blade. The twins didn't let up. They telekinetically launched an endless barrage of pieces of destroyed cars, hunks of concrete, and any other street debris they could assault H and Em with. The agents hunkered down behind the crumpled remains of the Jag.

In the maelstrom, Em spotted Vungus struggling from his overturned car. He looked even sicker than he had when they had deposited him in the back seat. He saw Em and reached out to her across the chaotic battlefield, "Em... Em..."

"Go on," H shouted, firing the big auto-blaster, "I'll cover you!"

Em dashed across the fractured landscape that only a few minutes ago been a quiet London street. She stumbled a few times, but somehow kept her feet. The hail of debris was all around her, but H was laying down withering blaster fire that was keeping the twins too busy to target her directly. She reached Vungus's side, firing a few shots from her own weapon and knocking one of the twins off his feet.

Vungus hacked up a glob of dark ooze that stained his lips. His color was all wrong, or at least she thought it was, for a healthy Jababian. Em had no idea what she was supposed to do now. "H," she called, "a little help here?"

Vungus groaned and shook his head. "No! Not H." Each breath he took seemed to hurt him. "He's... changed. I could feel it."

Em glanced over to H, who was blasting away at the twins, his eyes bright with excitement, not fear, as deadly debris hurled past him. H looked at Em in response to her call, blinking as if he were coming out of a trance.

H shouted something at her over the scream of blaster fire and the fury of the telekinetic storm the twins had summoned, but Em couldn't hear what he was trying to tell her.

Vungus slid a tentacle around Em's forearm. It began to sparkle as it had done when he had touched H. "I have to know… if I can trust *you*," he wheezed.

Em stared at the tentacle on her arm, almost holding her breath. He was *reading* her. She couldn't quite believe it.

"You… don't trust *anybody*…" Vungus seemed sad at the revelation. "You never have." Em felt like the hurricane of concrete and brick had fallen on her. The realization stung, but she also knew it was true. Since that night so long ago, when the world became a lie that everyone seemed to be telling, she hadn't trusted anyone. She still didn't.

Vungus's tentacle tightened on her forearm as he gasped in pain. "*Don't!*" he hissed. "Something's wrong in Men in Black."

With one of his hands, Vungus placed a small, rectangular box in Em's palm. Em grasped it. It looked like an alien version of an old Japanese puzzle box, covered in complex geometric patterns on its tiled surfaces. Vungus pulled himself closer to her ear. "Hide this." He struggled with each word.

"Vungus, what is this?" Em asked.

"*Trust no one, Agent Em.*" Vungus whispered. He made a few horrible grunting sounds, as he fought and lost his battle for another breath. Vungus lay dead on the ground. In shock, Em looked again at the box in her hand, and then felt the presence of other eyes on her. The twins were watching her—or, more accurately, they had locked on to the box. It was what they had come to Earth for.

They moved as one toward Em. She suddenly realized that H's suppressing fire had stopped. She fumbled for her own pistol, the one she had set down when she had been ministering to Vungus. She brought the gun up, knowing already that its firepower wouldn't be strong enough to stop the twins, to protect the box.

Standing by the trunk of the Jag, H now wielded a chrome, high-tech rocket launcher resting on one of his shoulders. H, from behind the targeting reticle, smiled at the twins as he fired the rocket. The explosion rocked the entire block. The force of the blast sent the twins flying halfway down the street. And suddenly there was a screech of tires and the roar of engines, and a swarm of MiB Lexus saloons came barreling around the corner and encircled them. Heavily armed agents jumped out of the vehicles. The twins exchanged a glance, speaking without words.

One twin stepped into the other, leaving a single figure. The lone figure glowed and scattered into a stream of tiny, staticky particles that disappeared into the air.

H dropped the launcher and rushed to Vungus's side. Em saw something cross H's face that she hadn't seen since meeting the cocky, charming agent—shock, grief, and sadness. H knelt beside her and gently closed his friend's eyes.

Em slipped the puzzle box Vungus had given her in her jacket pocket surreptitiously, remembering the dead alien's final words as she did.

14

If one word described Agent Cee's existence, it would be *order*. Cee awoke the same time every day; ate breakfast, lunch, and dinner the same time daily. He had the same thing for tea every day without fail. So when Cee's communicator buzzed several hours after his appointed bedtime, Cee's eyes popped wide open, and he snarled as he reached for the phone, already knowing the author of this disruption: H.

To Cee's mind, Agent H was a force of chaos. He should have been neuralyzed a long time ago and dumped back into that grubby little seaside town High T had found him in. It wasn't that H was an incompetent agent in the field, in fact, he seemed to thrive under pressure and in the presence of real danger. No, H's problem was he didn't think the rules applied to him, and in Cee's book, the rules applied to *everyone*, even heroes who had saved the world with only their wits and their Series-7 De-Atomizers. But H had a powerful ally in his former partner, High T. High T had personally selected Cee for MiB service as well, and Cee had enormous respect for his boss. High T's only flaw, in Cee's estimation, was his friendship with H. As long as High T put up with H's nonsense, there was little Cee could do about him, other than file the proper complaint forms and wait for the big goon to bollocks it up enough that even High T would see he was a liability to the service.

Exactly twenty minutes after receiving the phone call, Cee was at the crime scene, just as he had said he would be. MiB agents, in coveralls that announced they were with Southern Electric, were placing long, slender, metallic posts along the perimeter of the block. The street looked completely normal and quiet except for the "utility workers" and their trucks.

Cee parked his Lexus and strode across the street, ignoring the greetings of the agents. He walked between two of the poles, and reality shimmered and rippled. Cee now stood in the middle of utter chaos and destruction. The street had massive chunks torn out of it. In other places, the asphalt was frozen in rising waves and bizarre spirals. Cars along the street were crumpled and scored with energy weapons fire. Others were melted, overturned, or crushed. MiB agents were everywhere, scanning the debris with spectral analyzers. Cee looked up. An expensive car was partly embedded, upside down, in a brick building. Cee touched his temples, the freight train of an H-level headache already slamming into his brain.

His righteous anger overcame the throb in his

temples, and he scanned the scene for the source of his pain. Instead, he found the probationer, the American, Agent M. Cee strode up to her as she was circling one of the frozen splashes of asphalt, examining it in wonder. "Report," Cee snapped. Em was still in awe of what she was looking at, now that she had caught her breath.

"Remarkable," Em said to Cee, shaking her head. "They did this with their bare hands—turned solid to liquid and then back again. In thermodynamic systems, it's called 'phase transition.'"

Cee gave the crest a cursory inspection and then withdrew a fresh pair of latex gloves from his jacket pocket and put them on. He never left home without a good supply of latex gloves. He ran a gloved finger over the impromptu street sculpture. H had joined them, he noticed.

"Interesting." Cee was still examining the anomaly. He addressed H without looking at him or Em. "And what is she doing here?"

"'She' is walking you through the crime scene," Em said.

"Probationary agents aren't rated for field work—" Cee snapped off his rubber gloves and folded them precisely "—so she is not here at all."

"Well, clearly," H began, "she is here. I can see her." He poked Em, and she slapped his hand away. "I can touch her—"

"Yeah, she feels that," Em interrupted, "and she can speak for herself, thanks."

Cee turned to face H, having returned his perfectly

folded gloves to his coat pocket. "You had one job. To show some reptilian sleazeball a good time."

"He wasn't a 'reptilian sleazeball,'" H said, his jaw tight. "He was my friend."

"Who's now *dead*," Cee didn't bother to hide his smugness, "because of you."

"You need to watch what you're saying." H took a step toward Cee.

"Or what? We won't be friends?" Cee sneered. "Because being your 'buddy' didn't turn out so well for that guy." He nodded in the direction of Vungus's sheet-covered body.

H grabbed the smaller agent by the lapels and smashed him against the car.

Cee leaned in, closer to H's face. "Oh, I'm sorry, did I touch a nerve?" H reared back to punch Cee, but stopped himself. He let the senior agent go and turned away. Cee smoothed his jacket and looked to Em. "You were the last one with him. Did he say anything that would explain why he was killed? Anything at all?"

Em's hand dropped into her pocket where the hidden puzzle box resided. She recalled Vungus's final words and removed her hand, empty. She shook her head. "No, nothing."

Cee's scowl slipped away, and he found he was smiling.

"So, a high-ranking member of the Jababian royal family dies on your watch, murdered by assailants you can't identify, for reasons you can't begin to fathom." He turned to H, and the gruesome smile broadened. "Even the old man can't get you out of this one."

15

Em had never been to High T's office before, but it reflected what she knew of the London station chief: it was tasteful, elegant, and understated. While it shared the seventies futurist look of O's office in New York, High T had included touches like antiques in the corners and numerous oil paintings. High T was on the phone with the Jababian ambassador, explaining Vungus's fate. High T had a pained expression on his face, but his voice remained strong and serene.

"Understood," High T said, nodding.

Em examined the paintings more closely. She had thought they were classical at first, but they were actually scenes of moments in the history of the Men in Black. Em paused at a painting of a young MiB agent and an older agent battling a terrifying, gigantic bug on the grounds of the 1962 New York World's Fair. But another painting drew her attention: a heroically styled depiction of High T and H battling the Hive monster on the Eiffel Tower. Underneath, a small plate under the painting read: "…armed with only their wits and their Series-7 De-Atomizers…"

Em looked from the square-jawed, clear-eyed hero in the painting to the rumpled, hung-over reality of H sitting in the chair in front of High T's desk.

H was smiling as he watched his friend, former partner, and boss twist on the phone call. Em could hear the snarling, spitting language of the ambassador through the earpiece from several feet away. H gave High T a thumbs-up. The senior agent's frown deepened, and he spun his chair toward the window overlooking the MiB headquarters floor, away from H.

"I assure you, we will deal with this in the strongest possible terms," High T said.

That didn't sound good. Em caught H's eye, not trying to hide her concern. H waved a hand dismissively. He stood and walked over to Em, who still stood in front of the painting of H and High T.

"We'll be fine," H confided in a low voice. "He has to do the dance for the sake of diplomatic relations, but he'll probably just send them a fruit basket, and it will all blow over."

High T spun his chair around and hung up the phone. He did not look happy. "The Jababians want your heads… quite literally. Two heads sent by diplomatic pouch."

Em stayed calm, but her legs felt a little wobbly under her. He was serious. "What did you tell them?"

"He told them MiB aren't barbarians." H's usual swagger was back in full force. "We're not in the business of brutally sacrificing our own agents, right?" High T said nothing; he was seething. The look on High T's face finally began to sink in for H. "*Right?*" he asked again, not quite so confidently.

High T looked past H as Cee entered the office. Cee gave Em and H a dismissive glance and handed an MiB tablet to High T. "The forensics report you ordered." The tablet's screen announced it was "Eyes only, High T." High T held the tablet up to eye level, and the screen confirmed his unique retinal pattern and opened Cee's report. High T scanned it quickly, shaking his head several times.

"Well, this is troubling," he said, "very troubling." He lowered the tablet and made a grab-and-pull gesture in front of the screen. He followed it with a toss gesture to the holographic data column. Three-dimensional images of the twins appeared in the room, as well as coiled representations of spiraled DNA, with specific markers flashing red. "These are our suspects. A species called 'Dyadnum.' From a binary star system in the constellation Draco."

High T and H traded looks. H stepped forward and tapped a portion of the report hologram. A star chart appeared, filling a large section of the room. "Draco," H said, adjusting the focus of the map to zoom in on a twin star system in a distant constellation, "that's Hive territory. The entire sector fell years ago." The star map was covered in red dots representing territory held by the Hive.

"And as we all know, the Hive doesn't just destroy their enemies," High T said, grimly. "They subsume them, take them over from within." High T diminished the star map and enlarged the alien DNA sequences. Green indicator tags showed where the twins' DNA was squirming, shifting. "The Dyads' DNA. Riddled with Hive mutations."

"Meaning, whoever these two were," H said, "they're part of the Hive, now."

Em recalled the VR files on the Hive, and she had a sudden and terrible image flash through her mind: all of New York, all of London, all of the planet, consumed and enslaved by the relentless Hive. She pushed the thought out of her mind and tried to focus on the briefing.

"Yes," High T agreed, "but why would the Hive send them all this way to kill a Jababian royal?" He turned to H. "You knew Vungus better than anyone. Did he indicate why he was here? Did he want something from us?"

Em almost spoke up to tell High T about the puzzle box, but then Vungus's warning came back to her. *Something is wrong in MiB... Trust no one, Agent Em.* She stayed quiet.

"Something was wrong." H looked thoughtful. "He wanted to tell me, but he was distracted."

"He was distracted?" Cee muttered. "Or were you?" Cee stepped between the other two men. "Sir, if I may, this whole thing is a debacle, a farrago. A failure of this magnitude demands invocation of Article 13."

"Don't be a dick," H said. "Who says *farrago*?"

"Yeah," Em said, "don't—" She snapped her gaze to H. "What's Article 13?"

Cee drew back his jacket. On his belt he had a

little holster for his neuralyzer. It reminded Em of the old professors at college who carried their cell phones on their hips, next to their slide rules. "Immediate termination and neuralyzation, in that order!" the senior agent declared, whipping the silver wand out of the holster and brandishing it.

"Again?" Em stared in astonishment at all the senior MiB agents around her. "That's you people's answer for everything!"

"Sir," H said to High T, "you can't."

"Give me one good reason why not." High T's tone was grim.

Em saw the look on H's face. The words struck him like a punch. The reality of what might come to be in the next few moments seemed to suddenly fall on the other agent. Em felt sorry for H, in spite of herself and the trouble he'd brought upon her. He'd lost Vungus, and now his best friend was ready to fire him and make him an outcast. H was at a loss for words, for once, so Em decided she needed to step in.

"Because," she blurted out, "if you erase us, you'll never learn the *truth*."

"Can we just do this?" Cee implored his boss, still waving the neuralyzer. "They're obviously stalling."

"Hold on a minute," High T raised a palm to Cee. He looked at Em, and she could feel him sizing her up. "Go ahead, Em. Explain yourself."

"Well, sir, you see… if you think about it… *really* think about it," Em was tap dancing in a minefield. She didn't want to give up Vungus's final words or the box, not until she knew who she could actually trust in MiB. Wait, that was it! Finally, with some firm footing under her again, Em declared, "Vungus! How many people really knew he was here, on Earth?"

"The people in this room," High T said, "perhaps a dozen high-level agents, and Vungus himself."

"Right." Em nodded. "Exactly."

An awkward silence followed. H, of course, decided to fill it. "Keep going, Em," H said, "don't hold back. Tell him."

"I really think *you* should take it from here." Em gave H a significant glance to show that she needed some backup. "You have seniority."

"No, please," H said, completely oblivious to her silent plea. "You've got the ball; run with it." Em gave H a glare for an instant that fully articulated how much she wanted to knock the wits out of his head in that moment using his very own Series-7 De-Atomizer.

Em took a deep breath and continued. "Well, sir," she tried, "if those were the only people who knew where Vungus would be, and we assume it wasn't Vungus who leaked his own location to the killers, then... doesn't that mean it was, you know, someone... *inside* MiB?"

Cee, lost in neuralyzer revenge fantasies, suddenly looked up sharply. Em saw the lights come on in H's eyes as he *finally* realized the brilliance of what she had proposed. As per her previous experiences with H, his mouth went into gear scant seconds after his brain.

"Exactly," H began, "I put it to you, there is a *mole*, sir. Inside these very walls."

"Ridiculous." Cee was glaring at H again. "In all these years, we've never had so much as a leak."

"Sounds like something a mole would say," H said, nodding to High T.

"Don't be absurd," Cee said, appealing to High T.

"Classic mole talk."

"Mole 101," Em joined in.

"*Enough*," High T rumbled. He seemed to notice Cee's neuralyzer for the first time. "Put that away." Deflated, Cee holstered the memory-wiping tool.

High T walked over to the glass wall of his office, gazing down on all his agents and staff and the constant stream of aliens coming to and leaving Earth. Em thought she saw the senior agent slump a bit, but only for a moment, and then his impeccable posture returned. He spoke to the three agents at his back, still watching the bustling floor of MiB HQ. "If we've been compromised, it puts every citizen of this planet, both human and alien, at risk.

"Cee, track down these killers. Find the killers, we find the mole." High T paused for a moment, still facing the window. "Em, it appears you are as sharp as advertised. Work the case with Cee."

Relief flooded through her—she'd avoided the neuralyzer for the third time in her life. H was still standing before High T's desk, looking a lot like a lost puppy. Cee gestured impatiently for her to follow him, and he strode from the office. Em gave H a brief glance and then followed Cee out.

* * *

High T turned from the window and resumed his seat at his desk, ignoring H.

H stood silently for a few moments. Finally, he spoke. "Good move, sir. I assume you'll want me overseeing the case. A sort of supervisory role—senior management, as it were, right?" H said, fishing for any response.

High T sighed and lowered his pen, looking up at H. "I'm finished covering for you, H."

"But… you need me on this," H said. "I've dealt with the Hive before, sir, remember? With nothing but my wits and my Series-7—"

"No." High T's voice was cold. He pointed to the painting of their battle in Paris on the wall. "*He* dealt with the Hive before, and I don't know where the hell *he's* gone." High T walked around his desk to face his old partner. "I actually used to think you could lead this place. I was wrong about you. We're done here. That's an order."

H stood silently. The words, from this man—one of the finest men H had ever known—cut him deeply. He took a deep breath and stood his ground. "You weren't wrong about me, sir. You saw something in me once. It's still there. Give me a chance. I will fix this, T, I promise you."

High T saw a gleam of something in H's eye, something he hadn't seen in years, something he recalled always being able to count on. The guy in the painting? Maybe.

16

"It's not just a blade," Em said, examining the assassination weapon a bit closer on the computer monitor. The tiny weapon was on an elevated stage under the brightly lit ring of a magnification lens mounted on a rolling cart beside Cee's desk. The cart had been delivered and hooked up to Cee's computer by the two MiB forensic techs, who now stood by for orders from the senior agent and the probationary agent. "It looks like it carried some sort of poison."

On Cee's monitor there was a high-resolution magnified image of an intricate and wickedly curved and serrated blade. There did seem to be a tiny trace of a pale green substance on the tip of the blade.

Cee turned to the two MiB techs. "I want you to—"

The image on the screen blurred and was gone, leaving only the white light of the illuminated microscope stage.

H held the tiny weapon between his thumb and forefinger. "Sorry, mate, change of plans. High T decided he wants me to run point on this."

"Wait, what?" Cee spluttered. "I don't believe you!"

H was already making his way around the lab, and back toward the doors.

"Listen, I don't like it any better than you, but he kept saying something about 'relying on me,' 'needing our top agent,' that sort of thing. I don't make the rules, I just apply them. Take it up with him."

Cee's face grew purple, his lips, white. Before he could speak or explode, H turned to Em. She was watching him with an amused look on her face and her arms crossed. "And Em, he's keen for you to shadow me on this. 'Learn from the best,' he said," H parroted, trying to do his best High T impersonation.

H walked out the door, the tiny dagger in hand and a spring in his step. Cee was speechless. Em gave him a "What can you do?" shrug and darted out after H.

The two techs were silent in the wake of H and Em's departure. They looked at each other and then as quietly as possible shuffled away from Cee, who was sitting at his desk, speechless. Cee looked at the blank magnification screen and felt a familiar ice pick of pain sink into his skull.

Em fell into step beside H, as they navigated the bustling corridor. "Okay," she began, "and what's the *actual* truth?"

"You tell me," H said, "because for someone who hates lying, that was incredible. God, it was electric, wasn't it? The way we played off each other up there.

Did you feel it? 'A mole inside MiB...' Genius."

"I wasn't lying," Em said. "Think about it. It would explain a lot."

"The only mole around here is Hank in HR." H slowed as they passed a cubicle. Em glanced over to see an alien man-mole in a suit and tie reviewing a pile of paperwork at his desk.

The corridor opened into the busy mezzanine. H strode through the crowd confidently. Agents and aliens made way for him. "What do you have so far?" H asked her, holding up the tiny knife.

"I was about to run a molecular deconstruction on the substance," Em said, "and cross-reference it with all known toxins."

"Good idea." H put the tiny murder weapon to his nose and sniffed it. Em lunged at H to stop him. H's eyes popped open wide. "Holy fu—" He pulled the knife back away from his face. "I know what *that* is!"

"What are you doing?" Em hissed. "*That* killed a 300-pound Jababian!"

H handed the tiny dagger to Em, shook his head to clear it, and headed toward the stairs that led to the MiB subway station. "It's Zephos, pure grade. The wrong amount will kill you instantly, the right amount will keep you dancing, shirtless, on a nightclub table in Monaco for seventeen hours." He saw the expression on her face and quickly added, "Apparently. There's only one place in the world where they know how to mix it."

H descended the stairs while Em stood there looking at him, shaking her head. Was he an ignorant lunk-head?

All muscle and charm, no brains? He could work a room, work people, the way Em could juggle calculations in her head. It was almost as if something in H had been put to sleep, but now it seemed like maybe it was starting to wake up.

"Well, come on," H's voice echoed. The top of his head vanished from sight as he descended the staircase. "The world's not going to save itself."

For the first time since they met, Em saw the agent who had saved the world emerge, and she followed him down into the underground.

17

Beneath the azure crystal waters of the Mediterranean, a blur shot along inside a nearly invisible tube. Inside the MiB hyperloop car, Em studied the puzzle box Vungus had given her. So far it had defeated all her attempts to open it. H was across from her and soundly asleep, out like a light, the sports pages of *The Times* resting on his chest. The other passengers in the car were agents like them and a few others, including an alien in blue-and-yellow plaid PJs that looked a little like a clown fish with curled horns, who was sitting beside her, and an alien in a bright yellow sports coat with an elongated head crowned with sharp barbs and jutting eyes like a chameleon, who was a few seats over from H.

She felt bad for lying to H again, especially as he'd rumbled her so easily over the whole "claiming to be a Jababian wonk" thing, but Vungus's last words had been emphatic—*Trust no one, Agent Em.* With what she had seen at MiB London so far, the war between H and

Cee, the willingness of High T to let H slide on so many potentially dangerous and compromising procedural gaffs, she was starting to see why O had sent her... Unless O's plan had been just to shuffle her off from the New York office and make her another station's problem. That was the problem with not trusting anyone: you could come up with sinister motives for everyone.

Em slid the flat panels of the box back and forth, looking for patterns in the geometric designs or in the sequences of the moving pieces. She had beat the Rubik's Cube in eight seconds when she was eleven. She had done mathematical puzzles in her head to help her sleep at night for as long as she could remember. But with the alien box, so far, no luck.

She put the alien puzzle back in her pocket and regarded the sleeping H for a moment. After all the action, she could do with some company. She slid her foot forward and kicked H, "accidentally." He started. "I'm up."

"So I'm curious," she said, leaning forward in her chair. "How'd you do it?"

"Save the world?" H said as he yawned and stretched. "Easy. With nothing but my wits and my—"

"Your Series-7 De-Atomizer." Em finished the phrase for him. "No, how did you get in? How did they 'recruit' you?"

"I'd like to think it was my sheer, unadulterated, God-given talent."

"I'd really like to think so too." She didn't bother to hide the skepticism in her voice. "But what was it really?"

H looked from side to side, making sure no one was

listening in. He leaned closer to her with a smile. "I stole the wrong car."

Em was speechless. It wasn't what she had expected to hear.

H continued, "Vintage Jag—kind you didn't see much where I'm from. Mate of mine says, 'Bet you can't hotwire it.' So I do. Then I realize that there in the back seat, in handcuffs, is a Class-4 Gormorite."

"Class-4?" Em said, grimacing. "Reticulated or inverted?"

"Both, I think."

"Oh man. What did it do?"

"Ripped the roof off the car and ran straight for the guy I stole the car from. I see this big, chrome pistol on the seat, leveled my sights, and... boom."

"Purple guts everywhere?" Em shook her head, picturing the aftermath.

"All over him, all over me. So this guy—back then he was just 'T'..."

"Wait... you tried to steal *High T's* car?"

"Didn't try." H didn't attempt to hide his pride. "I *did* steal High T's car. So, T takes out his neuralyzer, about to wipe me. I tell him, 'Mate, around here, when someone does you a solid, you buy that man a pint.' One thing leads to another, and by the end of the night, he's offering me a job."

"So, you got the job because you committed a felony."

H was silent for a beat then retorted, "And hacking the Hubble telescope—the most secure closed system network in the world—what do you call that?"

Em smiled in surprise. He'd read her file. "Somebody did their homework."

"Now arriving," the automated voice of the hyperloop announcer boomed, *"Marrakech Station."*

H and Em made their way through the narrow, winding streets off the mercantile chaos of the Jamaa el Fna, the city's main square.

A large family passed them at an intersection, and Em caught a glimpse of alien ears spilling out from under the cap of one of the little boys. Em gestured to him quickly, and the boy gave her a grateful smile as he tucked his ears back under his hat and hurried to catch up with his family. As he moved away, Em spotted something daubed on the side of the building behind him.

"Check it out," Em said, nodding toward it.

A symbol about the size of a grapefruit was painted carefully on the wall. It was not an Arabic letter, nor part of any other terrestrial alphabet she'd seen.

H examined it, nodding. "A Cromulian tag. In their galaxy it's the symbol for 'balance'… or 'annihilation.' I can't remember."

"Actually it's 'harmony,'" Em corrected him. "On Earth it means we're entering an MiB safe haven." H regarded her oddly. "It's in the handbook. Yeah, the one you've never read."

Before he could retort, H caught sight of someone he recognized. "Great." The agent's voice dripped with weary familiarity. "Just who I wanted to see."

The street dead-ended ahead into a garage specializing in motorbikes.

There were partly assembled bikes and tools scattered everywhere in front of the shop.

A skinny man in a pair of Qandrissi trousers, sandals, and a black T-shirt crouched beside an oil-stained tarp, working on a three-wheeled motorized taxi bike, a tuk-tuk. However, it was clear to both Em and H, the tuk-tuk was some type of alien motorcycle, casually disguised as an Earth transport. The mechanic's back was to the street and the agents. He seemed to be having a hushed conversation with himself.

"You do not speak to the customers," he muttered as he turned a socket wrench. "That is *my* job."

A harsher voice came from the man. "And my job is what? Hang out here and shut up?"

"Yes, shut up," said the mechanic. "That is your job."

Em glanced over to H, but he seemed unconcerned by the voices.

"You know the rules, Nasr." H's eyes were on the tuk-tuk. "No visible alien tech. Don't make me write you up."

Startled, the man jumped to his feet and spun around, dropping his wrench in the process. His face was as narrow and gaunt as the rest of him. The most substantial part of him was his long, thick beard. He was covered in patches of grease, and the front of his T-shirt bore the logo for the rock band Motörhead. The bearded man quickly covered the alien bike with the dirty tarp at his feet.

"H!" Nasr said. "It's really you?"

"Who else would it be? Hey, Bassam." A small head popped out of Nasr's beard near his cheek. The tiny face smiled at H, and when it spoke, Em realized that this was the source of the gruff voice coming from Nasr.

"Hi, H," Bassam called. "Nasr said you were dead."

"What?" Nasr raised his eyebrows. "I never said that."

"You did," Bassam exclaimed. "You're lying."

Nasr grabbed his beard. He stumbled around the garage, twisting and wrestling with his facial hair. Bassam screeched in response.

"Why would I be dead?" H asked, putting a stop to the fight.

Nasr stopped attacking his beard and stepped back toward the agents. "Bassam misunderstood. We heard you and Riza had split up," he explained.

"Who's Riza?" Em asked.

H shrugged. "An… old friend of mine."

"Who runs the biggest criminal syndicate in the galaxy," Bassam added.

Nasr tried to cover for his beard. "We were so sad, H. What a lovely couple you were."

"You said, 'That psycho's gonna slit his throat,'" Bassam went on. "Your words. Not mine," the beard added.

"*Wrong!*" Nasr began smacking himself in the face. "*Rude!*" he bellowed. Bassam yelped and cursed as the two crashed around the garage.

Nasr punched his face with each word. "I… will… shave… you! I… will… shun… you!"

Bassam sneered in between grunts and cries, "You

wouldn't dare! You need me! You're *nothing* without me. *You have a weak chin!*"

Em turned to H as the mechanic and his beard struggled. Whoever Riza was, she sounded like exactly the kind of person the average MiB agent would want to arrest rather than get into a relationship with. But then again, if Vungus the Ugly was anything to go by, Em had already found out that there was nothing straightforward about H or his friendships.

"You *dated* this person?" she asked.

H actually blushed a little at the question, and Em could have sworn she saw a little hurt in his eyes—but just for a second. Then his feelings were hidden again with a nonchalant shrug.

H looked over to the aliens, still fighting. "Just keep it covered," he said as he walked out of the garage.

18

In the busy mezzanine below High T's office, Agent Eye, part of the MiB forensics tech surveillance division, approached Cee sitting at his perfectly organized desk. Cee was currently thinking up and organizing comebacks he should have said to H when he'd swaggered his way into the forensics lab and taken Agent Em off on another wild goose chase.

"What?" growled Cee.

Agent Eye handed Cee a plexi-tablet. There was some grainy black-and-white footage from the street battle with the twins on it.

"We were doing sweeps," Eye said. "Pulled this from a surveillance camera outside the club."

Cee saw in the jerky footage a brief exchange between Agent Em and the dying Vungus. Vungus handed something to Em. Cee paused the footage and rewound it, zooming in on Em and the Jababian. He froze the image. On the screen was an unusual alien puzzle box, pictured in the moment Vungus handed it to the young agent. Cee refocused the screen on the box, getting a clear capture of the alien artifact.

He looked up at Agent Eye. "You show this to High T?"

Eye shook his head. "You said everything goes through you."

"Good," Cee said. "I'll do it."

Eye nodded and departed.

Cee examined the image on the tablet, lingering on the alien puzzle box for a long time. Finally, he picked up his phone and began to dial a number.

H and Em arrived in front of the small curio shop just down the street from the sprawling Souk Semmarine. Em noticed the stack of Amazon packages piled beside the door; many of them had addresses located on other planets and even galaxies.

"Couple days' worth," she said, pointing at the packages. "No one's been out to collect."

Without further discussion, Em drew her pistol while H withdrew a sleek MiB-sanctioned lock-pick device. Em covered him and scanned the street while H knelt and applied the device to the doorknob. Needlessly, as it turned out. The door creaked open on its own, already unlocked. H put the picks away and drew his gun.

The doorbell jangled as they entered the dark room, guns sweeping, making sure each shadow was only a shadow. Dust hung in the air. The pair advanced toward the counter. Em paused, looking toward the floor. "H," she said softly. A pair of prone legs was sticking out from behind the counter.

The tall, lanky man must have been the shopkeeper. He lay face down; it was clear he'd been dead for several days. One of his long arms pointed behind him to the wall of shelves beyond the counter. Em looked at the wall, then to H, who nodded and covered her as she stepped over the dead man and behind the counter to examine the wall.

Em felt along the back wall, searching the sides and then the edges. On the bottom edge, she felt the indentation of a hidden button. She pushed it and then stepped back. The wall hissed as the pressure seal was opened and then hummed as it retracted.

They entered the hidden room, guns out. H parted the curtain, and they saw all the strange and wondrous alien artifacts that filled the room. Then they saw the chessboard. Tiny alien "pieces" were scattered across it, all dead.

"Chesixians," H said as they stepped toward the board. "I've heard of them but never actually seen them. Very ordered society, lots of customs to be followed precisely. Intricate caste and social system. It's strange, it always seemed very familiar to me, for some reason."

Em paused and looked at H, gesturing to the board. "Uh, chess?"

H frowned and nodded. "Always more a baccarat man myself, but yeah, I guess I can see that."

The agents stood over the board. They could see the Queen alone was still alive. Her tiny chest rose and fell in ragged breaths. She had been covered with a minuscule blanket, and a damp rag was on her forehead. A small cup lay beside her.

"W... W..." the Queen gasped, looking up at Em and H.

"Water?" Em said. She found a little cup that looked as if it was filled with water and lifted it to the Queen's lips. The Queen weakly raised herself to take a drink, but immediately spat the water out again.

"*Whiskey!*" the Queen demanded.

H holstered his gun and hunted around the room until he found a bottle. He filled the cup and helped her sip from it. Her color improved immediately; her eyes opened wide.

"Don't you fucking move," a loud voice said from a corner of the room. H instinctively moved to draw, but a howling laser blast of energy exploded, blowing a head-sized hole in the wall beside him. "Next one melts your face, pretty boy."

The agents looked up in the direction of the blast. On a high shelf, a tiny figure stood, clearly having the drop on them. The alien looked a lot like the Queen and the other dead aliens on the board. He was only a few inches tall, with dark green, scaly skin and features that reminded Em of a frog: no nose and a tiny slit of a mouth. He had big, amber eyes, and Em saw a sadness in them that he was trying to hide behind a tough exterior. The inches-tall warrior wore a conical helmet, a kite shield slung on his back, and pointed a forearm-mounted energy weapon down at them.

"Easy," H said. He opened his jacket slowly and removed his sidearm with two fingers. "We don't want trouble." He held it up for the alien to see and then placed it on the floor by his feet. He nodded for Em to do the same, and she set her own pistol down. "What do we call you, sport?"

The little alien looked offended. "A name? Why would I have a name? *Pawns* don't have names. We're pawns!"

"What happened here?" Em asked.

"We had a party," the pawn said, sarcasm dripping from every syllable. "What's it look like? We got our asses kicked!"

The Queen groaned; her color was fading again, and her breathing was becoming erratic.

"My Queen!" the pawn shouted. She began to wheeze. The tiny pawn jumped from the shelf to a tabletop and then to the chessboard, scrambling to reach her.

He knelt beside her, rubbing her forehead with the damp rag. She whispered something to him, and the little pawn took her in his arms, holding her tight. He began to cry, the sobs wracking his whole body. The pawn looked over his shoulder at the two agents. "A little personal space?" he asked.

H and Em, somewhat embarrassed, took a step back from the board.

"I'll never serve another; I swear it," the pawn said, gazing into his queen's eyes. "I'll plunge my dagger into my own body, pull it lengthwise—like this—through my vital organs, then up, like this, and leave it there. Until I'm dead."

The Queen seemed to take great comfort from the pawn's oath. She raised her arm weakly and touched her subject's face gently with her hand. She tried to say something to her loyal servant, but she no longer had the strength. With a final soft sigh, the Queen died, her arm slipping away from the pawn's cheek to lie still on her breast.

The pawn laid his fallen queen down and covered her body with the blanket. He drew his tiny dagger. Em immediately recognized it as a twin to the one that had killed Vungus. The pawn lifted up his breastplate, revealing his pale belly. He readied his knife to plunge it into his flesh.

"You're not seriously going to—"

"A queen's pawn without a queen is just… a pawn. A nothing. A loser. This is the noble rite. I must end my own life. In the most—" the pawn gulped as he struggled to pull out the words "—painful way possible." He pushed the blade to his stomach, gasping as it snicked his body. "Ow! That's sharp."

Em glanced to H and mouthed, *"Should we stop him?"*

H shrugged. "I think it's kind of sweet."

Below on the chessboard, the pawn had rallied and prepared again to commit alien seppuku. "Here goes, then," the pawn went on. "I'm going to do it." He was clearly stalling, now. "It's killing time." He cocked an eye up at the agents. "Yes? You said something, didn't you? One of you said something." When neither replied, the pawn extended his arms, preparing to give the blade a good plunge.

"Wait!" Em shouted, not able to let this happen and definitely not wanting to watch it. "I'm sure she... wouldn't want you to, you know, go through with it."

It was clear to Em that the pawn was definitely relieved, but he seemed bound to some custom or protocol that required a fuss. "Who are you to say what a queen would or wouldn't want?" the pawn said. "Are *you* a queen?"

"No, I'm... Em. Agent Em."

"*Agent*," the pawn turned the term over in his head. "Is that... a title?"

Em saw H's face light up and knew immediately that it was bad.

"It *is* a title, Pawny, old pal," H sang out. "A title of great eminence and stature. Em here is an agent, an agent without a *pawn*. If you see my meaning."

"Uh," Em said, "*I* don't."

The pawn stood proudly to his full four-inch height.

"Maybe you're right," the tiny alien said, newfound energy in his voice. "Maybe the best way to honor the dead is to go on living."

H nodded seriously in agreement. The pawn turned to Em. He fell to one knee and held his wrist blaster aloft.

"I swear loyalty eternal to you, Agent Em—*my* Agent Em—my one and only."

Em raised her palms, slowly shaking her head. "You really don't have to..."

"Such nobility, such grace," H said, smiling. "It's humbling."

The pawn continued despite Em's discomfort, "And if

you should die before I, I promise to end my own life, rather than suffer the shame of living one moment longer."

"In the most painful way possible," H added helpfully.

The pawn gave H a dirty look. "Of course," he said through gritted teeth, and then he lowered his tiny, helmeted head before his new queen and bowed.

The brass lamps that lit the hidden room flickered, and Em's eyes flashed toward the storefront. She put a finger to her lips and shushed H and the pawn. Carefully, Em pushed aside the curtain that separated the rooms and slipped back into the shop.

"Impressive," the pawn said, gazing after Em. "You and her a thing?" he asked H.

"All you, big guy," H whispered with a wink.

"We'll end up together," the pawn said, wistfully. "It's inevitable. When you protect someone, a closeness develops. Lines become blurred…"

In the curio shop, Em saw that all the lamps in the storefront were flickering. She remembered the lights in the nightclub doing the same thing… just before…

Throughout the marketplace, electronic devices and lights flickered as the twins strode through the quarter as if they owned it, seeking their prize. The many aliens in the area knew trouble when they saw it, and quickly began to close and shutter their shops as if a powerful sirocco were barreling in off the desert. The human shopkeepers followed their lead, and soon the Dyad twins were making their way through narrow, empty streets. They passed Nasr's bike shop, as the owner and his beard alien partner watched the lights flicker when the ominous pair walked by.

"Here comes trouble," Nasr said.

Bassam the Beard shifted as they watched. "I like trouble." Bassam hopped off Nasr's face and dropped to the floor. The hairy little alien looked a bit like a possum; and Nasr didn't look right at all without the beard.

Bassam looked up at Nasr. "You thinking what I'm thinking?"

An evil cut of a smile grew on Nasr's face as Bassam pulled his cell phone out of the reaches of his hairy body. "Yep," the mechanic said. "Call Riza."

19

Em stepped back into the hidden room behind the curio shop. She closed the wall-door behind her. "They're coming," she said to H and the pawn. "The Dyads."

The pawn activated his blaster, cranking the power dial up. "They killed my queen!" He tried to charge toward the door, but H held him back.

"Whoa! Easy, killer." H felt the pawn struggling against his hand as he knelt and retrieved his gun from the floor and tossed Em hers.

"H, I think we should go," Em said, glancing toward the CCTV unit in the hidden room that showed the storefront. The screen's black-and-white image was punctuated with static. "I know why they're here." The image on the screen cleared long enough to show the twins entering the curio store. They both stared straight into the camera and then the image drowned in static. H opened a back door that led to a side street. He gave Em a "to be continued" look and then stepped out, sweeping the street with his pistol. Em followed.

"My lady?" The pawn beseeched her with his big, golden eyes. Em paused, sighed, and plucked the pawn off the chessboard.

In the store, the Dyads moved toward the secret room. One of the twins picked up an antique iron candlestick. In his hand, it melted, shifted and flowed into a long, deadly sword. The other twin reached for the hidden catch to open the wall behind the counter. He looked to his brother. The sword-wielding twin nodded and moved to stand by the door. The wall slid away, and the twins stepped into the hidden room, pushing past the curtain. The room was empty.

H and Em, pistols in hand, rushed down the empty, twisting streets, heading to the next quarter, hoping to find a crowd to slip into.

H peeked around a corner. Seeing it was clear, he moved to head down the new street.

Em hunted through her jacket pockets for the puzzle box. "Look, I was going to tell you. I *wanted* to." But her pockets were empty, except for the little pawn, dodging her hand. The box was gone. "Where is it? Crap!"

H reached into his own pocket and retrieved the box. "You mean this?" he asked, waving it at her.

"You stole it from me?" She was obviously angry and hurt.

"No." H was still alert as they went, sweeping the street ahead of them. "I recovered evidence that *you* stole from a crime scene."

"Vungus said to hide it." Em caught up to him. "That I couldn't trust anyone."

H, his back to a wall, gun at the ready, psyched himself up to step into the street on the other side of the wall. "And you believed a Jababian lush you just met— rest his soul—over your senior agent?"

"In a word: yes," Em snapped back.

He took a quick glance and then slipped around the corner. The street opened into a busy square. This was another medina, an open market. There were people everywhere. Cars, beasts of burden, and motorbikes crept their way through the crowd. Merchants even walked up to the windows of the cars or accosted the riders to try to hawk their wares. H began to smile. It would be easy to slip into this churning throng and disappear.

"H—look." Em nodded at the crowd. Then H saw it too—the patches of black among the sea of colors. H's smile fell.

There were MiB SUVs at every major avenue that fed into the medina.

"There, too," Em said, beside him, spotting MiB agents, lots of them, spilling out of the Chevy Suburbans, scanning, searching the market. "What are they doing here?"

H's instincts were screaming that something was wrong. He spotted a good hiding place near a fountain and headed toward it. "Over here," he said to Em. The agents crouched near the fountain. It obscured them but still let them keep an eye on the majority of the Men in Black spreading out over the marketplace. H knew it wasn't a permanent solution, but it would give them a chance to regroup.

"Whatever that thing is," Em said, referring to the box, "Vungus died to protect it." She nodded toward the agents who were even now searching unrelentingly through the busy square. "He gave it to me so it wouldn't go to them."

Her urgency gave H pause. Staying close behind the fountain, he gave the other MiB agents a closer look...

High T stepped through the circular elevator doors directly into the special operations room. As he walked around the elevator tube, he found Cee and a group of agents reviewing live footage from a bank of wall screens. The footage was coming from agent body cams and from MiB stealth drones. The scene was an open-air marketplace.

"Could someone tell me what's going on here?" High T asked.

"Sensitive situation, sir," Cee told him. "In Marrakech. I thought it best to keep it quiet."

High T noticed that there were profiles of H and Em on one of the monitors, including their pictures. A dark banner declaring WANTED appeared below their faces.

"A word, Cee." High T stepped away from the other agents. Cee followed, his ever-present tablet in hand. "This is nonsense," High T said in a low voice once they were out of earshot of the others. "Despite your personal feelings to the contrary, H is one of the best agents ever to wear this suit."

"*Was* one of the best." Cee also kept his voice down. He clicked on the tablet. "He hasn't been the same since the incident with the Hive." Cee held up the tablet screen. "Look," he said.

High T watched the surveillance footage that had been recovered from the scene of Vungus the Ugly's death. He saw the alien giving Agent Ém the puzzle box as he died. Cee made a few gestures on the tablet screen, and the grainy image of the box was zoomed in on and enhanced, until it matched up with a schematic image of the box on an intergalactic bulletin covered in red symbols T recognized as the Jababian language. The Jababian royal family's crest and the seal of the Jababian military high command were prominent on the communiqué. "My sources say Vungus stole it," Cee said, "from the Jababian War Department, Advanced Research Division. He brought it here."

High T looked up from the data, his face pale with anger, his eyes dark. "You kept this from me?" His voice was rising, and the other agents were beginning to notice. "For how long? Explain yourself."

"Explain *my*self?" Cee said, not backing down. "Whatever that thing is, H and Em had it—in your office—and you let them go."

High T saw, over Cee's shoulder, that the other agents were all watching the power struggle intently. He regained his composure, but the anger didn't leave his eyes.

"Bring them straight to me," he said in a quiet,

commanding tone. Not waiting for Cee's reply, High T strode to the elevators and slipped his communicator out of his pocket. He began to dial.

As he studied the surrounding MiB agents from behind the fountain in Marrakech, H's communicator bleeped. *High T.* He answered, and a holographic image of High T appeared.

"Sir—" H began.

"H, listen to me," High T interrupted. "This isn't my operation. Get out of there. Get safe, then report."

High T, communicator in hand, stood at his office window, watching the agents and aliens below him. He saw Cee, flanked by a cadre of agents, walking swiftly across the main floor, obviously giving orders as he went. The agents scattered to perform their assigned tasks, and Cee paused, almost as if he sensed he was being watched. Cee turned and looked up at High T. The two men locked eyes.

"Em may be right," High T said. "There could be a mole in Men in Black."

20

T's hologram dissolved, and H put away his communicator, shaken. H led them through the periphery of the medina, keeping large clusters of people between them and the ever-tightening net of agents. H saw an agent make them. He cursed under his breath and led Em quickly toward a jam of people in a narrow street of the medina.

"Take this," he said, handing her the puzzle box. "They'll assume I have it." Em slid the box back into her jacket pocket. "Meet you in the main square in twenty."

Em took in the milling crowd, and her fellow agents— the people she'd spent a lifetime trying to find—closing in on her. "Not how I pictured my first week," she said. A ghost of a smile passed between them, and then they split, headed in opposite directions.

H moved deeper into the marketplace, closer to his pursuers. A group of MiB agents spotted him, just as he had meant them to.

"We're wearing the same thing," H called out to the agents. "What are the odds?" He bolted into the crowd, running like hell. The agents gave chase, and he could hear them calling out to more of their colleagues to close in on the renegade. H could see the other agents shoving their way through the crowd toward him. *Come and get me, boys*, H thought as he ran as fast as he could, the squad of MiB agents hot on his trail.

Em saw the agents leave their positions to triangulate on H and used the momentary opening to go with the crowd out of the marketplace. She ran until she was clear of the market, on a side street, and then looked back. No agents were chasing her. Em began to walk, keeping pace with the flow of pedestrian traffic and trying to blend in.

A light flickered near her, and she stopped suddenly, turned, and stared upwards. She saw no one on the roofs. Perhaps it was just a flickering light, and nothing more. She resumed her cautious walk, headed toward the rendezvous.

Above her, on the rooftops, the Dyad twins moved silently, shadowing Em's every move.

H ran, a pack of agents less than a block behind him. He knew they wouldn't risk using their sidearms in public unless he forced their hand—not against a fellow agent, at least. H banked as he saw a swarm of MiB drones closing on his position, ducking into a maze of streets so ancient, narrow, and twisting that aerial recon or even GPS wouldn't be much use. He'd had to use the same trick years ago when he was being chased in Marrakech by a swarm of Alcallian assassin bots.

His foot pursuers would have him back in sight in a few seconds. He saw his goal, Nasr's motorbike repair shop, and ducked quickly inside. A few seconds later, the MiB agents raced past the garage, talking into their coms as they tried to get some idea of H's location from their blinded air support.

H, catching his breath, turned to the surprised, beardless Nasr, who had been slurping a bowl of soup by a desk covered in greasy engine parts.

"Nasr, I need to borrow your bike! Right now!"

"As long as 'borrow' doesn't mean 'steal.'" The alien mechanic went over to the tuk-tuk. Nasr quickly and efficiently removed the wood and plastic camouflage from around the bike, revealing what the delivery cycle really was. H smiled. It was a big, muscly, alien hover-bike, just the sort he needed.

"Bassam!" Nasr bellowed as he disappeared into the other room of the garage, while H climbed on the hover-bike and scanned the controls. Nasr returned with a full water canteen, which he handed to H.

"You'll need this out there," the mechanic said. "It's hot."

H took the canteen and put it in one of the bike's storage boxes. He nodded to the controls as he flipped the main power on and the hover-bike growled to life.

"Seems pretty straightforward."

"Just like riding a bike," Nasr offered.

H hit the throttle, and the hover-bike roared to life, smashing through the closed garage door and careening into the wall of another building.

"This is actually not like riding a bike at all." He turned the handlebars hard, too hard, and hit a third wall on another building. He flew off and crashed into the street, face down, and the bike stopped, bobbing in the air next to him.

H groaned through a mouthful of pavement and climbed to his feet. A small crowd of locals and tourists had gathered around him and the strange, levitating, wheel-less motorcycle. H sighed and pulled out his neuralyzer.

The twins moved across the rooftops of Marrakech like parkour runners. They cleared the gap between two buildings and then dropped off the edge of the roof of the next building, landing on a ledge halfway down the wall. They pushed off the ledge backward and used their backs and palms to slide the rest of the way down the opposite wall, dropping ten feet in front of Em as she reached a four-way intersection of streets. Em froze. She knew, had seen, what the Dyads could do. Her Series-4 De-Atomizer sidearm wouldn't even slow them down.

A donkey cart, loaded with wares and led by an old, half-blind merchant, creaked across the street, blocking the twins from Em for a few seconds. When the cart passed, Em had vanished. The twins looked at each other, speaking without talking, and then split up to search the surrounding streets.

Em ran as fast as she could. She turned from street to street, ashamed to admit she was letting panic guide her path. She kept looking over her shoulder, expecting to see the twins, invulnerable, relentless, remorseless, on her heels. But they weren't. She turned onto an alleyway partially covered by a wooden roof. The shadows were deeper here, and Em felt a terrible sense of isolation and loneliness fill her. She tried to be cool, to keep her mind on the business at hand, but here, in this dark alleyway, she could die and no one would know, would really care. She was cut off from her partner and on the run from the very organization she had wanted to be part of her whole life. *You don't trust anyone,* Vungus had said, and he had been right. This was the downside to living the way she had. It was a two-edged sword. If you don't trust anyone, there's never anyone really close to you.

An electric streetlight in the dim alley flickered and then faded to black. She turned to retrace her steps and found a wall was in front of her, blocking her way. The wall's composition was odd, as if it were made out of the clay and tile of the buildings that made up the walls of the alleyway, but it was irregular, rippling, almost breathing. She remembered what the twins had done to the London street. *Phase transition.*

She spun around again, but one of the twins stood before her, his dark eyes locked on her, blocking any chance of escape. Em backed away as he came closer. *Draw your gun! Shoot him! Fight! Use the comm; call for help!* All her reason was choking on fear as the lone Dyad stepped closer. Her back brushed the dead-end wall that had materialized in her path. An arm of clay and tile grew out of the wall and grabbed her. Em gasped and struggled to free herself but to no avail.

A fireball of energy struck the arm growing out the wall, and it chipped and cracked, releasing Em long enough for her to move away from the wall. The other Dyad twin emerged from the wall, rubbing his arm but seemingly otherwise unaffected by the blast.

The pawn, peeking out of Em's shirt pocket, fired a second shot with his wrist blaster at the twin from the wall. "Not this time! Not this queen!" the little soldier shouted as his blaster howled and struck the twin. "Not this queen!" The injured twin seemed barely to notice the blast striking him. His brother, who was blocking Em from retreating down the alley, ripped part of an iron window grate off and transformed it into a nasty-looking, barbed, spear-like weapon.

The first twin raised the spear and stepped closer to Em and the pawn. Em's hand tightened on the puzzle box in her pocket.

The second twin moved menacingly toward Em, his skin still smoking from the pawn's blasts.

The twins closed on Em, and she was certain she was going to die. She pushed her fear away and reached for her pistol under her jacket. She might have failed in her mission, but these two Hive goons were going to know they had fought an MiB agent to her dying breath.

There was an explosion of sound and clay tiles, and

the Dyads' wall disintegrated, debris phasing through the second twin. H appeared on a roaring hover-bike flying through the fiery cloud, his smoking De-Atomizer in hand. The second twin had stabilized his form from the explosion just in time for H to run him over with the bike. The twin was smashed by the impact and then set on fire by the powerful exhaust of the bike as it passed him. H swerved the bike ninety degrees in the tight alley and stopped next to Em. "Jump on!" he shouted.

"Took you long enough," Em said as she climbed on.

"Had to learn how to drive it."

The first twin was coming toward them, dragging a living wall of matter behind him that consumed stone and clay, a tuk-tuk, everything in its path, hemming them in. A glance over his shoulder showed H that the second twin had rematerialized almost immediately. The scorching damage the fire and impact had caused were gone. He looked pissed. Like his brother, he raised a living wall, sweeping it toward the trapped agents.

There was nowhere to go—the Dyads still blocked them in, one on either side, and H no longer had the element of surprise. In unison, the twins brought their walls together; the street around the agents grew smaller and smaller as H hesitated. The second twin's wall caught a motorbike in its path; the twin grabbed a part of it before it vanished, and the metal morphed into a sharp, cruel-looking weapon.

H's eyes were on the wall ahead of them, and a high window with a closed metal shutter covering it.

H watched the ground seethe under the manipulations

of the twins on either side of them. The twins stood, their faces lit by the strange energies they had infused into the alley floor. The walls of energy they had summoned were closing in, and he didn't want to be around when they met. H jammed the throttle and the bike bucked and roared, the engine diagnostics jumped into the red, warning that the hover-bike was at maximum acceleration; the engines were pegged.

"Better hold on!" H shouted over the snarling engines. The hover-bike shot straight at the alley wall at maximum speed. H leaned back and jerked up on the handlebars with all his might. The bike reared up into a wheelie and then caught on the alley wall, rocketing up the vertical surface at a blurring speed.

The twins flipped, sending massive waves of molten stone at the spot where the bike had been only a second before. The deadly masses splashed into each other and rained down as the twins watched the hover-bike carrying the agents clear the roof, launched out of the medina.

At the zenith of the climb, all three passengers on the bike felt gravity and time abandon them. H hung onto the handlebars for dear life; Em, behind him, had flown free but was still above the bike's seat. Pawny was hurtling away from Em, his tiny mouth opened wide in a scream. Em grabbed H's belt, reaching out, straining, and managed to grab the tiny warrior, cupping him in her hand as the bike began to descend and gravity reclaimed them, hard.

The hover-bike hit a wooden canopy on the way down. H steadied the bike as it hit and shot off horizontally along the platform, jumping when the platform ended. H brought the bike down; its gravity suspension field dipped low but held as the bike landed hard on a busy market street several streets over from the alleyway. H looked back at his passengers. Em, cradling the visibly shaken Pawny, was gasping to recover the air that had been sucked from her lungs.

"I can't believe that worked," H said.

"H..." Em looked at all the startled and confused faces of the civilians on the street who had watched their descent on the alien hover-bike.

"Glasses," H said pulling out his neuralyzer. He spoke to the crowd. "If you would all please look—"

Em plucked the neuralyzer from his hand and slipped on her own sunglasses. "Just drive."

H gunned the engine and they shot off down the street. Turning back, Em pressed the button, and there was a flash of light—the bystanders in their wake had been neuralyzed. It wasn't quite how she'd imagined first using a neuralyzer, that was for sure.

H tried to get his bearings, looking for a gate out of the city, and feeling rather pleased with his skills on the hover-bike, when the empty street ahead of him was blocked by the sudden appearance of an MiB sedan. It screeched to a halt directly in front of them. H didn't think, only reacted, turning sharply left onto another street. Just as he righted the bike, another MiB car roared into view, moving to block the whole street.

H leaned in low and hard, nearly clipping the hood of the car. He barely made an extremely tight turn into what appeared to be a courtyard of reflection pools. A few tourists stood near the fringes, taking pictures with their phones. Beyond the courtyard, H saw the open roads and distant dunes of the Sahara, past the walls of the city. He grinned back at Em. The grin dropped when he saw another MiB Suburban, racing down the street behind them.

H revved the hover-bike and began to race over the pools, water flying in their wake, splashing the tourists. As they neared the portal, two more MiB vehicles roared into view on the other side, blocking the route to freedom. H hit the brakes, and the bike hung, unmoving, over the pools. Agents in tactical gear swarmed from the vehicles in front of and behind them, aiming their guns at the bike and its passengers. More Men in Black agents appeared on a narrow walkway on the walls of the courtyard, aiming down at them. They were joined by a swarm of MiB drones, hovering and flitting about the sky above. They were trapped.

"That's some escape plan, Blondie." Pawny stared at all the guns pointing at them.

Options sifted through H's mind; every one of them ended up with all of them dead or captured. He felt bad for Em, she was already a better agent than most he could remember. She didn't deserve this ending, this soon.

He scanned the hover-bike's console, seeking desperately for some hidden epiphany there. He didn't find one, but he did see something that set off his "what the hell" reaction. Close enough. He looked back at Em. "What do you think? Push the red button?"

"No way," Em said, peering over H's shoulder at the big, shiny red button on the top of the console. "You never push the red button. Everybody knows that."

H pivoted the bike, its massive repulsion vents still roaring. The MiB agents' guns tracked the slight movement.

"I think it's the hyperdrive," H said, nodding to the red button, ignoring the agents surrounding them. It took a lot for an MiB agent to shoot down one of their own, after all. He gunned the engines and shot straight toward the archway and the wall of guns.

"No, it isn't." Em shook her head, her hair fluttering behind her. "Hyperdrive is blue."

"Sometimes you have to trust your gut." H put his hand on the red button.

"*My* gut!" Em shouted. "Not *yours*!"

H pushed the red button. MiB agents flew everywhere as the hover-bike and its passengers vanished in a flash of brilliant light and a loud, earth-shaking *whomp*.

21

Em groaned and raised her head. All she saw in every direction was desert. She struggled to her feet and took in the scene around her. H was pulling himself up to a sitting position, brushing sand off his jacket. About twenty yards away, the mangled remains of the hover-bike jutted out of the side of a dune.

"Told you. Hyperdrive. Trust your gut," H said, standing.

"Yeah, yeah." Em got to her feet and turned her pants pockets out to empty the flood of sand.

Pawny's tiny green head popped up out of the sand between the two agents. "That was nuts!" he shouted, like a kid after his first time on a roller coaster. "We gotta do that again!" He saw the less-than-enthusiastic looks on his companions' faces. "What? I've lived my whole life on a chessboard. Anything new is good."

"Shhhh." Em heard a faint *snick-snick* sound and then a strange humming, like a machine powering up.

The sounds were emanating from the puzzle box, which lay a few feet away on the ground. It had fallen from her pocket in the hyperjump, and the tiles had shifted about in the crash, aligning themselves. It was humming, vibrating itself and the sand around it, as if it was desperate to pop open. She walked over to it, knelt, and carefully picked it up.

Pawny jumped up on the handlebars of the hover-bike to get a better view. "That looks pretty lethal."

Burning with curiosity, Em examined the pattern on the box, memorizing it so she could close it or open it again if needed. She slid the final tile into place, and with a click, the box began to expand in her hands, folding, shifting, and finally revealing a large, ominous-looking alien device, almost like a free-standing control panel. The device was as light as the box had been, so Em could hold it as if it were weightless.

At the heart of the device was a large sphere: a swirling maelstrom of light and darkness; a gasping, hungry maw that spun slowly, like some terrible cosmic predator, waiting patiently to be freed, to devour and destroy. The two agents stared at it. Em was mesmerized by the phenomenon inside the globe, the flaring light and deep shadow playing across her features.

"See the core," she almost whispered, "how it keeps emitting convective energy across the interior of the photosphere?"

H nodded quickly and tried to look like he understood what she was talking about. "Yeah, totally. The photosphere."

"Those are thermonuclear explosions."

"Hold on now—those are *what*?"

She tore her eyes away to look at H, as the magnitude of what she held in her hands unfolded to her. "I think we're looking at a super-compressed star. By its color temperature, I'd say a blue giant."

"Stellar super-compression isn't possible," Pawny chimed in. "It's a myth. Like alchemy, or a hangover cure."

The device had a series of markings on its side. The gauge started at .001 and ran all the way to a maximum setting of 10,000. H saw the eager look dancing behind the rookie agent's eyes; it was infectious.

"Why don't we find out what's possible and what isn't?" he said.

"You want to try a weaponized star just for fun?" Em nodded toward the seething core of the alien machine.

"And science. Fun and science."

Em's usually serious expression was now like that of a kid on Christmas morning.

"No better place for it." She set the device carefully on the ground. There were a series of field emitters on one side that Em suspected acted as the "mouth," or "barrel," for aiming the contraption. She pointed them out toward the endless dunes of the deep desert. "They don't call this place the Empty Quarter for nothing."

H leaned in. He had to admit, he was as keen as she was to see what this thing could actually do. For the first time, it really felt like they were in this thing together.

"Just at point zero zero one." Em sounded a little cautious despite her eagerness. She set the switch to the lowest setting. The whole device purred with seemingly endless energy. Em flipped the activator switch and... nothing seemed to happen. Everything remained quiet and normal. Both H and Em stopped holding their breath.

"Maybe try one notch higher?" H suggested.

Then the landscape in front of the device's mouth exploded in a howling vortex of wind and sand. H, Em, and even Pawny were knocked backward by the force of the sudden eruption. Through the stinging haze of dust and grit, H saw massive boulders sucked toward the device, only to be crushed to gravel and swallowed by the whirring machine. The storm covered everything in blinding, choking dust; and Em, H, and Pawny lost sight of one another even though they were only a few feet apart.

Finally, the howling winds quieted as the machine whined itself to silence. The dust settled, and the battered agents and tiny warrior climbed back to their feet.

They stood at the edge of a vast canyon, miles across. On the far side, the agents could see a very confused goat standing near the edge, its bleating echoing across the divide. It reminded Em of the time she and her parents had visited the Grand Canyon. This canyon, carved in moments by the machine, seemed nearly as large across and as deep as the one in Arizona.

H and Em stood, covered in desert dust, silent in disbelief. Pawny struggled up to the edge of the canyon, between the two agents. He looked back at the alien device, behind them.

"That was the *low* setting?" His voice echoed across the gulf.

22

Cee stormed into High T's office, his face pink with anger.

"They got away," he said coldly.

High T kept working at the stacks of reports on his desk. Finally, he paused and met Cee's glare.

"I believe the technical term is 'you lost them.'" His voice was calm.

Cee approached, placing his balled fists on the edge of High T's desk.

"They had help." Cee looked squarely at his boss.

High T didn't bat an eye at the veiled accusation.

"I know H," he said. "Whatever he's doing, there's a reason."

"Still protecting him." Cee shook his head. "What is it going to take?"

"I am *protecting* this institution." High T's voice hadn't lost any of the calm, but even so, there was suddenly an air of menace hanging in it, like the edge of a sharp knife.

"From whom?" Cee asked. "From me? Are you questioning my loyalty?"

"At the very least, your judgment."

Cee seethed but held his tongue.

"Is there anything else, Agent Cee?" High T asked.

Cee said nothing, a near-murderous glare in his eyes.

"No? Good." High T turned back to his paperwork. "Then you can kindly piss off."

The sun hung low, close to the dunes of the desert. The clear blue sky had deepened to indigo, bleeding crimson along the horizon. H, carrying the alien black-hole weapon, now once again tucked away in the puzzle box, approached the small camp fire they had made near the wrecked hover-bike. Pawny and Em sat by the fire, watching the light fade. H opened one of the metal "saddlebag" containers near the back of the bike.

"Vungus knew how powerful this thing is," H said, slipping the puzzle box into the metal container, "that it could destroy entire worlds." He closed the compartment. "But he gave it to you. Someone he'd never met." H sat down beside Em at the fire, leaning back against the busted bike. "Why would he do that?"

"Maybe he trusted me?" Em dragged a stick through the sand by her feet, not meeting H's eyes.

"I sang at Vungus's mother's funeral," H said. "I'm pretty sure he trusted *me*."

Em sighed and tossed the stick into the fire. She felt more than a little frustrated. "Okay, if you really want to know, he said you'd changed."

H shook his head, looking into the fire. "You know—" he sounded just as irritated as Em "—I'm actually getting pretty sick of everyone giving me this 'I've changed' crap."

"Are you saying you've always been obstinate, arrogant, and reckless?" Em asked.

H's voice started to rise. "Look, my job is protecting the Earth, and as long as I'm doing that, the rules are, there are no rules."

"Well," Pawny said, entering the fray, "that's a rule."

While the three argued, none of them noticed that the aluminum water bottle, partly buried in the sand near the hover-bike, was silently unscrewing itself.

"Okay," H raised a hand and tried to get back in control of the conversation. "The rules are there are no rules, apart from the one rule about there being no rules."

Bassam the beard pulled himself, dripping wet, from the interior of the water bottle. The drenched beard-alien looked around and was happy to see the agents and the pawn were busy arguing. He pulled a string and fished a small leather sack out of the water bottle as well. Bassam quietly slipped the pack on like he would a backpack, if he had actually possessed a back.

"So the rules are," Em cocked her head in mock-confusion, "there is one rule? That negates itself?"

"Yes." H sounded as if he had just won the argument.

There was a metallic click as Bassam closed the saddlebag.

"*Nobody moves!*" Bassam commanded, his deep voice unnaturally loud in the quiet desert. H, Em, and

Pawny all spun in the direction of the sound. Bassam was pointing a laser pistol at them. He held the puzzle box in another of his furry tendrils.

Bassam shrugged. "Sorry H. A beard's gotta eat."

"Bassam?" H said. "How did you get here?"

"I stowed away—" Bassam shook himself off again "—in the water bottle."

H made a face. "Euch. Really? We *drank* from that."

"I told you it tasted like soup," Em said, grimacing.

"Bassam, mate." H stepped forward, toward the beard. "Let's be sensible here. I don't think you know quite what that thing is capable of."

"Oh, no," Bassam said, backing away. "I definitely do, which is why she's willing to pay so much for it."

H reached for his gun, but the beard-alien yanked a cord on the harness of the small pack and a jet rocket unfolded from its confines. It launched Bassam into the night sky at a dizzying speed. H aimed his gun at the rapidly disappearing trail of the rocket, but Bassam was already too far away, too high up. H lowered his gun as the rocket's exhaust was lost in the canopy of stars overhead. Em walked up beside him and fixed him with a stare.

"Great work, hero," she said. "How could you not know he was there?"

"How is this my fault?" H holstered his gun. "Nasr gave me a water bottle. He said he didn't want me to get dehydrated." Em continued to glare at him. "You can't be too careful. It *is* a very dry heat."

"You go to an illegal alien chop-shop and ask a

weasel for help. What do you think is going to happen?" Em's voice was rising this time.

"Well," H snapped, just as loudly, "if you'd just told me about that box when Vungus gave it to you, we wouldn't even be in this mess."

"So it's *my* fault we lost the most powerful weapon in the galaxy?" Em shouted back.

"You said it," H barked.

Em stepped back and shook her head at H, too angry and hurt to speak. She walked away from the camp fire into the darkness.

Pawny looked up at H's expression, then raced after Em.

Alone, H stood alone by the crackling fire with no idea of what to do to make any of this right. And, for once, with absolutely nothing to say.

23

The moon was high and full over the dunes as H and Em, stripped down to their tank top undershirts, worked silently to repair the hover-bike. The day had been blistering. As the desert cooled, it felt wonderful. They knew that in a little while it would become uncomfortably cold; but for now, it was a relief.

The two hadn't spoken in a long while. Pawny stood between them while H worked at repairing the hover-bike's power supply, repulsion array, and engines. Meanwhile, Em worked on repairing the extensive damage to the bike's onboard computer systems, control panel, and system software. Occasionally, the two agents sneaked furtive glances at each other's handiwork, both impressed by the other's aptitude, but unwilling to admit it.

"Pawny," H said, his back to the small warrior and to Em, "ask her to pass me that torque wrench."

"'*She*' has a name *and* a title," Pawny muttered gruffly, "and I would thank you to use it." Despite his objection,

Pawny turned to Em and relayed the message. "My lady, the jackass needs the torque wrench." Em reached into one of the saddlebag compartments on the back of the bike and fished out the torque wrench. She handed it to H without a word, and resumed her work with her back to him.

"Pawny," Em said, "tell him the sooner he restores power to my drive console, the sooner I can figure out how to program it."

Pawny turned to H's back. "My lady says you're a cloth-brained ass clown whose gullible idiocy has threatened the very existence of the planet."

H stopped working and turned to the little warrior. "She didn't say that. She didn't say *any* of that, so—"

"No." Em was still working, not even looking around to H. "But he makes a good point." Pawny smiled. H dropped an oil-spotted rag over him.

It took H a few more moments to reinitialize the power core, but when he did the bike's engine hummed to life. Em's console lit up, streaming with alien symbols.

"Tell your lady she now has power."

"Tell him I said thank you."

"Really?" Pawny sounded incredulous. "Do I have to? He'll mistake your kindness for weakness."

H turned away from the engine and wiped his hands with the rag he had dropped on Pawny. "I know where the weapon's going," he told Em, "and I know how to get it back."

Em looked up from her work. "I'm listening," she said.

"Okay," Pawny asked, "so am I opting out of this now?"

"Bassam has only one real buyer," H went on. "He said so himself. Riza Stavros."

"Is this the Riza you used to go out with? The intergalactic alien arms dealer?"

"You dated Riza Stavros?" Pawny exclaimed, turning to H. "The Merchant of Death? Are you insane?"

H ignored the pawn and focused on Em.

"I didn't know she was an arms dealer when we met. I got distracted by her feminine wiles, her intoxicating beauty. We weren't interested in labels," H went on, rolling now. "We were interested in our hearts. And if having a big old heart is a crime, then shoot me."

Pawny raised his blaster, aiming it at H's skull, unbeknownst to the agent who was waxing poetic. The tiny warrior, standing on the bike's seat, looked up eagerly to Em for permission to fire. Em shook her head. Pawny frowned and reluctantly lowered his gun.

"You're telling me you've never just abandoned logic for passion?" H asked.

"Not once," Em said calmly as she continued to type lines of code into the bike's operating system. "Physical attraction is just serotonin and neuropeptides. Chemical reactions in the brain. You can't trust them."

H paused in his labors and held his arms out to encompass the vast mosaic of stars above them. "The whole universe is a chemical reaction," he declared. "It's still real."

Em was silent.

Pawny sat back on the bike's seat, taking in the profundity of H's words. "That's... actually kind of deep."

H made a final adjustment to the power flow. "Okay, that should do it. Power her up."

Em tapped in some commands on the console keypad and the hover-bike's engines grumbled to life. The bike jerkily raised itself off the desert floor, its suspension field generators working again. The massive thruster-engine exhausts glowed with power as the sand on the ground swirled under the hover-bike. Em and H let out a cheer. The two agents smiled at each other. It felt like the hard night and the harsh words were all forgotten in the smooth thrum of the bike's engines.

"I know Riza," H said to Em. "She may be a merchant of death, but she does have one weakness." He looked down to Pawny. The small soldier glared back at H. "You ready to be a hero, little guy?" Pawny opened his mouth to give H a vulgar reply, but the agent kept going, "Great! Because we're going to Naples!"

As if on cue, the hover-bike's engines began to seize and choke. The power core failed and the bike dropped. Pawny grunted as he tumbled off the bike seat and thudded to the sand below.

H and Em regarded the dead bike sadly. Em gave H an "atta boy" slug on the shoulder. "Maybe you can fix it," she said with smile, "with your big old heart."

Despite her words, Em went back to work on the interface, checking for shorts or bad connections to the console. H picked up the wrench and started again on the power system. He gave his partner a faint smile as he picked up the water bottle.

It was a long way to Naples and Riza, over three

thousand kilometers, H mused, figuring their odds. Even if they got the hover-bike's hyperdrive fixed up again, every MiB station in the world would be on the lookout for them. But as he watched Em work, he suddenly felt something he hadn't felt in a very long time—hope. Real hope.

He took an absent-minded sip from the water bottle, and immediately spat the soup–Bassam-flavored water out, disgusted.

24

The ancient port city of Naples was dappled with color. Brightly painted buildings of yellow, red, blue, and green were clustered around the bay. The waters of the Tyrrhenian Sea were like blue glass, sparkling in the sunlight. In the distance the slumbering volcano, Mount Vesuvius, filled the eastern skyline, as beautiful and majestic as it was deadly. In the old town by the harbor, a long line of Vespas, looking like they belonged in the film *Roman Holiday*, were parked near the cluster of cafes and bistros that filled the narrow streets.

With a rumble and a growl, the alien hover-bike appeared in the street, Em, H, and Pawny aboard. They clambered off the big muscle bike, and after a few hurried minutes of arguing and gathering packing boxes from outside storefronts, they constructed a makeshift cardboard camouflage for the vehicle. Despite their efforts it was barely concealed, incongruous in the long line of Vespa scooters; but nonetheless, the three weary passengers left it there, heading for the rows of stores along the winding street.

Em, still in her MiB uniform, waited with Pawny outside a men's clothing boutique. H had said he needed new clothing for their next task.

"It'd be a real shame if something were to happen to H out there," Pawny reflected.

"H is a pro." Em glanced back toward the store and then at her watch. MiB was looking for them and every second they delayed made the likelihood they would be spotted increase. "He'll be fine."

"I'm just saying, if the worst *did* happen. We *are* in Italy. We could grab a little Prosecco, a little pasta…"

Pawny stopped as H came out of the clothing store. He was wearing a loose white linen button-down shirt, untucked, and a pair of pale pink pants. He'd completed the look with dock shoes and no socks.

Em made a face. "Wow, that's… bold."

"Thank you." H headed in the direction of the dock and they walked across the street together. "Good with the plan?"

"Great with the plan." Em tried to sound her most enthusiastic, though she had some doubts about H's strategy. "You?"

"Seeing my murderous, arms-dealing ex? Sure." H paused at a port-side vendor's booth. He paid the man in cash for a jar of fresh sardines, and then headed down the dock, unsealing the jar as he went. He dumped the fish into a trash can but kept the jar. "We will need one of these—" he scanned the port and nodded to Em "—

and one of those." H was looking at a beautiful wooden speedboat that was moored to the pier and was bobbing gently in the crystal-blue water.

"For the record," Pawny interjected, "I am not a fan of this so-called plan."

Riza Stavros's office was a large, luxurious room, the epitome of wealth and taste. The decor was traditional Mediterranean style, with a few nods to modern aesthetic. Rustic hardwood floors and stairs were set off by older columns and walls of rough-hewn stone and block—"souvenirs," or more accurately, loot, from the ancient ruins of the Neapolitan countryside.

Stone arches—some open to the air and sunlight of the sprawling patio outside, others windows and doors decorated with intricate wrought-iron latticework—encircled the room. Elevated marble-floored walkways between the central columns. Expensive and tasteful antique furniture dotted the room, including pieces of Grecian statuary, an armoire, and an old, heavy iron, multilevel birdcage. Stone stairs led down into a sunken conversation pit with a lovely view of the living cypress tree that grew up out of the wooden floor and whose leaves received sunlight through a square skylight.

The room was also a museum of death, a showroom of destruction. Several transparent panels stretched from the floor to the ceiling, lined with "samples" of various weapons from millions of different worlds and galaxies, lethal instruments of all imaginable shapes and sizes.

The ugly truth marring the beauty of the room was that Riza's business was selling slaughter. The occupants of many worlds across the universe had paid the ultimate price in blood for her to live in such opulence.

"This one here," a slender man with a razor-thin mustache was saying, "is the prize of the lot." The man looked human. He spoke English with a thick French accent. Only the curve of his ears and the mirror-like quality of his eyes gave away that he was not a native of Earth. Riza's desk was a sheet of glass held aloft by two chromed columns beneath it. On the desk in front of the man was a small plastic cage. Inside the cage was a small, cute pink creature. The animal looked a little like a hairless badger with a small, furry horn on its forehead. "Forget its size, it's a killing machine," the man went on. "One prick—" he indicated the creature's horn "—and you are dead before gravity takes you to the floor." The man gestured to the creature in the cage, with a flair of showmanship. "A Medoosean bark mole. *Beyond* endangered. He is the absolute *last* of his breed."

Riza regarded the little pink creature and the alien salesman. On Earth, nature often warned of the danger of another organism by marking it bright, colorful, and beautiful. The same warning applied to Riza Stavros. She was breathtaking in her beauty and unmatched in her cruelty and madness. Riza had long, straight hair that fell to her shoulders. It was pale blonde in color with black horizontal stripes that made one think of a tiger's coat. She wore a bare-shouldered diaphanous dress with a tropical pattern of blue and turquoise with gold highlights. The dress showed a lot of well-shaped leg through a long slit. She wore a cape-like wrap that matched her dress.

Her eyes flicked up to the salesman and all the affection vanished from them, like someone flipping off a switch.

"The very last? Do you have a certificate of extinction?" Before the salesman could reply, the small earpiece in Riza's perfect ear gave off a tone notifying her of an incoming call. She held up a finger to silence the salesman. "So sorry," she said, "I've been waiting for this." She tapped the earpiece with her exquisitely painted and manicured nail. "Hi. Klim, bit of a problem. The plutonium in the Eviscerator you sold me was C grade."

The salesman could faintly hear Klim on the other end of the call, protesting his ignorance and innocence in a language that sounded equal parts Khoisan, Dutch, Arabic, and Auto-tune. Riza shook her head as she listened. "You had no idea? Yeah, well, here's the problem: if people aren't getting vaporized, that reflects poorly on *me*."

As Klim retorted, sounding a bit annoyed, Riza nodded toward the bark mole, and spoke in a slightly lower, much sweeter, tone to the salesman. "He *is* cute, but is his little horn crooked?" Her voice switched abruptly to cold and angry. "*Klim!* I *know* plutonium, I *love* plutonium!"

Riza ducked down behind the desk and picked something heavy off the office floor. She returned to the salesman's sight holding a large and dangerous-looking rifle—the Eviscerator in question, clearly. She cradled the gun like a child and chambered the weapon with a loud *cha-chock*. The gun's breach was open, a sickly green light spilling out. She never took her eyes off the salesman. "And I know when something doesn't smell right."

The salesman swallowed hard as Riza bent her head down to sniff the open chamber on the gun deeply like she was smelling wine, or doing a line of cocaine.

"Okay, Klim, here's the deal. Some associates of mine are going to stop by." The salesman actually thought he heard Klim make a frightened "*eeep*" sound over the earpiece. Riza continued as if she had heard nothing. "My advice is not to resist. Less splatter for someone else to clean up."

The salesman heard Klim frantically babbling, pleading. Riza tapped the earpiece and disconnected the call. She placed the rifle on the desk in front of her and looked up, all malice gone from her eyes and voice instantly. She cocked her head slightly. "Now, where were we?" She looked from the clearly rattled salesman to the little pink animal. "Ah, yes. My little chubby bubby with the crooked horn," she baby-talked at the creature as she opened the plastic cage's door and reached inside.

Riza scooped up the badger-like animal and carefully lifted it out of the cage. She stroked the little creature's back and then looked up to the salesman as she flicked the fake horn off its head with a single finger. The salesman paled visibly.

Riza looked back to the badger. "Oh. Oh dear. Did

the bad man crazy-glue a pipe cleaner to your head?" She set it on her desk and took up the rifle again, bringing it humming to life with the push of a button. She aimed it at the salesman, who curled away in terror.

"Speaking of extinction..." Her finger tightened on the trigger, preparing to fire.

An alarm tone sounded from one of the half-dozen tablets Riza had on her desk. She glanced over at the tablet clamoring for attention. On the screen she saw live security camera footage of a sleek speedboat approaching her island. She reached out to activate the web of underwater mines that encircled her island, but paused when she got a better view of the man at the helm of the boat. It was H, Agent H. *Her* H.

Riza looked back to the hapless salesman who had been seconds away from pain and oblivion. "I'm *so* sorry," she said to the terrified man, her voice once again pleasant and businesslike. "Can we do this another time? I have a visitor."

25

H piloted the classic, wooden speedboat toward the private island of Riza Stavros. He knew from personal experience how intricate and expansive her security was, and he was certain she already knew he was coming. Physically, the island was beautiful and intimidating, just like the woman who owned it. The crumbling but still-formidable walls of an ancient fortress ringed the lower approaches to the island. Riza's guards patrolled those walls and the boat docks, making unseen approach and infiltration impossible. There was one possible exception to that—the jagged, vertical cliff on the back side of the island. Riza's multimillion-dollar villa was the crown on the highest peak of the island, nestled among the still-majestic ruins of a crumbling twelfth-century castle and an abandoned monastery, with its basilica dome still intact and shining bronze in the sunlight. H cut the engines and drifted in, closer to the dock and pier complex.

He put on his most charming smile and blew a kiss toward the villa.

From dozens of different hidden emplacements among the rocks, large turrets bristling with alien weapons appeared, their barrels extending, all trained on H.

H's smile fell and he hastily pulled out a handkerchief, waving it above his head wildly.

"Riza, don't shoot! It's *me*. It's H!"

There was no response for several very long seconds, as H's voice echoed through the stone canyons. Then the gun barrels retracted and the turrets descended below the rocks once again. H sighed with relief and steered the boat toward the dock.

Beside Riza's yacht, a fleet of speedboats, and an assortment of small pleasure craft, H also saw Riza's personal bodyguard, a hulking, eight-foot-tall Tarantian brute named Luca, waiting for him. Luca was all gray muscled skin and scowls. He had a mane of blue hair that fell to his shoulders. From his forehead to the tip of his nose formed a tapered, almost arrowhead shape of thick bone plating. His eyes were shaded over his massive brow and looked small and cruel. H waved at Luca and the two-armed alien guards that flanked him, as he tossed the big Tarantian his bow line. Luca handed it off to one of his subordinates who quickly tied the line, securing H's boat. H stepped onto the dock, covered by the other guard. He carried a multicolored gift bag, tied closed with a ribbon. H walked up to Luca.

"Hey big guy," H said, looking up into Luca's angry eyes, "miss me?"

"No," Luca rumbled. The bodyguard shoved H in the direction of a path at the end of the docks that led upward into the broken rocks of the island's mountain face. H followed the path, Luca at his shoulder, the two guards pointing their guns at H's back.

Just to one side of the path, a door embedded into the rocks of the granite island was set partially open. This was supposedly an old boathouse, H remembered—but he'd always suspected it was more than that. He peered in as they passed, careful not to show his escorts that he was scoping out the place, and was rewarded with the sight of a bank of high-tech security monitors at the back of the dark room. He let out a breath of relief, which cut short as he looked up at the alien gun mounts that surrounded the path. They seemed to be tracking him as he moved. He really hoped that was just an automatic setting. Riza wasn't the type to forgive and forget.

"That's the worst thing about breakups," H said as they walked closer to the villa, "losing those friendships. We had some good times, didn't we?"

Luca was silent.

"Well... Riza and I had good times. You just sort of lurked."

The winding path brought the party to a flatter patch of land, still some way from the main villa, in which a large orangery nestled. Luca punched in a code to the keypad beside the orangery's door. The door hissed open and Luca shoved H inside, then followed him in, leaving the other guards to wait outside.

Luca led him to a clearing in the massive glass dome.

There was a tranquil pond and trees from hundreds of alien worlds scattered around the clearing. There were also orange trees among the alien flora, giving the whole place a lovely scent. H watched the silver and blue lilies on the pond's surface drift lazily about. Then he saw the "lilies" rise up on the water's surface—each alien on thread-like legs of silver—and skate, almost weightless on the surface tension of the water. They circled and danced in increasingly complex and beautiful patterns.

A tiny, orange alien hummingbird darted up to H's face. The agent was able to see that the bird had a small face like a lovely woman wearing an ornate, purple masquerade mask. The long, needle-like "nose" of the mask was actually the bird's beak. H smiled at the flitting creature, which was just out of his reach. The little face smiled back and seemed to be trying to say something with its minuscule mouth below the beak.

A woman spoke from behind him. "Wonderful, isn't she?" H would know that voice anywhere. It filled him with a jumble of emotions, from anger to desire to fear. He turned as Riza, as striking and lovely as ever—no, she looked even better—walked toward him, like a sleek panther, out of the foliage. Luca, ever-present, lurked a few paces behind her.

Riza stopped inches from H's face. "I love dumb, beautiful creatures."

Her hand shot out to slap H's face. H caught her wrist. She swung with her other hand and H caught that one too. Then her third hand flew up and slapped his cheek with a loud crack that made all the nearby birds screech and scatter. "Ow," H muttered. He released her other arms, rubbing his stinging cheek.

Riza gave him an up-and-down look, noticing his lack of an MiB-sanctioned black suit. "MiB finally showed you the door?"

H bristled a little at that. "Showed myself out. Some horses are born to roam free."

"And others," Riza added, "they just get shot."

H lifted up the gift bag, and produced a jar from inside. "Peace offering." He held it up for Riza to see.

A wide, almost manic, smile spread across her beautiful face. Inside the jar, which had air holes punched in the lid, Pawny, minus his armor and weapons, capered about trying to look like a docile, mindless creature.

"Meep, farble," Pawny babbled, eyeing H and secretly wanting to punch a bunch of air holes in the MiB agent. Riza made cooing sounds.

"He's cute," she said, glancing up at H, "in an ugly sort of way." Pawny began to sneer and make a very un-docile, un-mindless, finger gesture at the arms dealer; but H shook the jar, just slightly, and Pawny's face fell against the glass and slid down a little at a time like a rubber mask.

"Blaaah," Pawny said, teeth clenched behind his bucolic smile.

"Last of his kind." H offered the jar to Riza.

She melted a little at those words, holding the jar in two hands and placing a third hand on H's chest. She looked up into his eyes. "You always knew the way to my heart."

"And you always knew how to make mine beat that little bit faster." H placed his hand over Riza's on his chest.

"Can I turn my earpiece off for this part?" Em's voice said in the tiny transceiver in H's ear.

On the jagged rocks below the villa, Em was slowly struggling her way up the cliff face, a comm unit in her ear, too. She'd sneaked out of the boat when H was being taken up the path by the henchmen—all the cameras she could see had tracked his movement along the path as she'd bolted for the cliffside and its camera-free climb. This Riza woman was clearly still holding a grudge, or obsessed, and H had been right that his presence would prove a good distraction.

It was too hot, and the work was too hard for formal wear. She'd ditched her MiB jacket, shirt, and tie back at the boat, and now wore only her black sleeveless undershirt and black pants and shoes. She was almost to the level where she had spotted the gun emplacements popping out of the rocks. It was slow going, but she knew she had to make sure every rock was really a rock, not a booby trap or panel that would trigger an alarm system. The wind had picked up a bit as she climbed higher, but it was a cool breeze off the water, not strong enough to be a risk of blowing her off the rocks and sending her falling to her death. She looked out across the perfect blue water, the sun flashing on its surface.

If it weren't for the nauseating lovers' reunion playing out in her earpiece, and the likelihood of imminent discovery and death, this would actually be a pretty fun way to spend an afternoon.

"Oh, H, I was looking forward to watching my guns tear you to pieces." Riza stepped away from H. "But then I saw that sweet little grin of yours, and I had to know."

"Know what?" H asked.

"The truth. Was any of it real? You, me?"

"Uh-oh." Even though he couldn't see it, Em's voice gave away her grin. *"This is going to be good."*

"I knew who you were from the start," H said. "My job was to gain your trust; and when the opportunity came, take you down. That's the truth."

"You said you didn't know she was an arms dealer!" Em snapped in his ear.

"What happened along the way—" he cupped Riza's perfect chin, and raised her head to meet his gaze "—me falling for you? That was real."

Riza's cautious countenance softened and the two former lovers looked deeply into each other's eyes. There was nothing else, no one else. The time, the angry words, they all fell away.

"There's not a neuralyzer in the world that could make me forget that one," Em said.

"Thank you, H." Riza's voice was both earnest and vulnerable. "For giving me closure."

She carried Pawny's jar over to a small wicker table between a pair of matching lounge chairs near the pond. She set the jar down on the table and turned back to address Luca, not H. When she spoke, her voice was detached and businesslike. "Get rid of him."

"Hold on," H said as a smiling Luca grabbed his shoulder in a vise-like grip. "I've got feelings too! Don't I get closure?"

"Oh, and H," Riza added, as he was being manhandled out the door by Luca, "here's a tip—next time you come with a peace offering, don't make it on the same day I come into possession of the most powerful weapon ever created."

H grabbed hold of the door frame with both hands, struggling against the inevitable pull of Luca's biceps. "This has nothing to do with that!" He disappeared from Riza's view, save for his fingertips, still curled around the frame. His head and torso popped back into view. "It's just an insane coincidence!" he shouted.

H vanished again—this time fingertips and all—as Riza's Tarantian bodyguard finally yanked the agent free. The door hissed shut behind them.

Riza watched the door for a moment. A lone tear rolled down her flawless face. She dabbed it away with her third arm. Then she blinked, and it was as if the sadness had instantly left her. A weird smile came to her lips. She began to hum "I Will Survive," as she picked up the jar with Pawny inside and made her way back to her office.

26

Luca had deposited H with the two guards waiting outside the orangery, and now they were walking him down the path back to the jetty, one on each side of H, blasters leveled at him. The agent babbled on as they descended closer and closer to the beach and, he guessed, his impending violent demise.

"I think that went pretty well, guys." They were nearing a tight bend, where the path hugged the mountain on one side, with a sheer cliffside drop on the other. "What do you think? Do I have a chance?" They entered the turn and H kept talking. "I mean, has she been seeing anyone seriously?"

One of the guards pushed H again with the barrel of his rifle. H spun as soon as he felt the faintest touch of the gunmetal against his back. He grabbed the barrel with one hand and jerked the blaster out of the guard's hand. He drove the heel of his palm into the guard's chin with a crunch, sending the alien flying back over the side of the cliff.

As the other surprised guard raised his blaster to fire, H swung the gun in his hand, like a club, smashing it into the side of the guard's head. The second guard followed his partner over the cliffside, a look of horror on his face as he fell. H looked around the narrow passage, making sure he had been correct when Luca had led him through here on his way up the path to the villa. This was a camera and sensor blind spot. The absence of alarms confirmed it.

He slung the blaster over his shoulder and hurried down the path toward the old boathouse, keeping his head down.

The door was still open, just as it had been when he'd passed it earlier. Somebody was slacking on the job, clearly—or perhaps the guards just thought nobody would be foolish enough to dare to sneak about an island bristling with alien weapons, under the nose of an array of cameras. He crept in cautiously and pushed the door to behind him.

There were several speedboats dry docked here in various states of disrepair, as well as boat maintenance equipment and supplies, workbenches, spare anchors, tools, and engine parts. The other side of the boathouse had been converted into a control station for at least part of the island's security network. H scanned the banks of monitors, levers, and buttons. He found the motion sensors and central power supply to the hidden gun emplacements. He snapped that series of switches off.

* * *

"Em," came H's voice over her earpiece, *"you're all clear."*

On the cliffs below Riza's villa, Em saw the gun turrets rise up out of their hidden alcoves all over the rocks above her. The guns then drooped and grew still as their power was cut.

"Copy that," she replied.

She smiled and began to climb again, as quickly as she could toward the villa.

In the boathouse, H watched Em ascend on one of the monitors. He turned to leave just as he heard the door click open behind him. It was Luca. The big Tarantian was across the room much faster than H had thought he was capable of moving. Just as H was swinging around, Luca drove a powerful kick into H's chest, knocking the wind from his lungs. The agent flew across the room, smashing into—and then wedging him into—one of the wooden boats stored there. The rest of the boat crashed down onto H. He struggled to free himself from the shattered boat debris.

"H, you okay?" Em's voice sounded worried in his ear.

"Yep." H began hurling winch hooks, wooden boards, and anything else that looked like it might hurt, at Riza's bodyguard. "Got him right where I want him."

The barrage of debris bounced harmlessly off Luca's hide, not even slowing him down as he stepped forward and flipped the power to the cliff-face guns back on.

* * *

Em was still scrambling up the rock face when she heard the exposed turrets all hum back to life. They were scanning for moving targets in their zone of fire, and Em was right in the middle of it. She froze, her fingers gripping the tiny stone handholds as best she could. Several of the guns snapped in her direction, their ugly barrels searching every inch for any overt signs of life. If her grip failed her, she'd fall to her death, unless Riza's guns blew her into particles long before she hit the beach.

"What's happening?" she said into the comm. The line was silent.

Luca heard the sounds of splintered boards and debris shifting across the room, and turned to see if that jackass of an MiB agent was still awake and struggling to free himself. The bodyguard was surprised to find H was already standing behind him. He had a heavy, wooden oar and was in mid-swing when Luca turned. The oar smashed into Luca's head, cracking and breaking as it did. The Tarantian crashed into a wall, sending down shelves full of paint cans and tools on top of himself.

H strode over to the security consoles and once again deactivated the guns.

"Nothing's happening," he said to Em. "Stick to the plan."

* * *

Em watched the searching guns suddenly go silent and slump again into inactivity. Hesitantly, she pulled herself up to a narrow shelf of a ledge. She wiggled her numb fingers, looking for her next point of ascent and trying to keep her eyes on the guns, in case they jumped back to life.

"You sure these things aren't going to kill me?" she asked as she began to climb again.

"One thousand percent," H said confidently, an instant before Luca erupted out from under the mountain of heavy paint cans, sending them flying like missiles crashing into everything, even smashing and wrecking some of the security monitors and controls.

Luca snarled and launched himself at H, a blur of rage, a juggernaut of anger. He spun and drove a tree-trunk-sized leg into H's side. H groaned as he was punted through the air, snapping through solid wooden rafter beams and crashing into another wall and the contents of its shelves.

Luca hit the button again.

The guns next to Em snapped to life. She narrowly avoided the blasts and debris by ducking behind another outcropping of rock for cover.

"There's no such thing as 'a thousand percent!'" she shouted.

* * *

H shuffled back toward Luca, keeping on the balls of his feet, bobbing left, then right, his arms up in a classic boxer's guard. Before H could close in to throw a punch, the eight-foot-tall brute spun with surprising agility and snapped a kickboxer's roundhouse kick. H tried to block it with his forearms, but the sheer force behind the kick broke through his defenses and connected with the side of his head. H's guard fell as he struggled to stay on his feet. Luca windmilled around and drove another devastating kick to H's jaw, sending the agent reeling backward and smashing through a thick support column. "Don't worry, I got this!"

H was on the floor, struggling to rise again. He spotted a carpenter's hammer on the floor and reached out, almost willing it to his hand. Nothing happened. Gathering the last of his strength, H scrambled to his feet, grabbing the hammer and hurling it at Luca with all his might. This seemed strangely familiar to H for some reason. The alien bodyguard grabbed the hammer in mid-flight and tossed it aside. It was the distraction that H needed. With a snarl, the MiB agent charged in, his shoulder low, and plowed into Luca. The Tarantian stopped H cold and lifted him over his head before body-slamming him onto his back, cracking the wooden floor.

"*What was that?*" H heard Em's voice in his ear, over the roar of weapons fire all around her. "*It sounded painful.*"

Luca pulled H's battered form from the floor and raised him again, above his head.

"Stick. To. The. Plan," H growled through gritted teeth. As Luca began to swing H back to throw him across the room, the agent hit the button with the tip of his shoe's heel, shutting down the guns. H flew like a rag doll across the boathouse and collided with a wooden rowboat with bone-jarring force. He saw bright, painful light strobe behind his eyes.

Em kept climbing, listening to the sounds of the fight playing out in her earpiece. She was getting closer to the top of the cliff on the side that the back of the villa faced, putting more space between herself and the guns.

She pulled herself up a jagged outcropping near one of the deactivated turrets, paused to catch her breath, and then kept scaling the rock, trying not to think about H. *The plan... stick to the plan.*

H reached out as he fought to stand. Not beaten yet, his fingers found a small boat anchor and chain. He hurled it low at Luca's legs like he was doing an Olympic hammer toss. Luca dodged the anchor but his massive legs got tangled in the chain.

Fighting to stay conscious, H yanked the chain with all his remaining strength.

27

On the cliff face, Em finally made it past the deadly maze of once-again silent guns and moved quickly toward the villa. "Okay," she said into her comm, "I'm through. Pawny, do you copy?"

At that moment, Pawny couldn't respond. He was busy acting like a docile creature in his jar prison. Riza had taken him from the orangery to her villa, some way away, and was now carrying him through a series of brightly lit, well-appointed corridors and then cave-like passages carved out of living rock. She paused at a sealed door and tapped a code into a small console on the wall beside the door. The door hissed open and Riza took the tiny warrior into her cavernous office.

A series of arches opened up to give a view of the grounds; the other side gave a breathtaking view of the tranquil, sky-blue Tyrrhenian Sea, the tiny dots of island chains, and distant Vesuvius. A large aquarium tank took up a prominent place in part of the room. Pawny recognized a few of the alien species gliding through the waters of the tank. Others, like the thing that looked like a cross between a coelacanth, an electric eel, and a wasp, Pawny didn't know and didn't want to know.

Two Elcidean smoke treaders padded silently around Riza's office, most of their attention on a large, ornate, and heaving-looking birdcage full of alien avians. The exotic alien pets were roughly the size, and had features reminiscent, of Earth cats. Pawny felt the smoke treaders' eyes, each with two brilliant, orange pupils, track him as Riza passed, before they turned back to their hungry patrol of the cage. Pawny wished he still had his blaster, or at least his dagger, when he saw how the smoke treaders looked at him.

The walls surrounding Riza's desk were covered in racks of weapons from across the universe. Riza sat down behind her desk and set Pawny's jar beside a vaguely skull-shaped diamond sitting on a small pedestal. Riza turned Pawny's jar around so that she could study his face. Pawny tried to act as mindless as he could. He had decided to use Agent H as his inspiration for this performance and so far it had gone off like gangbusters. "Now what am I going to do with you?" Riza cooed to Pawny. "I just want to eat you up, yes I do!"

In his tiny ear, Pawny once again heard his queen, Agent Em, speaking. *"Pawny, do you copy? Pawny?"*

Riza's earpiece comm chirped, announcing a call. Her looming face shot up and away from Pawny's jar as she tapped the comm to answer the call.

"Sebastian? Kisses. How would you like to be able to

destroy entire solar systems without leaving the house?" Riza wandered over to the far end of her office. Her voice grew distant.

Pawny let out a sigh and answered Em, keeping his voice low. "It's hard to copy when you're being slobbered on by a psychopath," he told her.

"You see it?" Em asked over the comm. She crouched among the rocks, just below the wide opening in one section of the cave office.

After a moment, Pawny's voice came to her. *"Yeah. I see it."*

She breathed a sigh of relief. The puzzle box was in Riza's office, just as H had said it would be. "Everything depends on you, now," she told him.

"Define 'everything,'" the tiny alien whispered.

Pawny inspected the lid of the jar. Besides making the air holes, H had been sure not to tighten the lid when he put it on. Pawny reached up and began to unscrew the lid from the inside. He was acutely aware of Riza on the far side of the fish tank, the murmur of her sales pitch rising and falling almost pleasantly, as if she were selling anything other than weapons of mass murder. He was glad he couldn't hear what she was saying.

The lid came loose and clattered as it fell onto the desktop. Pawny peeped out, his big eyes above the rim of the jar. Nothing. No indication the arms dealer had heard anything, and no sign of the alien cats. He spotted the rough-hewn corridor he was going to make a run for. With a grunt, the small soldier pushed his former prison to the edge of the desk and with a final shove let it fall.

The glass jar shattered and Riza's head popped into view at the noise. She spotted her newest pet scuttling as quickly as his tiny legs would let him down the access corridor that led to the sauna and torture chambers. Pawny disappeared from sight. Riza rolled her eyes in frustration and sighed as she followed him out of the room.

The office was silent except for the burbling of the massive fish tank. Em appeared, climbing up the last of the rock face and entering through the open wall. She looked around the huge office and then spotted the puzzle box on the table on the other side of the room. Quietly, she made her way to it, picked it up off the table, and stole back to the window.

"And here I thought H worked alone," Riza said. "Poor you."

Em turned slowly. Riza was by her desk, Pawny standing on her shoulder.

"It's been a steep learning curve," Em said.

Riza picked up a weapon off her desk, an ugly energy pistol with a compact, wide barrel. The intergalactic criminal held it up for Em to get a better view. "Snub-nosed Karzig Annihilator." Riza aimed the gun straight at Em. "Know what it does to a human body? Boils it from the inside out."

"Cute," Em said. "Know what a Pawny does to sadistic alien arms dealers?"

"No," Riza scoffed. "What's a Pawny?"

"*I'm* a Pawny, psycho!" The tiny warrior on Riza's shoulder bit down into her flesh as hard as he could with a snarl. Riza screamed and fired, but the blast missed Em and blew out the window next to her. The agent ducked for cover, clutching the puzzle box. Riza grabbed the snarling Pawny and hurled him into an adjoining room. She fired again on the fleeing Em, who vaulted over an antique chest to avoid the second blast. The chest burst into flames and cracked apart as Riza's blast missed her.

Em kept moving, ducking behind and jumping over various pieces of furniture in the office to avoid being hit. Riza fired again and again, but couldn't hit her.

Em launched herself off a settee and flew toward the opening and escape. Riza howled and launched herself airborne as well, corkscrewing her body in midair to lash out and punch Em solidly with her third arm. The punch sent Em crashing to the ground, tumbling across the expensive tiled floor. She lost her grip on the puzzle box and it clattered along the floor, ending up near the aquarium.

Riza landed in a crouch, all three of her arms outstretched to stabilize her landing. Her eyes were bright with crazy. Em groaned and pulled herself to her feet as Riza stood.

Em looked around for something, anything, she could use as a weapon. She spotted a chair only a few feet from her.

She considered bashing the chair into the aquarium and letting the hundreds of thousands of gallons of water that would pour out give her enough of a distraction to grab the puzzle box and make for the cliffs. However, it would most likely kill the beautiful and strange creatures inside the tank. No, she wouldn't kill innocent creatures for her own benefit—that would make her too much like this lunatic.

She feinted away from the furniture and then took a quick step toward it, picked up the chair with both hands, torqued her hips to gain extra energy in the swing, and hurled it at Riza with all her might. The chair tumbled toward the arms dealer's head. Riza fell into some kind of martial arts stance and deftly deflected the chair with all three of her arms, knocking it with a crash into a tree.

Em recalled everything she could from every Jason Statham movie she'd ever watched. She pulled her arms in tight and up at the elbows to guard her face. Riza saw the agent's inexperience and laughed. She came in fast and hard, driving a punch to the side of Em's head, bypassing her stiff guard and lack of footwork. Em's arms dropped and Riza followed up with some hard jabs to Em's face with one, then another, of her three fists.

Angry now, Em swung hard and wild. Riza blocked it with her third arm. Em charged in to try to tackle the arms dealer. She landed a glancing blow on Riza's cheek, before Riza used Em's own momentum and leverage to toss her across the room and into a bookcase. Em hit the floor, landing on her backside among a rain of antique books tumbling from the shelves.

Em's hand searched about as she stood up. Her fingers

touched the cool pewter of an antique candlestick that had been on top of the bookshelf.

Em grabbed the candlestick, brandishing it like a club, and came at Riza again, swinging with everything she had. Two of Riza's arms came up, almost crossing, and blocked the stick. Her third arm shot out and plucked it from Em's hand. Riza tossed the candlestick aside and brought her two blocking arms down, one on each of Em's shoulders. The pain was so great, Em's legs buckled.

Before she could fall, Riza spun her around and smashed her into the desk, pinning her down. Riza's hand raised above Em's head, ready to come down with lethal finality.

28

In the corridor to one of Riza's antechambers, Pawny climbed to his feet and shook his head to clear it from the impact. He could hear the sounds of fighting in the office, and heard Em gasp in pain. Pawny reached for his grapple gun and aimed it toward the rock surface of the wall above the distant doorway to the office and his beleaguered mistress. *I'm coming, Em.* Suddenly, Riza, grinning and in a fighting stance, came into sight past the doorway. Pawny lowered the gun slightly, taking aim on the unaware arms dealer's temple.

Just as he was about to fire, a dark shape that had been scuttling silently in the shadows sprang toward the little warrior. Pawny fell, the hairy thing on top of him. For a second, he prepared to feel the claws of the treader ripping at his armor, but then he realized this was no alien cat that had jumped him. It was Bassam; Bassam the beard.

"Time to taste my wrath, pawn!" the beard sneered,

its hairy tendrils entangling Pawny, keeping him from firing his wrist blaster.

"I eat beards for breakfast, Bassam!" Pawny said as the two small combatants found themselves locked in mortal combat.

Back in the office, Em, pinned to the desk and about to die, struggled to find any way she could out of Riza's vise-like grip. Her scrambling hands found a ceramic bowl on the desk. She grabbed it, smashed it, and held on to a large, jagged piece of the pottery. Riza swung down to end the agent's life, and at the same time Em slashed out at the arm pinning her down, leaving a wide, bloody cut.

Riza hissed at the pain, released her grip, and pulled back her arm. Em drew her legs up and drove them hard into Riza's stomach, knocking her backward, stunning her, and almost knocking her down. Em came up off the desk, a fierce look on her face as she pressed her attack, grabbing the arms dealer by the throat with both hands and squeezing with all her strength.

Riza's hand shot out and wrapped itself around Em's throat, choking her as well. Riza's other two arms came up and grabbed her by her wrists, trying to pull her hands off Riza's throat. They struggled silently for moments. Em could hear her own blood thudding in her ears, like a muffled drum. White spots of light danced before her eyes. *How can she be this strong?* Em thought, her lungs screaming for air.

Riza was too strong, even with a badly cut arm. Slowly, Em felt her grip on Riza's throat loosening as her opponent won the tussle. Then a moment of new, sharp pain, as Riza kicked her, hard. Em flew backward, crashing into the desk again, and collapsed to the floor, gasping for breath.

Em must have looked worse than she felt. Riza didn't even bother to come after her to finish her off this time but instead walked away, her attention on the puzzle box that lay undamaged on the floor.

Em sprang up. Images of what Riza and her monstrous clients could do with the black-hole weapon pushed her past her pain and exhaustion. She launched herself at Riza. Without even looking, the arms dealer caught the battered agent by the throat again and hurled her dismissively into a Grecian statue of a semi-robed woman near one end of the conversation pit. Em crashed into the statue with a groan, destroying it, but went right back at Riza again, running on nothing but desperation and anger.

Riza took a swing at Em and the agent ducked, dodging the blow. Em snapped a punch back as quickly as she could, and connected, but Riza hardly seemed to notice. She grabbed Em under the arm and by the hair, twisted and lifted her off the ground, and slammed her hard onto the floor, shattering and scattering several of the pieces of marble floor covering. Em felt the wind forced from her lungs with a *whoosh*. Her awareness dimmed and she fought to stay awake and aware.

* * *

In the corridor, Pawny struggled to free himself from Bassam. The beard was beginning to slide more hair around Pawny's chest, getting him in a position from which Bassam could constrict and crush him to death. Pawny heard the sounds of Em and Riza's battle and guessed things were not going well for Em. He had already lost his first queen, he wasn't about to lose his second. He wriggled, and managed to bring his arm up from Bassam's pin. In a moment, Pawny stood over Bassam, and punched Bassam, over and over again, until the beard no longer fought back.

Pawny looked in the direction of the office and the sounds of Em's distress. He ran as fast as he could toward the sounds of battle.

What could be better than learning the truth about the universe? Molly heard a younger version of herself ask, through the semiconscious haze of the beating she had taken from Riza.

You are, her father had said, putting his arm around her mom, the two of them smiling at her. Mom... Dad. Riza was somewhere far off, laughing, taunting. If she let herself slip off into the painless darkness of oblivion, that horrible weapon would get used, maybe even here, and a lot of innocent people—humans and aliens— would die. It was funny, she had spent so many years convincing herself that human attachment was just a bunch of chemical reactions that messed with your head, she had forgotten how much she really loved her mom and dad, and how much they really loved her.

What had H said? *The whole universe is a chemical reaction...*

Wake up, wake up!

Em's eyes popped open. She had only been out for a second and Riza was still standing above her, mid-gloat. Em began to sit up, and as she did she swept her leg out, tripping the surprised Riza. The arms dealer went down hard on her back with Em, also on her back, on top of her. Em drove her elbows back into Riza, fighting like the life of every being in the universe depended on it. But the arms dealer blocked her blows.

The two rolled around the floor of the now-demolished office. Riza fended off Em's flurry of blows and began to choke her again. Em found her hand on a rope from the destroyed statue and got an idea. As they struggled, she managed to tie the rope around a serpent bangle that Riza wore on her third arm. Em jammed the rope under the metal of the jewelry and secured it as best she could while still struggling with the now furious, and quite insane, crime boss. Riza seemed to have no focus, no awareness of anything other than killing Em. In her frenzy, she seemed to have forgotten even the puzzle box they were fighting for.

But Em hadn't forgotten that box, nor what was at stake if she lost this fight. Her lungs were burning like they were filled with acid, and her throat ached, but the rope was secure. She guided the direction of their rolling floor brawl toward the large birdcage. As they got almost beside it, Em released her grip on Riza and rolled away, at the same time kicking out and sending the heavy cage crashing down on top of Riza, freeing a flock of beautiful and terrified alien birds. The cage had pinned Riza's third arm under its weight.

Em, with great effort, made it to her feet and limped toward the puzzle box.

In a lunatic's display of strength, Riza pushed the birdcage aside and rushed to intercept Em.

The rope attached to Riza's already badly damaged third arm snapped taut as she stumbled toward Em. Only now did Riza realize she was attached to a pulley. The tension on the rope jerked her back across the room and smashed her into a large twelve-foot-tall bookcase. She hit the floor with a loud slap.

When Riza raised her head and looked up, she saw Em standing beside the bookcase. The MiB agent grunted and pushed with all her might and the case wobbled, tipped over, and then crashed with a thunderous boom on top of the arms dealer. Riza moaned and Em punched her again and again and again until she stopped moving or making a sound. She was soundly unconscious. Em stood up, groaning at the effort.

"That," she said, walking over and retrieving the puzzle box from the floor, "felt good."

Pawny was there, back in his armor. For some strange reason a few large, stray hairs poked out of his clothing.

"Hold onto that feeling, my lady," Pawny said. "Cherish it." He was looking at something past Em. "And then you might want to turn around."

Pawny jumped from the floor to the overturned

bookcase to Em's shoulder as the agent turned around.

Riza's big alien bodyguard, Luca, stood there by the main entrance to the office. He held a huge gun in one hand, pointed at her and Pawny, and a slumped, seemingly unconscious H in the other.

29

H groaned, and Luca tossed him on the floor in front of him. H rolled over and saw Em and Pawny looking at him. He summoned a smile. "Don't worry," he said, "all part of the plan."

Em heard a rumble and a crash behind her. She closed her eyes and sighed even before she heard Riza's voice.

"Well, H," Riza remarked, "you've always been slightly delusional."

Riza walked over and plucked the puzzle box from Em's hand. Em looked at H, who was trying feebly to punch at Luca's tree-trunk-like legs.

"I got him right where I want him," H declared. Em shook her head.

"'Peace offering,'" Riza said.

Em took a step toward Riza, her hands raised, palms open.

"Look, Riza, you don't know me," she said, "I don't know you. We're not even from the same galaxy, but here we are, on the same rock. Turns out the universe is pretty small." Em walked toward the arms dealer. She thought of her folks back in Brooklyn, ignorant of all of this, who had no idea she'd even left the States; she thought of Guy, her fellow probie at MiB London, and all her colleagues there who she'd barely had time to get to know; and she thought of all the people who were going to die if that box, that terrible weapon, got away from her. She nodded toward the box in Riza's hands. "That weapon can swallow entire solar systems. Maybe, one day, Earth. It's your home, too."

Silence fell over the room. H nodded to Em. It was clear he was proud of what she had said.

"Mic drop," Pawny said.

Riza seemed lost in contemplation of Em's words, her eyes unfocused on the here and now. The focus returned and she looked at Em thoughtfully.

"You're absolutely right." She pulled the box tight to her chest with all three arms. "You don't know me." She nodded to Luca. "Kill them." She pointed to H. "Him first. Make it hurt."

Luca reached for the battered and exhausted H, knocking aside his attempts at defense as if he were a small child. He picked H several feet up off the floor by his throat and began to squeeze the life out of him. Em rushed toward Luca and H while Riza, nearly beaming with joy, enjoyed watching the show.

"*Stop!*" Em shouted. H, growing red, his eyes bulging, put up a final effort, slapping and punching Luca, to seemingly no effect. "You don't have to do this," Em beseeched the gargantuan alien.

"He does," Riza happily offered. "He's under contract."

H tried boxing Luca's ears, kicking him in the chest, even going for his deeply hooded eyes with his thumbs. He had no strength left in him and everything was too bright and dimming at the same time. A strange feeling passed through H, like he hadn't accomplished anything real in his life. It was the same feeling that had been dogging him, that he had been hiding from for years, since Paris. *My life is meaningless*. Even saving the world seemed hollow, unimportant, in this final moment. He felt like letting the bodyguard get on with it, but another older, stronger part of him refused to do that, and kept fighting the darkness, even though he didn't know what the point was. "Let... me... go," H sputtered hoarsely, driving his fist uselessly into Luca's expressionless face, "you... Tarantian thug!"

Em blinked. H's words set off a memory, one so integral to her core that she hardly even examined it or thought about it anymore, like ignoring the details on the wallpaper in your own home after years of walking by it. "Wait," she said. "Did you say 'Tarantian?'"

"Yes, my lady, he did," Pawny said from his perch on Em's shoulder. "They tend to be single-minded when it comes to killing. Brains the size of a pistachio nut."

Luca growled a bit at the remark and redoubled his efforts to wrench H's head off.

"You're... not... helping!" H gurgled.

Em stepped closer to Luca, examining every detail on the brutish alien's face. There was something there, something familiar. She was ten years old again, in her bedroom with an ugly little alien with a wild mane of turquoise, green, and purple hair sprouting up above big, innocent, ping-pong-ball eyes.

"I know a Tarantian," Em pleaded, talking straight to Luca, trying to reach him. "I met one once. I helped him."

Luca looked over to Em and she thought she saw something behind his tiny stone-like eyes, a flicker of awareness. Luca seemed to shrug it off, however, and raised H even higher, squeezing tighter. Em glanced over to H. He was no longer struggling, hanging limply from Luca's hand. Em felt something cold slither through her stomach. H's chest was still rising and falling but his breath was ragged and shallow. She recalled the MiB agent's words that night, so many years ago: *"He's cute now, but when these things hit puberty, they turn into real monsters."*

She was sure she was right about Luca. There had to be something, anything, she could say to the Tarantian to make him stop killing H. The tumblers of her memory turned and clicked. She looked up at Luca and shouted, *"Kabla nakshulin!"*

Luca started, as if he had been hit by something stronger than H's most deadly blow. His grip on H loosened. H's bloodshot eyes opened, feeling Luca pause at Em's words.

"Yeah," H gasped, "what she said!"

Luca looked down at Em. "How do you know that?" he asked her.

"He said it to me," Em told him. Luca searched her

face now as intently as she had examined his. His cold
eyes warmed with recognition.

"Molly?" Luca asked.

Em smiled and nodded. "It's *you*," she cried.

Luca dropped H to the floor and lowered his rifle.
The agent, red-faced and gasping, rubbed at his throat.

Riza threw all three of her arms up like she had just
heard the worst umpire call ever made in a championship
game. "You're shitting me," she shouted. "*Really?*"

"Who's delusional now?" H smiled at his furious ex.

Riza reached to grab Luca's gun, but Luca trained it
on her and she froze in her tracks.

"Give her the box," Luca ordered.

"Luca, you can't." Riza's voice was honeyed and soft,
pleading with her bodyguard. "Haven't I been good to
you? I let you kill anyone you want."

Luca gestured with the gun at the puzzle box. Riza
glared at Em as she tossed her the box.

Em smiled at the puzzle box, safe in her hands. "*Kabla
nakshulin*," she asked Luca. "What does it mean?"

"It means, 'One day I will kill whoever you choose
in the most gruesome way imaginable,'" Luca said.
"Rough translation."

"Or..." Em nodded at Riza thoughtfully, "just keep
her here for a while."

30

Em, H, and Pawny made their way down the winding mountain path from the villa to the docks below, toward the heart-aching beauty of the sea and the sky. Em was practically vibrating, still high from the adrenaline rush of everything they had just done.

"Now that was a rush!" Em said.

H nodded, exhilarated despite his bruises. "When a good plan comes together, there's nothing like it." Em glanced back at him and they both paused in their descent. They held each other's eyes for a second longer than they should, and something passed between them. Pawny didn't like their new-found camaraderie, not one bit.

"I'm pretty sure the plan went wrong," Pawny interjected, "in every conceivable way."

H and Em ignored his attempt at buzzkillery as they continued descending the path.

"So it's Molly," H said.

"You're not supposed to know that," she replied.

"It's only fair you know mine."

Em shook her head. "I don't *want* to know."

"It's Horatio," he said, and laughed when he saw the look on her face. "No it's not, it's Harry," H blurted out. Em looked over at him and they both laughed. They smiled at one another and again Pawny saw the connection between them was strengthening.

"I'm Steve," Pawny announced.

"Steve?" Em glanced over at the little warrior on her shoulder. "I thought pawns don't have names."

"We don't," Pawny told her. "I was feeling left out."

As they neared the final turn and the steps to the dock, H paused.

"What's wrong?" Em asked warily.

"Nothing," H said, looking out across the crystal-blue waters dotted with distant islands. The bare peak of Vesuvius seemed to reach heavenward to the very edge of the endless, unmarred sky. Em saw the look in his eyes, and got it. After so much danger, so many chances to die, she joined him and they watched the beauty before them and recalled silently why their jobs were so important.

The whole island began to rumble and quake. Both agents were pulled from their reverie, and scanned the ground at their feet. There was a sound like the planet was being shredded and a wide fissure tore through the ground. The crevice ripped toward them at a furious pace.

Em grabbed H's hand and pulled him aside as the massive opening in the earth shot past them, and the land between them and the stairs and the dock below caved into the sea. A second fissure, moving just as fast and as improbably as the first, tore another deep valley between them and their way back up the path on the mountain. They were cut off. The nearest part of Riza's island groaned, creaked, and then collapsed, breaking up and tumbling into the ocean below. They were stranded on the edge of a very tiny strip of land, high above the Mediterranean Sea.

At the far end of the island strip, two glowing, faceless, amorphous beings knelt low to the ground, energy pouring from their bodies into the warping and trembling earth. The two aliens began to flow and shift into a pair of humanoid figures as they walked toward the agents.

"So what's the plan this time?" Pawny asked. "I'm open to anything."

The figures solidified and became the Dyad twins as they came closer.

"We must have it," the first twin announced.

"For the Hive," the second twin finished the thought.

Em cradled the puzzle box, looking around for any way out, any escape route. All that was behind them was a crumbling cliff, a deadly drop into the water with the jagged teeth of rocks below. When she saw H's face, she was surprised to see a new look in his eyes. He'd been beaten, shot at, bruised, cut, and he was exhausted. He was seething.

He caught her glance and nodded sternly at her, then took a few steps toward the twins, his eyes steely and set with determination.

He called out to the twins. "I don't know if you've heard, but we are the Men in Black… the Men *and the Women* in Black. So if you think we're going to just let you hand this thing over to the Hive, you don't know who you're dealing with. See, we protect the Earth and everyone and every *thing* on it. No matter where they came from. So let's go."

Quite suddenly, the twins stopped. They took a step back. His speech had *worked*.

H stood a little taller, and thrust out his chest and jaw a bit more at the effect his words had had on the Dyads. Then he heard a faint, mechanical whir behind him and looked back to see that Em had the stellar compression weapon out of the puzzle box and in her hands. She had powered it up and the weapon's mouth was aimed straight at the twins.

"One more step," Em called out to the Dyads, "I obliterate this whole island and everything on it."

"*Including* you and me," H murmured in a low voice. "You could have said something. I gave a speech and everything."

"It was a very good speech," Em said, glancing over to H. "You with me?"

H was silent for a second, then, "I'm with you," he said. Turning to the twins, he called out, "We'll do anything to save our world."

For a moment the only sounds were the wind whistling through the canyons on every side of them and the whoosh and crash of the waves. After a moment of silence, the twins glanced at one another, silently communicating.

"So will I," the twins said in unison.

Em and H looked at one another, confused by the reply. The twins began to advance toward the agents again.

Em's hand fell to the activation switch for the weapon as the Dyads came closer. She had it set to the minimum power setting, the same one that had annihilated miles of desert. She looked to H. H swallowed and then nodded. *Do it.*

But before she could press the button, there was a loud humming and the hiss of static electricity, then two loud cracks as bolts that looked and sounded like purple lightning struck the twins, disrupting their human façades, turning them into out-of-phase humanoid silhouettes of glowing white particles. Right on top of the disrupting lightning came twin fireballs of brilliant golden energy that struck both twins and sent them scattering into millions of particles of white energy, each particle going dark and falling to the ground, remaining still, unmoving, dead.

Both agents looked in the direction of the discharges. On the other side of one of the crevasses, standing on a high rock outcropping, was High T. A massive MiB weapon that was a bit like an over-under double-barreled bazooka was slung over his shoulder.

"Nothing in this universe is unkillable," High T said, patting the side of his weapon, "with the proper voltage." He grinned and gestured for H and Em to join him on the other side of the rift. By the time they had taken a good running start and crossed the crevasse, T joined them near the stairs to the dock.

"Are you both all right?" High T asked.

H nodded. "Yes, sir. Never better."

Em's attention was on all the dark, dead particles scattered on the ground. She looked back to T.

"But, sir, how did you find us?" she asked, obviously puzzled.

"'Experience,'" High T said, then tsked and shook his head at H. "Riza again, H? When are you going to learn?" H looked sheepish, and High T placed his hand on his protégé's shoulder, no explanation needed. "I knew I could count on you," he said more softly, "that in the end you'd pull through."

H beamed like a boy given a kind word by his father.

"Yes, sir," he said.

"You too, Em," High T said. "Agent O had a feeling about you and she was right. The universe has a way of leading you to where you're supposed to be at the moment you're supposed to be there."

Em stepped away a few feet as H and T talked. She wasn't trying to distance herself from their conversation, far from it, but she just felt... off. The stellar compression gun was folding and retracting itself back into the puzzle box in her hands. She looked back again at the remains of the dead Dyads. Something felt wrong, like an important page in a book was stuck to another page, or she had skipped over a critical part of a mathematical equation. Maybe life was just more messy and chaotic than that, not always fitting neatly into some formula. Maybe this was just the crash from the adrenaline high—perhaps she was just finding out, after so much had happened, that she wasn't fully ready for it to be over, to go back to what had been before all this.

"Shall we go home?" High T asked. He paused a moment and scrutinized H's once pristine, expensive new outfit. Now it was rumpled, torn, and bloody. "Better clean up first."

31

It was night when they arrived in London. H and Em, cleaned up and back in their black suit uniforms, were greeted on the main floor of MiB headquarters by thunderous applause and a standing ovation from all the agents, support staff, and aliens. High T walked behind them, the massive Dyad-killer gun slung on his back by a strap, Vungus's puzzle box in his hand.

An agent and a forensics technician approached High T, Em, and H. The tech carried a high-tech, evidence-room strongbox.

"Let's keep these safe," High T said, handing the huge gun to the agent and the puzzle box to the forensics tech, who secured it in the strongbox. The two hurried away to carry out their duties.

H had an easy grin on his face.

He drifted through the crowd like an old pro, exchanging high-fives, fist-bumps and thumbs-ups as he made his way through. Em was overwhelmed by the attention and the accolades. She smiled, nodded, and waved awkwardly a few times, but all the time she was trying to find a way out of the crowd. In the churning mass of people, H and Em were pulled in different directions. It reminded Em of that one time her bestie in school, Stephanie Kepros, had talked her into going to a club to see a bunch of punk bands at an all-ages show. The crowd had been too much for her and when people started stage diving, and pulling her toward all that churning chaos, she was out.

Em made it through to the other side and was thankful to draw in a cool, uncrowded breath. Her escape had been helped by the fact that H was still at the center of the crowd, soaking it all in, gracious, and cool, just like when she first met him.

High T was behind her, watching his protégé receive his laurels.

"Quite the first assignment for a probationary agent," High T remarked. "Marrakech, the Empty Quarter, Naples. Imagine what you'll accomplish when you're one of us."

She saw H among his colleagues and it felt like nothing that had happened on the mission had been real. He seemed to be back to the same old H, glad-handing, shallow, and superficially charming. It was like he was made of Teflon, no real emotion or feeling could stick to him. It made Em's growing feeling of apprehension even worse, and she felt very alone again. That surprised her. When had she stopped feeling alone, started thinking of herself and H as "us," as a team?

Without turning to High T, Em said, "Thank you, sir."

"Enjoy this moment, Em," High T said. "They never last." Was that wistfulness in his tone? He walked away before she could ask, and was quickly lost in the traffic of people bustling through the main floor.

Em glanced back to H. He was sitting on the edge of his desk, surrounded by fellow junior and senior agents. An agent at an adjourning desk withdrew a bottle of Glenfiddich from his desk drawer and started pouring the scotch into plastic cups and passing them around. Em slumped a little. Suddenly she was back in high school, watching the cool kids' table in the lunch room from her lonely vantage point, eating alone, save for the company of one of Michio Kaku's books.

Even Pawny was fitting in and had an audience. A group of office workers was crowded around the small warrior. He was on a desk, using a stack of books like a stage. "So we're on the edge of this cliff and H is cowering in front of the Wonder Twins, like, 'No please, don't kill us!'" Pawny was doing his best H impersonation. "And I'm like: 'Man the F up, H.'" His audience was eating the story up. "So I turn to these guys and I say, 'Dudes, either you back off, or you're not going to know what hit you.'"

Em did a double take when Agent Cee joined the circle of agents around H. He took up a plastic cup of scotch gladly and with a smile.

Cee held up his cup to toast H. "Well, H, I don't know how you keep doing it," the fastidious agent said, "but somehow you keep doing it." The other agents laughed.

H glanced over and saw Em's alien cubicle buddy, Guy, had joined her and was taking a picture of himself and Em with a selfie stick. Nerlene photo-bombed the two. Guy and Nerlene laughed, but Em had a serious and distracted look on her face. They exchanged glances from across the room of celebrating people, and H knew that Em felt something wasn't right, either.

"I mean, what are the odds?" Cee was droning on. "That you'd save the Earth from total destruction twice in so few years?"

H managed to get a word in over Cee's monologue of praise. "I don't know, Cee, what are the odds?" Before Cee could wind up to address the question, H set his empty cup on the desk. "Excuse me."

He met Em at the center of the room.

"Is this what saving the world is supposed to feel like?" Em asked. "Because I'm not feeling it."

"Me neither," H replied. "What if we got this all wrong? The Dyads... When I said we'd do anything to save our world—"

"They said they would, too," Em finished the thought.

"They told us they wanted the weapon 'for the Hive,' but what if we misunderstood what that meant?"

"Maybe they wanted it to use *against* the Hive—to save *their* world."

"Which could mean they were never Hive at all."

"What about the DNA, the mutations?" Em shook her head. "High T showed us the sample."

The two agents navigated the celebration in their

honor and managed to politely disengage from numerous attempts to pull them into conversation. H sat down at the closest desktop computer terminal. He keyed the voice recognition microphone in the keyboard.

"Agent H." The computer chirped as it authenticated his voice print. "Bring up the Dyad forensic report."

The report's title page appeared on the screen. Across it in bright red lettering was the word: DELETED.

An awful connection formed in both their minds. The nagging, irritating sense that something was just out of mind's reach bloomed inside. It flowered into a cold, heavy fear in both their stomachs as a terrible realization settled on the two agents.

"Who has the authority to make a case file disappear?" Em whispered. Both agents turned and looked up to the window of High T's office. Then, as one, they bolted, sprinting side by side toward the evidence room, and the stellar compression weapon.

Cee had managed to pull himself away from the celebration—it was all very well snatching victory from the jaws of the Hive, as it were, but there was always business to attend to; somebody had to keep an eye on things. He knocked on the entranceway into High T's office and entered. High T was sitting in his chair facing the oil painting of himself and H at the Battle of Paris. For a moment Cee thought he heard the station chief muttering to himself over and over again.

"My name is Terrence Pemberton Wood...

Terrence... Pemberton Wood... I am a senior officer in a non-governmental agency... My name is Terrence Pemberton Wood..."

"Sir?" Cee said, the concern evident in his voice. "Did you say something, sir?"

High T spun, surprised. "I didn't hear you come in." He stood up and pulled on his overcoat. "You have the helm, Cee. I'm not feeling myself."

High T strode out of his office. Cee stared after him, utterly freaked out. He turned back to the chair his boss had been sitting in, staring at it as if at a loss, then raised his eyes to the painting of the Eiffel Tower, wondering.

"And what about Naples?" Em asked breathlessly as they bolted down the hallway, dodging agents and aliens. "How did High T know we were there? He mentioned the Empty Quarter to me. How did he even know we were there?"

"He was doing his job," H replied. He knew it was a weak answer. Everything pointed to High T as the traitor within MiB, but his instincts told him that was impossible. There was no way the man he knew—his friend, his mentor—had sold out.

"Does his job include tracking us?" Em side-passed H the compass she had received from High T on her first day on the job in London as they skidded into the corridor that held the evidence vaults. "He gave it to me as a gift. There's a chip inside."

They slowed and H examined the compass as they

walked together through the polarized glass doors that led into the evidence room. The same technician who had secured the puzzle box from them when they returned sat behind a semicircular desk with illuminated white panels. Past him was a room that contained smooth, flat, near-infinite walls of lock boxes of all imaginable sizes and dimensions. The attendant sat a little straighter when he saw two such legendary agents enter.

"We need to see the confiscated Jababian weapon," H announced. There were no hints of charm, no pleasantries. He was all business.

The attendant shook his head. "Not possible."

H bristled. "I'm the senior agent on the case." Em had never before heard the cold steel in H's voice she heard now. "Show me the weapon."

Cowed, the attendant reached for the evidence case that was sitting on his desk, sliding it over to them. It seemed odd to H that it would still be lying out and hadn't been logged in and put in a secure box on the walls.

Em and H spun the case around and the tech keyed in the code to unlock it. The case was empty.

"High T signed it out just before you got here," the attendant explained.

H felt like he had been punched hard in the gut. As much as he wanted to fight it, to deny it, there was no other theory that made sense.

H and Em stepped out of the elevator onto the mezzanine level of the station.

"I think he's been after it this whole time." Em could see H's world was turned upside down, but she needed him to step up now. She tried again. "*H*. High T's the mole. He has to be."

"A mole for who?" H shook his head, like he was trying to clear it. "Where is he taking it?"

"My guess would be Paris." Cee came out of High T's office. "There's something not right with him," he added, acknowledging what they were all thinking.

"Paris." Em remembered the pictures of Guy's family and the old alien depot in the Eiffel Tower; she thought back to the breached gate she had seen in the VR archives record about H and High T's battle with the Hive monster in the same place. "He's taking it to the portal."

Cee blocked H's path before he could get away. "All this time I thought he was covering for you, but he was hiding his own tracks, wasn't he?"

H didn't know what to say. If High T was guilty, another terrible consequence of that betrayal fell on H like a wall of bricks. In typical fashion Cee didn't give him time to answer, anyway. "I'm going with you."

"No—"

"This isn't about you, H," Cee snapped, a little of his old snark returning.

"No, it isn't." Em couldn't recall seeing H look so sad, or so determined. "If word gets out that T—the most highly decorated agent in MiB history—is a traitor, the agency will never recover. We stop him and no one will ever have to know."

"And if you don't?" Cee asked. H set his jaw. He

banished the pain from behind his eyes and met Cee's own gaze with a steely resolve.

"Tell them it was me. Tell them *I* was the traitor. Trust me, the agency will believe you." He paused, and then said significantly, "*You*."

Cee looked at H in a way he never had before. He nodded and stepped out of H's and Em's way, letting them pass.

They stopped only to rescue Pawny's captive audience from any more tall tales; he climbed gladly back into Em's pocket.

"What phase is the moon in?" H asked, as they headed for the elevators. Em looked at him, confused. Had the new discovery tipped H's senses over the edge? "Sorry," he added, "you seem like someone who would know that off the top of your head."

"Full," she said. "It reaches its perigee tonight."

"The portal can only be opened during a full moon." He checked his watch. "In one hour and thirteen minutes."

"You think High T's opening the portal? To give the weapon to who?"

"What does your gut tell you?" H asked, grimly, as he walked to the window overlooking the main floor, where the celebrations had broken up and everyone was back to their jobs.

The agents entered the elevator, headed for the underground garage, racing against the rising moon.

3 2

The elevator doors hissed open on the MiB garage. H and Em stopped cold in their tracks as they turned the corner into the alcove that housed H's Jag. The vintage Jag looked more like a crumpled beer can than a car, having been demolished in the first battle with the Dyad twins on the streets of East London.

"Oh, right," H said. "That happened." His gaze travelled away from the mangled heap to a vehicle covered by a tarp sat next to the corpse of the Jag. H walked over to the car and pulled the tarp off, revealing a sleek, black, brand-new Lexus. An MiB-issued replacement for the Jag.

"Now we're talking," Pawny said, from his place in Em's pocket.

H tried his key fob and was greeted by a loud *bloop* as the car's alarm was disabled. Em strode past him and snatched the keys from his hand on her way to the door.

"I'm driving," she said as she slid into the leather seat.

She looked over at the steering wheel on the opposite side and at the smiling H as he slid into the driver's seat of the UK-configured car, and plucked the keys out of her hand.

"I'll never get used to that," she said as H turned on the ignition and the Lexus growled to life. The car screeched as it took the tight turns of the garage. As they hit the hidden garage entrance, H pulled a power turn, tires drifting. Then he floored the accelerator, and the car shot down the street, London streetlights flashing by. The chronometer on the car's flat screen control panel said they had about an hour till perigee.

H flipped open the armrest compartment between him and Em. There was a set of very nice cup holders inside the compartment. That was it.

"There should be a big red button around here somewhere." He pointed down into the compartment.

Em tapped the computer screen set in the dash between them, jumping quickly from menu to menu, until she stopped and cleared her throat. H glanced over. There was a menu on the screen: AUDIO, BLUETOOTH, RED BUTTON. Both agents smiled.

"Found it," Em said.

She selected the "RED BUTTON" option and was rewarded with a graphic of a red button. She pushed the button and the graphic changed to an overhead schematic of the Lexus that rapidly began to shift before their eyes. There was a loud electronic hum and a sharp *clack-clack* as the car shifted into rocket-car mode. Wings and massive engines deployed, unfolding virtually seamlessly from the body of the coupe. There was a series of not-terribly-exciting tones, like you might hear on an airplane, notifying you to buckle your seat belt and place your tray table in the upright position. H and Em glanced at one another, a little disappointed. Then, several Gs of acceleration hit them square in the chest and both agents gasped and yelped a little as the rocket car bucked and lifted off. Pawny screamed as he flew off Em's shoulder and splatted against the rear windshield, looking a bit like a piece of gum that had been spat out.

Em saw the beautiful lights of London, the dark mirror of the Thames reflecting and distorting the flare of the car's jets. She recalled what it was like to have a mystery come into your life, to show you there were secrets and wonders in this world. She remembered that night, all those years ago, when the young Tarantian had stolen into her house and the agents in black had stolen her parents' memories, and she was glad she had never stopped chasing her star. She wondered if some kid down there in London was watching right now, and dreaming of another world.

Pawny struggled to pull himself free of the rear windshield as the MiB-sanctioned rocket car roared into the night, rapidly becoming a new star burning in the sky, bound for Paris.

33

The brilliant full moon was not alone in the sky above the City of Lights. Heat lightning flashed above the Eiffel Tower, and distant thunder rumbled, a warning of the storm to come. H's sleek, black Lexus rocket car came in at hyper-speed on final approach toward the Eiffel Tower. H wrestled to keep the wheel straight and on course as the winds grew stronger over Paris. He saw distant, dancing red lightning and it brought him back to the last time he had been in Paris.

"Strange, isn't it? How history repeats itself," H said.

Em murmured a reply, watching the streaming lights of the city beneath them. It was beautiful, like a city made of jewels.

"It was a night just like this," H continued, "when High T and I went up to face the Hive with nothing but our wits and our Series-7 De-Atomizers."

Em glanced over at him. "You know you tell that story the same way, every time?"

"That's how it happened," H said.

Several stray ideas started banging into one another inside Em's head. Once again, she got the feeling that something was not right. The ideas collided into an awful thought. For now, she kept it to herself.

The rocket car landed on the street, merging flawlessly into the evening traffic on the Quai Branly, the street running on the side of the tower, facing the Seine and the Trocadero. The Lexus pulled to the curb as the rocket and wing components melded back into the body, turning it back into a car again. The two agents got out of the car, illuminated in the blinding headlights, and looked up. Strange, reddish heat lightning was surrounding the apex of the tower, like a crown. Pawny popped up out of Em's jacket pocket and regarded the iconic structure.

"God, I love Paris," he said.

The agents slung their rifles as they strode across the plaza toward the banks of elevators, and approached one that was labeled STAFF ONLY. H keyed a code into an old-style keypad next to the slightly rusted steel trellis doors.

The door to their elevator slid open, and H and Em entered.

As the elevator lifted the agents closer and closer to the portal at the apex of the tower, Paris, in all its radiant beauty, showed herself to them.

"Ah," Pawny reflected, "Paris. The City of Bicycles."

They were silent for a moment as the car took them higher and higher.

MEN IN BLACK INTERNATIONAL

Em kept looking at H. She decided she needed to test her theory, and now was better than later. She hoped she was wrong. She took Pawny off her shoulder and slid him back into her pocket.

"I'm sorry," she said, "but do you mind telling me one more time? How did you beat the Hive?"

"What?" H looked a little annoyed. "Em, we have no idea what we're about to face up there. Let's focus on the now, shall we?"

"Just humor me."

"It was three years ago," H said, hurriedly. "High T and I went up to face them with nothing but our wits and our Series-7 De-Atomizers."

The sick feeling Em had began to show on her face. H looked confused.

"Yes, but how did you beat the Hive?" she asked again.

"Are you serious?"

"Curious," she replied. "How'd you do it?"

"I *told* you," H started again, "with nothing but our wits, and our..." H paused. A look of horror and betrayal fell on his face, as the realization came to him, finally. Em wished she hadn't been the one to put it there, but he needed to see, needed to know, the truth. "My God," he said. "I'm repeating myself, aren't I?"

Pawny popped up out of Em's pocket. "Word for word," he blurted out. Em made a gesture for Pawny to hush.

"Over and over," Em said.

"It's actually kind of freaky," Pawny added.

Em wished Pawny wouldn't be quite so keen to have

the last word sometimes. H had already had a rough night with the revelations of T's treachery, and now this. She glanced over at the old-style floor indicator, above the elevator's doors. Its needle was edging closer to, almost at, the top.

"H," she said, unslinging her gun, "I don't think you beat the Hive that night. I think… I think you were neuralyzed."

H didn't want to believe it, any more than he wanted to believe High T had betrayed MiB, but the truth was relentless. Em could see him trying to fight it, hanging onto the shreds of the man who had been his partner, his friend, and in many ways, his father.

But then Em saw H accept the truth—her idea made an awful kind of sense. He hadn't saved the world, not really. He'd just become part of the lie. The elevator shuddered as it neared the top and the abandoned portal depot.

They turned to face the door as it slid open, guns raised. Outside the feeble light of the elevator car, there was darkness and silence.

The two MiB agents chambered their De-Atomizers. They stepped together out of the light and into devouring darkness.

3 4

The pregnant moon, burning with silver light, was nearly overhead. The agents made their way across the silent, empty deck at the top of the tower. Off in an alcove, there should have been a black door marked STAFF ONLY. The massive metal seal that had once covered the opening had been ripped off and lay crumpled on the floor. An emergency access light above the door was a silent, red, blinking star in the darkness. The light blinked rapidly, paused for a moment, and then blinked again. The seal had been broken.

It would have taken strength far beyond a human's to tear off the covering, and then fold it up in the process as if it were made of aluminum. But there were indentations on the torn seal that resembled human handprints. Beyond the broken seal, through the opening, was a spiral staircase leading upward.

This was where it had all gone wrong for H, Em thought, and in the very moment of victory. He'd thought he'd finished off the threat, all those years ago, but it was quite the opposite. It had been the beginning of the Hive's campaign. And perhaps that hidden memory, under the surface, was the thing that had changed him— made him date arms dealers, go for the highest stakes, live on the surface.

Em took the lead, stepping through the circular doorway and cautiously ascending the stairs, her De-Atomizer aimed up them. H was right behind her, watching left and right, gun leveled as they climbed. The stairs led, H knew, to the antechamber of the portal room. They reached the top, now side by side, sweeping every corner, every dark shadow of the long, dusty, cobweb-covered room. Em had visited Ellis Island once with her parents as a child and the depot reminded her very much of the island. There were rows of processing booths and desks, where new arrivals to Earth would wait in line to begin their new lives. An extraterrestrial Ellis Island.

As dangerous and unnerving as the situation was, Em felt a sense of wonder fill her as she imagined the depot over a century ago, bustling with life and color, like the MiB headquarters in New York, or London. She paused before a wall with departure and arrival times scribbled in chalk on old slate tablets. Surrounding the timetables were ancient framed photographs, black and white and silvered, faded with age.

Em recognized Gustave Eiffel, the builder of this very tower, in one of the photos. He was with a group of men dressed in what was apparently the height of nineteenth-century fashion. They appeared to be standing on the construction site for the tower. All the men around Gustave Eiffel were dressed head to toe in black and wore smoked lenses. Em touched the dusty glass covering the photos. Other photos showed lines of aliens, dressed in Victorian garb, variously smiling, waving, and stern-faced as they were processed in this very room. H couldn't help but smile at Em's wistful reaction. He could hardly recall the last time he had felt wonder, real wonder, in this job. It was nice to see the world through her eyes, even for a second.

There was a loud thump from the other side of the depot, and the two agents snapped their heads in that direction. The noise echoed through the stale air. H and Em began to advance, their Series-7s moving back and forth before them as they went past the booths and desks, making sure each one was empty before they moved. Pawny had even come out of hiding from Em's pocket and had his small, but powerful, blaster aimed— covering his queen. They moved as silently as they could past wooden benches and rusted, skeletal luggage carts.

The far end of the depot contained the portals. They were just as H recalled them, three circular arches, each sealed by a heavy, metal slab of a door. The size and shape of the arches reminded Em of subway tunnels. There was a circle on the floor of the chamber. The edge of the circle was surrounded by a ring of alien symbols interspersed with pictograms that represented the cycle of all the phases of the moon. Directly over the circle was a round skylight and the huge, brightly lit moon was almost dead center in the skylight, edging ever closer to perigee.

Large cables snaked along the floor between the portal archways and among strange box-like contraptions of brass, leaded glass, dials, and meters. The arches were labeled in roman numerals, I through III. Below the numerals was an old-fashioned power meter with what looked like a pressure bar, half red and half black. The brass arrow-like needles for each indicator were currently in the red.

"You came to say goodbye. Good lad." The voice was High T's and it echoed in the ancient air of the depot.

There was a loud snap, the sound of electrical current, and a whining hum like a turbine powering up. Em and H looked up to see High T standing behind a pedestal on the catwalk above the three portals. The controls for the portals were on a pedestal made up of three circular, equidistant panels, covered with dials, levers, switches, and glowing glass-covered meters. The rogue agent manipulated the switches and dials of the consoles, bathed in the blue, ghost-fire glow of the meters that he had just powered up. Lights encircling the middle portal's door came to life, indicating the sequence to activating Portal II was underway.

"You can feel the history here," High T said, looking down on the two agents, who had split—H left, and Em right—into the shadows of the depot. "Can you feel it? Eiffel discovering the wormholes, gangways to other civilizations. The first alien migration." H and Em climbed the ladder to the catwalk as quietly as they could, weapons at the ready.

"And we made history here, too, didn't we, H? With only our wits and our—"

"No!" H shouted as he leveled his weapon at his old friend and former partner. "We didn't."

Em, on the other side of the catwalk, also covered High T. Pawny, on Em's shoulder, also aimed his blaster at the rogue agent. H moved closer, cautiously. High T glanced from side to side, seeing he was surrounded. He didn't seem concerned in the least.

"We never beat the Hive," H almost snarled. "The Hive wanted the most powerful weapon in the galaxy. They knew Vungus would bring it to the Men in Black. So, what, you made a deal? You'd wait and when it came, you'd give it to them?"

High T responded by turning a large knob. There was a deep bass throbbing that rose in intensity. "You have no idea. There's no stopping this. There never was." The moon had reached apogee through the circular skylight. Portal II began to rumble open. Brilliant white light spilled out from the retreating aperture as the wormhole yawned open.

H advanced. Only a few feet separated the two men. "You neuralyzed me," H said. "Made me a hero, 'the guy who saved the world.' But I was just your prop, left alive to sell the lie." H's massive gun barrel was inches from High T's face. "What did they promise you?" he asked. The rage came off him almost like heat off a desert road. "What *could* they? To make you betray everything you ever stood for?"

High T winced, seemingly physically pained by H's

wounding words. He let his gun fall to the floor. H kicked it away.

Below them, Portal II yawned wide open. Though it was difficult for Em to see it from her vantage point, she had a horrible vision of what waited across the frozen gulf of space on the other side of that door. Hive Space: the worlds invaded and consumed by the Hive.

It was a swath of death and destruction that scarred the universe, like an ugly wound, like a cancer. Em knew hungry, terrible entities waited to pour through that gate and do to Earth what they had done to so many other vital, living worlds. The only thing that stood between the Hive and her beautiful little blue-green world was Em, the tiny alien pawn, and H.

T removed the puzzle box from his pocket and held it so Em and H could see it. "They wanted this. I said no. You were there."

H's gun wavered for a moment as he struggled to find some scrap of memory. Em took a step closer, worried for her partner.

"They... take you over... from within," High T said. "Until whoever you were, you're not that anymore."

High T looked into H's face, his eyes. "You were always like a son to me." His voice became deeper, his body convulsing.

"H..." Em began, but the warning died on her lips.

"You were always... like a son to me," High T said again. He sounded like a record skipping, stuck in one groove, one strong memory. His skin began to split like rotted cheesecloth. His body began to twist and grow. T's voice dropped several octaves. "You were always like a son to him." His hand morphed into a Hive hand made up of tentacles—disposing neatly of H's gun as it did so.

And then the man who had been known as High T exploded, his body popping and shredding, countless tentacles erupting from within. H and Em jumped back in utter horror.

For the second time in his life, H found himself standing before a great Hive monster, a gigantic mass of nearly indestructible, wrapped muscular tissue strands. Whirring, super-humanly strong, rope-like tendrils shot out of the thing that had only seconds before been High T.

A mass of tentacles slapped into him with the same kind of strength that had ripped and crumpled the seal to the depot, smashing him into a wall. Em opened fire, hitting the monster in his back several times, but apparently doing no damage. A group of lash-like tendrils shot out of the Hive creature's back, knocking her for a loop and sending her crashing to the floor below, and skidding toward the portals.

Pawny went sprawling as well; his tiny armored form flew free from Em's shoulder and he bounced a few times before coming to a stop. As Em struggled to her feet, a rain of slithering Hive tendrils spilled over the catwalk and began to wrap themselves around her feet. She struggled to scoot away from them before they got a firm grasp on her, scrambling for her De-Atomizer.

Above, the monster ripped away a piece of the catwalk's steel rail and stabbed it into the portal control panel. The panel erupted in sparks and smoke.

On the ground by the portals, Em, blasting away the encroaching tendrils, saw Portals I and III grind partway open and she couldn't help but look.

The first portal opened onto wonder. It was a vast vista of deep space, icy oblivion smeared with thousands of subtle colors from a nearby nebula. A violet star radiating a crown, a golden corona, and beyond it, millions of distant lights, pinpricks of ancient ghost light, filling Em's eyes from the depths of the birth of time. Crystalline mountains floated in the obsidian deep—asteroids made of sapphires, rubies, and emeralds flashed in the scattering rays of the purple sun, refracting the light of the star. Drifting islands of pure diamond with castles, temples, whole cities carved into them. Em saw their ghostly, gaseous inhabitants flying from place to place among the glittering spires.

A quick glance at the second portal showed a lush world of seemingly endless vegetation, plants and trees of every imaginable color thrived under twin yellow suns. Em was shocked and delighted when she saw several of the "plants" uproot themselves and begin shambling along, seeming to join limbs to communicate as they walked, or perhaps they were just holding hands.

Em pulled her eyes away, but she didn't want to. The swarming flesh-ropes of the Hive reminded her that the universe could be an ugly place too.

The Hive monster made sure the puzzle box was tightly secured inside its fibrous body. Its long mission complete, it launched itself toward the portal that would allow it to leave this chaotic world of undirected individual lifeforms and disharmony, and take it home to the silent, undulating unity of the Hive. It launched itself off the catwalk and straight toward Portal II. H, his back to the wall he had just been smashed into, clambered to his feet, knowing what the thing that had been High T was planning to do. He ran full-tilt down the narrow metal walkway and launched himself at the monster, knocking it off course and causing it to crash to the main floor of the depot. H bounced off and tumbled into a pile of old debris from the depot's active days and lay still.

35

Em's gun didn't seem to be stopping the Hive tendrils. She began to wrestle with the snake-like tentacles, ripping them off her legs as quickly as she could. Pawny helped by blasting them with his own gun, which seemed to drive them off, if not actually hurt the Hive's writhing fingers.

She was dimly aware that H was back on his feet again, and that he had gone toe-to-toe with the Hive monster, swinging a broken two-by-four at the thing's almost mummy-like head. The creature slapped H into an open nest of metal gears and springs underlying the metal grillwork floor near the portal machinery. H was cut, burned, and crushed in a spray of sparks and metal.

Free of the burden of H for the moment, the Hive monster spun, giving Em its undivided attention. A barrage of new tendrils lashed out at the agent and Em scooted back and tried to roll out of the way of the living, squirming onslaught. Several of the strands hit Em and knocked her down into the same open mechanical trenches that resided under the depot's main floor. On her way down, she saw that H was currently climbing back out of one such pit.

Em fired wildly as she fell, blasting a few strands. She hit a series of pipes and they broke her fall, but her De-Atomizer was jerked from her hand and clattered down into the darkness beyond the pipework. Fortunately, the pipes she landed on were insulated. One of them had broken when she hit it and a howling blast of steam was spilling out of it. She could feel the heat coming off the pipes. It was lucky she was behind the curtain of scalding air. *Of course, this place is steam-powered*, she thought as she struggled to reach the edge of the trench without getting burned.

A mass of Hive strands slithered down in pursuit of her, and Em, out of desperation, swung the broken pipe in their direction. Em watched as several strands shriveled and seemed to die under the blast of steam. The others crawled back up, making a hasty retreat to the Hive monster that spawned them.

Em wrestled the broken end of the pipe back up to the depot floor as best she could and aimed at the retreating Hive strands, and the Hive monster itself. Where the steam hit them, the strands shriveled and died. Many rejoined with the Hive creature, wrapping themselves about the monster like extra muscle fibers. The Hive monster howled in pain for the first time as the steam enveloped it. It staggered out of range of the blistering cloud and glared with hatred at Em. It began to shift and change, growing larger, more muscular and massive.

Pawny, who stood on the edge of the pit Em had fallen into, watched the Hive thing grow and glanced over at Em. "I'm not sure that helped."

The now larger and meaner-looking Hive creature spun to confront H, who had just made his way back up out of the gear nest. H, panting, and not looking too happy himself, held a large metal gear in one of his hands, gripping the center of the cog. Each of the gear's teeth were pointed and very sharp. The Hive monster charged at H, sending a swarm of its strands ahead of it. H spun, grunting as he sliced tendril after tendril. He fought his way closer to the Hive creature that had been his best friend. Just as he was about to reach the range to strike, the Hive thing used its superior reach to drive a jackhammer of a punch at H's jaw. The agent flew backward and smashed into one of the support posts for the catwalk, sliding to the ground.

As the monster moved in to finish off H, Em let out an angry cry of defiance from behind it, and charged, wielding a piece of metal pipe. Em thrust with the pipe, trying to impale the monster, but it shifted and opened its body to allow the pipe to slip harmlessly through it. However, doing that freed the puzzle box from within the creature's chest and it clattered to the steel-grate floor of the old depot.

Em's satisfaction was short-lived. The monster tightened its body's grip on her pipe and ripped the weapon from her grasp. The next thing she knew, the pipe was coming at her too fast to dodge. A cloud of pain enveloped her, and then blackness.

36

H let loose an angry bellow as he saw Em fall and lie unmoving on the floor. He was dead on his feet, but he summoned up his strength again and drove a few powerful uppercuts into the Hive monster's rope-like abdomen, and then a devastating right hook that would have shattered a human's jaw. The Hive monster didn't even seem to flinch. It drove its winding fists down like a hammer onto H's skull. The agent's legs buckled and he fell beside his incapacitated partner. He was relieved to see Em had come to, but they were both too stunned by the Hive monster's blows to move.

But they couldn't just lie there. Even as they watched, the Hive monster recovered the puzzle box from the floor and affixed it to its chest with a mass of ropy strands. It lumbered toward Portal II and home. H and Em helped each other pull themselves to their feet and leaned on one another to stay standing. The thing that had been High T had its back to them, ignoring them as it made its way to the portal. From their vantage point, H and Em could see into the Hive's world. They both wished they couldn't.

In contrast to the other planets on the other side of the portals, teeming with life and light, the home planet of the Hive was a desolate graveyard of cold rock with a sky of starless void, punctuated by ghostly streamers of wan, red light from some distant nebula. The crimson glow gave the whole landscape an infernal look. The surface was moving, undulating, and for a moment Em thought it might be the surface of some black, oily ocean. But then she realized what it was, and real terror clawed its way up her throat from her stomach. The surface of the planet was covered, teeming in billions of Hive monsters, like the one they were facing now. The horrific mass had spotted the portal on their side and let out, en masse, a terrible, frenzied shriek. In that nightmare window, H and Em saw Earth's future, and knew they couldn't stop now.

H staggered after the Hive monster, grabbing a big, rusty wrench off an old shelf. "I'm going to get it back."

"H—a plan?" Em called after him.

H hurled the wrench at the back of the Hive monster's head. It connected with a loud thud, and bounced off. The monster turned and glared at H.

"High T," H began, "that's who you are. There's still some of you left, there has to be."

The monster closed the distance between the staggering MiB agent and itself in less than a second. It grabbed H violently and pulled him closer. H searched for something, anything, in the creature's eyes.

"I was like a son to you? Well, you were like a father to me."

Em could feel—could see—this all going badly very quickly. She looked around for anything that might harm the Hive monster. It was hard to stay upright. Her head was pounding and she was pretty sure she had a concussion. She heard the hissing of the steam pipe and looked over to see one tip of a piece of steel rebar rod had been heated red-hot by the broken pipe. Em picked it up by the other end.

H was still trying to reason with the thing, trying to find High T in there somewhere.

"You wanted me to take your place," H said. "Remember?" For a moment, there was an echo of T's face, his features, in the twisting, writhing face of the creature. Then it was gone.

"And you will," the Hive monster replied in a rumbling bass. The thing grabbed H by the head and forced him down to his knees. Smaller, vein-like strands slithered free from the thing's hand that clutched H's skull. They slid over his face and slipped down into his ears. H began to convulse, his eyes rolled back in his head as the Hive began to devour him and change him, from within.

It's trying to do to H what it did to High T, Em thought as she charged at the monstrosity, wielding the red-hot steel rod. She began to swing at it, trying to sever the tiny threads invading H's body without harming him, but the monster slapped her with its free hand and sent her flying through the air. She bounded against the ramp in front of Portal I and fell through the other side of the wormhole gateway.

She was drifting in the void. What had she said to O, back in that interrogation room? *"I want to know how it all works."* Well, she was seeing it all now. Flaring stars and swirling clouds of living art. It was so beautiful, and she was so small, Earth was so small. There was a drumbeat in her ears, her lungs were freezing, her eyes too. Her heart was going to burst. She was made of ice, but her blood was lava, ready to erupt. She thought she heard something from so very far away. Em's body spun in space, so that she was facing back the way she'd come. There was the warm light of the portal door. A tiny figure stood in it.

"My Queeeeeeen!" The impossible cry seemed to come from far away—too far to save her. But the figure was coming closer now, moving at great speed. It was Pawny. Em was fighting to not pass out. On the back of his armored breastplate was a small jetpack that he was using to maneuver around her.

He was wrapping her in a snug sling of wire line. He used the last of the pack's fuel, apparently, to give her mass a nudge toward the portal entrance. Then, when they had drifted close enough, he raised a tiny grapnel gun with a motorized spool and fired it in the direction of the portal. The line went taut and Pawny clicked on the motorized spool. They shot at great speed toward, and then back through, the portal.

Em coughed and gasped. Her lungs were on fire. Had

all that really happened? She couldn't have been out there very long or she would have been in much worse shape. Em rolled over and blinked as her blurry vision began to clear. Back to the nightmare.

H was being devoured by the Hive.

37

H convulsed. His thoughts, his memories, maybe even his soul, were being sucked away and replaced with a squirming, ugly entity. It was the Hive and it knew only hunger and conquest. H heard Em and Pawny behind him. He fought to stay him; he fought the minds of the trillions of things all across the galaxy that had been converted into that one, terrible, blunt thing.

He focused and saw the puzzle box held by a few squirming strands on the Hive monster's chest. H summoned every last drop of his humanity and willed his arms, his hands to act.

What are you doing? the Hive buzzed inside him.

He grabbed the box and ripped it free before the monster could strengthen the tendrils. He threw it to Em with all his remaining strength. It was up to her now. That thought comforted H a great deal as he swirled down into horrible, humming darkness.

* * *

The puzzle box skittered across the floor and right to Em's feet. She bent and picked it up, fighting to not pass out. She looked up to see that the Hive monster had retracted its tendrils from H and tossed him aside. It charged at her, at full speed, back from the brink of Portal II.

Em's fingers worked of their own accord. She ought to be terrified, but she wasn't. The stellar compression weapon unfolded in her hands just as the Hive monster launched a mass of tendrils to grab it, grab her. She had a second, tops. Em slid the power scale to maximum as she keyed the trigger.

"Bye, T," Pawny said.

There was no wait, no buildup like there had been in the desert. An annihilating beam of near-infinite energy ripped through the Hive monster that had been High T. Nothing remained of it. The beam kept going, reaching its maximum discharge range on the other side of Portal II—Hive space.

The Hive home world ceased to be just as quickly and as completely as the Hive monster had. And still the beam kept going until it released all of its energy at its maximum range, destroying world after world, system after system, until the entire Hive sector of space was empty and silent. No world would ever again have to fear the threat of the Hive.

Portal II crumpled and collapsed in a shower of sparks and shattering metal. Outside, the night sky became as bright as day for just a moment, then the stars regained their dominion.

Pawny hopped up onto Em's shoulder. It was almost enough to knock her over. The stellar compression weapon folded itself back up into the puzzle box and Em put it in her pocket.

"Nice grab, Pawny. You served your queen well."

"Thank you, my lady. It was nothing really. Just timing, and aim, and extreme bravery."

H staggered to the spot where the Hive monster— once the man who had been his friend—had died. There was nothing left of the thing that had taken over High T—the thing that had tried to take him over, too. Portal II was nothing but scrap metal and a gaping hole, through which there was a new view of the City of Lights. Despite the destruction, the view was still beautiful.

Em joined him. She knew exactly what he was going through and she knew that, for once, he didn't need to talk. She put her hand on his shoulder as they looked together at the radiant city and remembered, again, why they did the job.

3 8

The sky lightened with the rising of the groggy sun. As Em and H walked away from the Eiffel Tower, they saw a fleet of MiB-sanctioned Lexuses and a containment truck parked around H's new car. There were Men in Black stationed at every vehicle.

"She as tough as they say?" asked H.

A smile of recognition came to Em, and she quickened her pace and straightened her posture as they approached the Men in Black.

"In a word?" she told him. "Yes."

Agent O stood at the edge of the street, projecting an authority that made it seem like all the monuments surrounding her were there because she willed it to be.

"Well," O said to Em as she and H approached, "you didn't screw up."

"Yes, ma'am," Em replied.

"There were some bumps along the way," H said, summoning Classic H, "some friction at the start…" He stopped when O gave him an impatient look. "Sorry, ma'am." He cleared his throat. "Yes, we didn't screw up."

Em spoke up again. "You said, 'We may have a problem in London.' You *knew*."

"I hadn't trusted London branch for some time. I never would have guessed why." O's stern face softened for a moment. "T lived for this organization. He was the very best we had to offer. He will be missed."

O took a moment to collect herself and then turned to Em, extending her hand. "Welcome to the circus, Agent Em." Em shook her superior's hand. "You're no longer probationary."

H smiled at Em. "Well, my work is done here—"

"You are," O said, cutting him off.

H nodded in agreement, then did a double take as O's actual words sank in.

"I'm sorry," he said, "what's that, now?"

"Probationary head of London Station," O said.

Em could see the surprise and the pride cross H's face. The raw emotions were quickly hidden away behind his usual carefree façade.

"*Probationary* head?" he asked. "Did I just get demoted and promoted at the same time?"

"Several years ago, before all this," O explained, as she, H, and Em took in the MiB clean-up and containment operation going on around them, "T mentioned to me an up-and-coming field agent who possessed certain leadership qualities." She gave H a look as if she were judging the very qualities of his immortal soul. "Was his faith in you misplaced?"

H stood tall, his demeanor serious, as if he were before a Marines sergeant major. "No, but there are other more experienced agents better suited for the job."

"Yes, there are." O nodded. "And you have the support of all the senior agents. Including Cee."

H looked over at a group of his fellow senior agents. They were not-so-subtly eavesdropping on the conversation with O. They nodded their support.

Serious now, he turned back to the New York station chief, sounding more solemn than Em could recall. "Thank you, ma'am."

O spun on her heels and addressed Em. "You'll need to tidy up your affairs in London. You report to MiB New York on Monday."

O saw the look that passed between H and Em at the news. It made a distant part of her heart, that she had long ago promised to seldom visit, wince. She thought for a moment of K, of what might have been, could never be. She ordered the feelings back into their box, and they departed as quickly as they had come upon her.

"Congratulations, probie," Em said, summoning a smile. She extended her hand to H. H took it and shook it. Already his mask was slipping back into its old, comfortable place.

"Congratulations to you."

They were both all smiles. O noticed they both held the handshake a second too long and then reluctantly let go.

"You'll want to go brief your agents," O said to H, waving him on to his duties, and he turned away. "Walk with me," she added, to Em.

O walked Em away from the bustle of the crime scene until no one was in earshot of them.

"You wanted to know how it all works," O reminded her. "Now you do."

Em didn't answer O. She didn't want to. She glanced over to H addressing his agents. *His* agents. H's put-on confidence had been replaced by a true authority, one she had only glimpsed in him before this moment. It suited him, like he had been born to it. In a very short time she had come to think of her universe always having an H in it. He challenged her, complemented her, made her laugh, and kept her thinking about what she believed and why. She *trusted* him. She willed H to look over at her, but his back remained turned, busy with his new job, his new responsibilities.

"But, as you may have divined," O went on, "there's a price."

O moved on to assess the scene and see where they stood in the process. Em fell into step beside her.

With his circle of agents around him, H explained High T's fate as delicately as he could. The men were visibly shaken by the revelation and wounded by their leader's loss. As they moved away, H turned to Cee.

"Thank you," H said.

"You've got *so* much paperwork coming your way," Cee said, a little of his old wicked smile returning.

"Which I'll send to you," H replied without missing a beat. Both men laughed. For now, the hatchet was buried.

H turned to see if he could catch up to Em but she and O were already gone from the spot, moving quickly away, engrossed in their work. She never looked back.

Pawny popped up from H's jacket pocket. The little warrior looked like H felt.

"How long have you been there?" H asked.

"Long enough."

H walked away, into the breaking Parisian dawn, carrying Pawny with him.

39

Most of the larger MiB stations around the world had a room tucked away that acted as a memorial for their fallen. The London office was no exception. The walls were black marble and, as you approached them, the code name of each fallen agent and their dates of service glowed to life. The names they had been born with were not present. The walls were covered with glowing names, and like any agency that valued secrecy, there was no mention of how these men and women had died, or where.

A row of square, marble pedestals lined the wall you faced as you entered the chamber. The pedestals were white and bore only the code name of the few agents who had been elevated to command of an MiB station. High T's pedestal was the newest addition to the room.

Atop each pedestal was a transparent crystalline bust of the station chief. H shook his head and gave a dry chuckle when he examined High T's bust. Even though it had been laser-cut using the 3-D holographic image from High T's service record, H thought it didn't look like the real High T. It reminded H a bit of the busts of Roman emperors that usually served vanity more than historical accuracy. H was pretty sure T himself would get a laugh out of it. Maybe he should ask him.

Embedded in the crystal of each bust was a monomolecular quantum AI storing a complete brainwave print from the deceased, made sometime prior to death. It was maintained and updated on a regular basis throughout the agent's life. While it wasn't immortality, and often wasn't even accurate, touching the bust would let you "visit" with the dead through a telepathic interface. H didn't think he was ready for that, not right now, so he just did it the old-fashioned way.

"Well, here we are, old man," he said, his voice echoing in the empty vault. "I never thought you were serious about me taking your place." He looked down at the marble floor. "That night we bumped into one another the first time, in Bridport? Well, it was pretty much just another night for me. Working a job to pay the bills, pub, a few too many, then either over to the Cod for a quick sober-up meal or just home to get up and do it again the next day."

H paced in front of High T's bust, feeling like he really was talking to his old friend. "That had been good enough for my mates, not a bad life, you understand. I just always wanted... more, felt there was more out there, just hiding a bit out of reach."

H looked at the bust. "You believed in me, T, when I didn't even believe in myself. I just wanted to say thank

MEN IN BLACK INTERNATIONAL

you. Thank you for seeing something in me, when no one else could. You were always like a father to me. I hope some part of you knew that."

H took his flask out of his jacket and began to unscrew it. "Here's to you." He paused for a moment, considered the flask, and then tightened the cap and slipped it back into his jacket. "Maybe later," he said. "Goodbye, T." He turned from the bust and strode toward the doors. "I've got a train to catch."

40

Em sat alone in the hyperloop depot on the lower level of the MiB London Station. She was waiting for the train that was going to take her home, back to New York. She had tried reading *The Hitchhiker's Guide to the Galaxy* on her MiB-sanctioned tablet. She'd read it several times in her life. Her dad and mom had even read it to her when she was a kid and it always delighted her. H had told her that a lot of the book was more travelogue than fiction, and that had made her want to read it again with different eyes. But she couldn't focus to read right now.

She glanced at her watch and then to the empty escalators. No one was coming to say goodbye. He wasn't coming to say goodbye.

But when she looked away from the escalators, she found H sitting on the bench next to her. Pawny, in a new suit of black-and-white armor, reminiscent of an MiB uniform, was sitting on his shoulder.

"You were going to leave without saying a proper

goodbye." A half-smile was playing on H's face.

"You were going to let me," Em said, her eyes brightening.

"No... I just hate long goodbyes."

"No kidding," Pawny said, checking the watch on his gauntlet. "Her train leaves in, like, seventy-four seconds." H picked up Pawny and stuffed him back in his jacket pocket, patting it gently.

"I'm sure we'll bump into each other," Em said. "Sometimes cases intersect, right?"

"Not often." The disappointment was evident in his voice; he didn't want to be the bearer of bad news. "Issues of jurisdiction and all that." His face brightened a little. "Unless there's a mole in New York."

It coaxed a smile out of Em.

"You're the boss now, aren't you? You could always make something up."

"Well, *probationary* boss," H said. "Whatever that is. I mean, talk about an oxymoron, right? 'High PH?' Sounds like some kind of skin condition—"

"Is there something you wanted to say?" Em asked, cutting him off.

H was awkwardly silent for a moment. Then, "About what?"

"You did come all the way down here," Em reminded him.

"It's not so far." H pointed up toward the main floor beyond the escalators. "I work just up there."

Em sighed.

"Pawny?" Em said.

The little warrior popped up out of H's pocket.

"Yes, my Lady?"

"Will you tell Agent H he's almost out of time?"

Pawny looked up at H. "My Lady says, 'Spit it out.'"

H was silent for a heartbeat, then he leaned forward, his elbows on his knees, his gaze on the floor.

"When High T was High T," he told her, "he had this thing he'd say about how the universe has a way of leading you to where you're supposed to be at the moment you're supposed to be there." He met Em's eyes, stared deeply into them. "You came right when I needed you. And I just wanted to say—" he wrestled with so many things he wanted to say, but knew it was better if he didn't "—thanks."

There was a loud *whoosh* that echoed through the empty station. The train was suddenly there, the doors hissing open, the automated conductor announcing the stop and the next station.

Em leaned closer to H.

"I wanted this suit more than I ever wanted anything," she began, knowing she only had seconds. "I always thought there was nothing I couldn't happily walk away from." She let the words hang in the air. She wrestled with so many things she wanted to say, but knew it was better if she didn't. "Okay... I'm going to walk away now." She held her gaze on H one more moment. "Take care of him, Pawny."

"Is that an... order?" Pawny asked.

"That's an order," Em said, as she stood and walked to the train's doors.

H stood, too. He took a step toward her, but only a step.

"Goodbye, Molly," H said.

She turned back to him. "Goodbye, Har... Can I just call you H?"

H smiled and nodded.

"Goodbye, H," she said.

Em entered the train and took a seat. She looked back at H, one last time through the window, and smiled. The doors closed and the train rocketed away, immediately out of sight. She was gone.

H and Pawny stood alone on the platform. The wake of the train faded and was gone. H began to walk toward the escalators.

"H," Pawny sighed sadly, "I think this is the beginning of a really annoying friendship."

OPEN ARMS

A SHORT STORY BY R.S. BELCHER

A vintage Jaguar glided toward the churning chaos of the crime scene that stretched the length of Elcot Avenue. *Well*, thought Agent H as he parked near the border of the blue-and-white police tape, *2012 is off to a brilliant start*.

It was early March, and already MiB London Station had seen an alien attempt to assassinate the royal family, a "plague" of microscopic aliens called Millicrons joyriding around in the bloodstreams of unsuspecting humans, and now this—whatever *this* was.

H climbed out of the Jag and ducked under the police tape. He was tall, athletic, blonde, square-jawed, and clean-shaven. He wore the standard issue "uniform" of the Men in Black: a crisp black suit, white-collared shirt, and black tie. Being nondescript was part of MiB's armor. The covert international agency oversaw extraterrestrial activity on Earth and secretly protected the planet and all its inhabitants from any threats that came from among the stars. And that meant protecting the inhabitants from that knowledge too.

There were MiB personnel everywhere. Teams of agents like H were busy using their neuralyzers—small, silver, pen-like devices—to erase and replace the memories of the bystanders and police who were swarming everywhere in the aftermath of what had happened. Other MiB support personnel were gathering forensic evidence, while at the same time destroying any traces that anything involving aliens had gone on here.

"Oi!" A burly constable came at H, all swagger and authority. "Get back on the other side of that line! This isn't some tourist attraction; it's a crime scene."

"You could have fooled me, mate," H said. "All you need is a few jugglers and someone selling roast chestnuts." H gestured to a fellow agent who had just spotted the altercation between him and the policeman. The other MiB agent, wearing sunglasses even though it was night-time, stepped up and put the neuralyzer in the cop's face as H looked away. The small wand gave off a flash of light, and the constable stood frozen and vacant-eyed.

"Evening, H," the agent said with a smile. "Catch the match last night?"

"Not much of it." H walked toward the heart of the scene. "Enough to know I lost a bet."

At the center of activity was the man who had called him out here in the middle of the night—the recently appointed head of the MiB London Station, H's boss and former partner, High T. High T was a tall, slender man, decades older than H, with close-cropped, salt-and-pepper hair and a neatly trimmed beard. He carried himself with an air of gravitas and a hint of menace lurking under all that civility.

"Peckham's gentrified a bit since I was last here," H said. The street was lined on either side with neat, terraced houses, expensive cars parked in front of them.

"It has. Still a little rough around the edges, though." High T beckoned him to the side of the road, and H followed. "Unfortunately, a few gangs claim parts of the neighborhood as their territory. Two of them ran afoul of each other here this evening."

The ground was dotted with bodies covered by white sheets, blood-soaked islands in a sea of concrete. High T knelt and drew back a sheet. "One gang had knives, crowbars, their fists." Underneath the sheet was a puddle of goo with some clothes floating around in it. "The other group had Capellian De-Valenizers." He covered the remains again. "It was a massacre." High T's voice grew cold, sharp, and angry. "They killed several bystanders, too, ripped them apart at the molecular level…"

"How did they get their hands on Capellian military hardware, T?"

"An excellent question," High T said. "One which you are going to answer. I've seen reports from numerous MiB stations all over the world with the same problem: alien weaponry making it onto the streets. I want you to track it, H. I don't just want the dealers, I want the source."

"Yes, sir."

"You want me with you on this one?" High T asked.

H shook his head. "You're not getting away from that desk you chained yourself to that easily. I'll work it alone. In fact, I have a good idea of where to start looking."

The Boar and Crown was well past its glory days. Back in the 1960s, the pub had been popular with London's most infamous gangsters. But it had faded alongside its customers. A few low-level mobsters, old men now, sat at the bar or played darts in the back, but times had changed enough that when H pushed into the pub, wearing scruffy jeans, a leather jacket, and a five o'clock shadow, they barely lifted their eyes.

He saw the man he wanted right away. "Whistler never takes his coat off," his informant had said. "He's always ready to run. Horrible acne, too. You'll spot him a mile away." And there he was—younger than the card-players, with dark hair and bad skin. He wore a wool coat and his eyes were glued to the Millwall match on the pub's TV.

H blocked Whistler's view. The arms dealer's eyes flickered over him. "Unless you plan on being more entertaining than this game," Whistler said coolly, "clear off."

H opened his coat and dropped a heavy pistol with a scope on it onto the table with a loud thud. Several of the pub's patrons looked up quickly and then got back to minding their own business. "Galadorian neural shredder," H said. "Silent, no visible beam trace. A tri-optic bio-tracking scope. Guaranteed kill on most lifeforms, up to class three, from a thousand meters. Makes that Capellian army-surplus stuff you sold the Peckham crew look homemade."

Whistler reached over and picked up the pistol.

"Okay, you got my attention, Mister...?"

"Hern. Just Hern. That's just a sample. I heard you were the man to see about out-of-this-world weaponry."

"Who told you that?" Whistler gestured for H to sit.

"People who want to do right by me." H wasn't about to give up his informant, an alien whose brother had died in a gang shooting not long ago.

"I'm guessing you're not here to buy," Whistler said, "so what you got for me?"

H slid a piece of paper across the table to Whistler. The gun-runner shook his head as he read it, a smile coming to his lips. "What'd you do? Rob an arsenal?"

"An MiB arsenal, to be specific."

Whistler looked up from the list. "You... you ripped off MiB? Are you insane?"

"Came across a shipment of confiscated weapons en route to be destroyed," H said simply. "Now they're mine."

"How—?"

"The whole shipment's for sale. One deal, in and out. I want to be long gone before MiB comes calling."

"So, what's your price?" Whistler nodded at the list.

"Oh, no." H chuckled. He reached across the table and picked up Whistler's scotch. He took a sip from the glass and leaned back in his chair. "I spent the last two years setting up this score. There is no way I'm dealing with some middleman. There is enough death on that list to make you and me wealthy for the rest of our lives. All you have to do is get me in a room with your boss."

"Okay, tough guy," Whistler said. "You're on. You got a passport? Only my boss doesn't hang out in old boozers like this. Get yourself to Saint Tropez, three days' time. We'll find you. And you'd better be what you say you are, *Mr.* Hern, or my boss will eat you alive."

"And who is that?" H asked. "So I can be appropriately fearful."

"The Merchant," Whistler said. "The Merchant of Death."

"The Merchant of Death," High T said. "We've been after him for a long time." His new office was an oval, elevated above the constantly swarming main floor of MiB London Station. Both men stood at the glass wall, surveying the hive of activity below them.

"I'll need a sample case with real, working weapons." H was back in his suit, every inch the MiB agent. "The nastier, the more illegal and exotic, the better."

"Done."

"What do we know about the Merchant?" H asked.

"If there's a conflict occurring anywhere from the Milky Way to Centaurus A, some of the Merchant of Death's products are in use. He's one of the largest arms dealers in the universe."

"What's he doing on Earth selling weapons to London street gangs?"

"Perhaps expanding his operation. He has a massive

distribution network, and operatives like your friend Whistler across known space. No job too small."

"Background?"

"He's believed to be an alien that goes by the name of Nirous Stavros," High T said. "His home planet is not known, but the story is that he was a warlord there who ended up on the wrong side of a rebellion. He fled his world with his family and a freighter full of weapons. He's wanted for illegal arms dealing in several galaxies."

"Well, we can extradite him after I shut him down."

"Let me back you up on this one," High T said. "I can have a strike team ready to move at a moment's notice. This is no ordinary criminal you're dealing with, H."

"Precisely. He's the kind that will smell a strike team a parsec away. Thanks, T, but I'll be all right."

High T rubbed his well-trimmed beard as he gestured to H's shadowy stubble. "You seem to be enjoying the undercover lifestyle."

"It's just for the job," H said with a laugh. "I won't make a habit of it."

Nights in Saint Tropez were bright: lights, motion, and music. The wealthiest people on Earth, and from other planets, came to dance, gamble, and drink in the luxurious clubs and casinos of the Côte d'Azur.

Shortly after he'd checked in to the exclusive Byblos Hotel, a note arrived from reception: *Tonight at ten, Les Caves du Roy—Whistler*. He hadn't noticed being tailed from the airport, which both impressed him and made him a little nervous.

Les Caves du Roy was the nightclub in the grounds of the hotel, and just as exclusive. He dressed in a suit that was more expensive than he liked to think about, wondering for a moment if Whistler would still be wearing his drab coat. He slipped on a shoulder holster with a sleek, deadly alien blaster in it and hit the club early.

Music thundered around H, and lights rained down on him as he made his way across the crowded dance floor toward the bar. A stripy-haired woman, dancing with several other beautiful people, shared a guarded smile with him, and then she was lost to the crowd and H was at the bar.

Whistler was nowhere to be seen. H ordered a drink and settled down to wait. Someone sat down beside him, and H glanced over to find it was the stripy-haired woman. "You play hard to get," she said, sipping from a €20 bottle of water.

H smiled. "I'm not playing." He tipped his glass toward her. "Hern."

"Just 'Hern'?" She raised a perfect eyebrow.

"I'm building my brand."

"One word." The woman nodded. "Must make it easier for you to remember. I'm Riza."

"Just Riza?"

She was breathtaking, with hair that was a pale blonde with black horizontal stripes. It fell down to her shoulders. Her skin was pale with a hint of a citrine undertone. Her eyes, pale blue like the Tyrrhenian Sea, shone with intelligence and wit.

"No, but 'Riza' is all you get for now." A playful smile came to her face. "So, Man With One Name, you here for business or pleasure?"

"It was strictly business, but now I'm thinking, why limit my options. You?"

"My father has business here," Riza said, "so while he works too hard, I'll play hard for both of us."

"He's lucky to have such a devoted daughter."

"I try to live up to his expectations. You have pretty eyes, Hern."

Before he could respond, H spotted Whistler moving through the crowd like a threat of smoke. A smaller, greasy-looking man in a bright yellow jacket kept close to his side. The gun-runner nodded to H, and H gave him the faintest of nods back.

"Sadly, my business has caught up with me, Riza," H said, "I truly wish it hadn't." He was a little surprised at how much he meant it. "Perhaps—"

Riza put both her arms around H's neck, pulled him to her, and kissed him deeply. His confusion rapidly became pleasure, and he returned the kiss just as passionately.

Breaking the kiss, she danced back into the crowd, calling, "Good luck with your business, Hern."

H touched his lips, still tasting her on them. He walked over to Whistler and his companion.

"Who's the girl?" Whistler asked.

"I wish I knew." Now that H was closer, he saw the man in the yellow jacket was a Luboshian: he had two tiny pairs of gills on his cheeks, either side of his nose. To a casual observer, they looked like scars. "Who's this?"

"Skeeze." The man had a thick, slurring accent. "How you doin'?" He offered his hand to H, who did not take it. "Okay, okay," Skeeze shrugged.

"Skeeze works for the Merchant in these parts," Whistler said.

"We got a car waiting outside the kitchen service entrance," Skeeze said. "This way."

Whistler stopped H from following Skeeze by placing a palm on his chest. "Hold it. Where's your sample case? I told you to bring it."

"I'll show you outside." H pushed the hand away and followed Skeeze toward the kitchen doors.

An oversized black Range Rover stretch limo was idling in the parking lot. As they reached it, Skeeze shoved H against the car and began patting him down.

"What the—!" H spun and pushed Skeeze away. The Luboshian fell.

Whistler aimed a laser target pistol of elegant design at him.

"You don't get in the car until you're searched," Whistler said calmly. "Boss's orders. Now, you can let Skeeze do it, or Luca can search you."

"Luca?" H looked around. "Who's Luc—?"

The whole limo lifted suddenly as a massive amount of weight departed its back seat on the side opposite H and the others. An eight-foot-tall alien loomed over the roof of the car and regarded H. The alien had dark green skin; it was gray in a few places. His body was muscled well past the point of caricature. He had a shovel-shaped face with a massive, fanged jaw that was drooling a little.

His eyes were like cheap, green, glass marbles.

"Whoa." H took a few steps back as the giant alien approached him. "You're a Tarantian, aren't you?" The alien glowered, and continued to advance. H glanced over to the smiling Whistler and Skeeze. "You have yourselves a Tarantian, don't you?"

"That," Skeeze said, rubbing his jaw, "is Luca. He's the boss's personal bodyguard. Now, you going to behave and let him pat you down, or do you want to see what he does to rude clients?"

"Not looking for any trouble, big guy." H raised his hands and leaned against the car to be frisked. Luca growled a little and shoved him against the car, hard. H and the whole limo moved under the Tarantian's one-handed shove. The big alien searched him roughly for hidden weapons. He felt Luca grab at his shoulder holster under his jacket and then the leather snapped as if it were made of twine. Luca held up the holster with the blaster and tossed them to Skeeze.

"Get in the car," Whistler said. H complied, and Luca squeezed into the opulent compartment beside him. Whistler and Skeeze got in on the other side, facing H and Luca. Skeeze examined H's pistol and then leveled it at the agent.

"Sample case," Skeeze said.

"Where's Stavros, first?"

Skeeze thumbed the power switch on the blaster. "Where'd you get that name?"

"If you think I don't look into the background of those I do business with, you're dumber than he is." H jerked a thumb at Luca. Luca bared his teeth.

"Stavros don't come near any deal until we give the green light," Skeeze said. "The man's got heat on him, *intergalactic* heat, not to mention the MiB."

"We've run checks on you too, 'Hern,'" Whistler said. "Not much to find; you're a big question mark."

"Good. I paid a lot of money to stay that way."

"The point is, Stavros pays us good money to take the heat for him."

"So, you deal with us," Skeeze said, "or we don't deal at all. Now, where's your sample case?"

"Here." H had crossed his hands, so each was touching one of his cuffs. He put a finger on each of the jeweled cufflinks he wore. There was a soundless flash of light, and H now held the handle of a sample case in one hand and a squat, flattened grenade in the other hand. He squeezed the grenade, and a red display light came on.

"What is this?" Whistler barked. Skeeze brought the gun to H's face.

"This—" H held up the cylinder "—is an active vortex grenade. I take my hand off this, everything, everybody, in a half-block radius gets compressed into a space the size of a Tic Tac."

"How did you do that?" Whistler asked nervously.

"Toscolan Phase gems in my cufflinks. Keyed to teleport specific items to my hand as they burn out. In this instance, my sample case—" H handed the black, featureless metal case over to Skeeze "—and my insurance policy." He held up the grenade.

"You're crazy, Hern," Skeeze muttered as he flipped open the case. He and Whistler inspected the half-dozen weapons, and H could tell they liked what they saw.

"Okay," Skeeze said, "supposing we're interested, I'm thinking—"

"I'm thinking this is above your pay grade," H replied. "I will sell the whole arsenal to Stavros for the price I already tendered. No bargaining and no intermediaries." He opened the limo door and climbed out. "I'll be staying here for the next week if your boss decides he wants to do business. I think I'll work on my tan." He gestured toward the ripped shoulder holster and gun. "Keep it; it's deactivated." And then he tossed the vortex grenade into the compartment. "This is, too... I think, anyway." He slammed the door on the limo and walked away, smiling, as the car convulsed with frantic shaking and angry shouts.

H made his way back to his suite. Everything had gone as planned. Well, except for meeting Luca... and Riza. H felt a pang of regret that the encounter had been so brief. He'd send High T a message to update him on the evening's progress and then go to bed and try not to think about how wonderful that kiss had been. He expected it to be a long night.

Thoughts of Riza faded when he noticed the door to his suite was ajar. H opened it silently. Nobody there. He crept quietly into the main room and removed a small alien handgun from its hiding place. He swept each room, moving cautiously, wondering if perhaps Stavros had sent assassins, his way of saying the deal was off.

A creak from the bathroom. He took the three steps that led up to the raised pedestal section of the suite's floor where the bed and master bath were located. H waited behind a column. Someone was padding lightly across the bathroom tiles. He stepped out from hiding and leveled his gun at the intruder. It was pointing straight at Riza, who was wrapped in a towel, her hair wet.

"I was sweaty from dancing." She was unfazed by the gun. "I decided to take a shower and freshen up. I hope you don't mind." That last part wasn't a question, more a challenge. H put the pistol away.

"Not at all. I don't suppose you'd care to tell me how you got in here?"

"When we were kissing, I took your room key. That's why I left the door open a bit, so you could get in without it. Key's over there." She indicated the key card in the wall holder.

"You're good. I didn't feel you lift it."

"I'm good at all kinds of things," Riza said. H turned. She was now wearing a sheer black nightgown, her long hair pulled back from her face in a loose ponytail. H walked toward the pedestal, shrugging off his jacket.

He ascended the steps to her. She slipped her arms around his neck again, pulling him close. H put his arms around her waist and pulled her even closer. The kiss felt like the continuation of something old, something perfectly in sync, powerful and preordained. When they broke the kiss, they were already in the bed. Riza was pulling H's shirt off him, kissing his lips, neck, and then chest as she did. H cupped her face and took one of her hands in his own.

"Why?" H asked.

"That's really not the question to ask after the train's left the station, darling," Riza said, her hands busy freeing H and herself of their clothing. She sighed. "Because how often in life do you meet someone that you can kiss the first time you meet them and it feels like a lifetime full of kisses? You don't let that get away from you." She kissed him again. H fell into the kiss until his brain told him something was weird. He was holding her hand, but she was undressing them with two hands.

H pulled back for a second and looked at Riza. "You... you've got three arms!"

Riza smiled. "Brimming with biceps and brains, just the way I like them."

"You're a Tribrachian!"

Riza nodded as she laughed. "Guilty. Half the people in that club were aliens. I figured that with that Klothonian hardware you were packing in your shoulder holster when I snatched your key, you were either not from this zip code or a local who knew the score."

"I'm local. Jury's still out if I know the score."

"I know better than to ask why you're carrying a gun. But I do have to know, is the third arm a deal-breaker? 'Cause it can come in... handy. Pun totally intended."

H pulled her down with him onto the bed. "It is not a deal-breaker," H said. "Far from it. In fact, I think it adds a great deal to your already dis-arming charm."

"Oh," Riza moaned, partly from the pun, partly from the kiss. They fell into each other. The night was tangled and torrid, soothing and sweet.

The next few days were a blur. It felt to H like a different life, or maybe a dream. Whatever it was, H feared pulling at the seams of it too much, in case it dissolved. He and Riza were inseparable. They boated, swam, and danced the evenings away in the hottest nightclubs along the coast. They spent the days lazing on white beaches. All the while, there had been no word from Whistler.

Riza's personality swung like a pendulum, from a playful side that harbored a childlike attachment to small animals, to a more mature and much more aggressive side. He saw tiny flares of a cold, cruel anger show up in Riza, too, like when one of the waiters got her drink order wrong, and Riza tore him apart verbally, to the point H feared she was going to do violence to the man. Then, like a light switch being turned, she was sweetness and light to the man again.

The shifts in personality should have been a red flag for H, but he wrote it off as the powerful personality of a passionate and complicated woman. He was happy with her, happier than he could ever recall being in his whole life, before and after MiB.

On the fourth night, they were walking alone along the beach. The waves smashed themselves to foam, and the cool wind, coming off the ocean, raced unchecked along the dunes. H paused in their stroll and looked up.

He held Riza's shoulders and she leaned against him.

He pointed to the star-scattered sky. "There," he said. She squinted to see what he was pointing at. "About 37 million light years away. Your home galaxy." The cold spray of water rushed in and tickled their feet.

"I don't remember it."

"Why did you leave?"

"I'm an army brat," she said with a smile. "My father was a soldier. He fought in wars and police actions and rebellions across the universe, and he dragged me and Mom along."

"Sounds like you didn't care for it."

Riza shrugged. "It was exciting for a while—new worlds, new people. I learned a lot about cultures, languages. But every mission Dad took killed Mom a little bit more. There were so many nights I heard her crying, heard her praying he'd come home alive and in one piece. I started to hate it."

"I'm sorry."

Riza laughed. It sounded a little sad, a little broken, and very wrong.

"When Mom died, I considered setting off on my own, finally, but my dad was starting to slip. He was making mistakes, forgetting things. I couldn't just abandon him. Then one day, I discovered that spending my life idolizing and then caring for a risk-taking, emotionally distant man had marked me more than I had ever dreamed. I have a thing for dangerous men. Men like you."

H didn't want to lie to her anymore. "I'm not—"

"Please," she said, "don't tell me what I want to hear.

I know your type, Hern, I know you're going to hurt me in the end. I don't care. You're worth the pain." Their lips brushed against each other, and H pulled her to him.

"I'd never hurt you, Riza." They kissed again, and the kiss became hungry, insistent.

"Is your name really Hern?" she gasped, momentarily breaking the kiss.

H almost told her then. "My name starts with an H."

Then they were lost to the embrace, and there were no more words.

The note was waiting for H at the front desk when he and Riza returned to the hotel the next day. It was from Whistler, saying they were on for tonight and they would pick him up at eleven. The meet was set for an old, defunct shipyard complex on the coast near Nice.

"Your 'business' came to find you," Riza said, sadly, seeing his expression. H nodded. He took Riza's hand and walked her over to an open-air patio bench just outside the lobby.

"What if I told you this was my last piece of business, ever?"

"What? Why?" she asked.

"I found something more challenging to take up my time." He looked into her dark eyes.

Riza's smile was like the sun breaking out from behind the clouds. "You... you really mean that, don't you?"

H nodded. "I'll finish this up tonight, and tomorrow we start making plans for whatever comes next."

Riza laughed and hugged him, and H found himself laughing too.

"Go back to your suite," H said. "I'll call you when it's finished."

There was a knock at H's door. He opened it to find High T dressed in the white formal wear of the hotel's kitchen staff. "*Bonsoir, monsieur,*" High T said in impeccable French. "The champagne and caviar you requested." H's mouth opened and then closed, as High T wheeled the waiter's cart into the suite and then closed the door. He held a black, plastic capsule about the size of a small Bluetooth speaker. He clicked the button on it and dropped the fake accent. "Where have you been?"

"Are you out of your mind? The suite could be bugged."

"If it is, this—" High T pointed to the capsule "—buys us about ten minutes of privacy. Report."

"The deal's on tonight. They're picking me up in about twenty minutes, unless they show early."

"Don't worry; I'll be gone in five. Where?"

H gave him the location of the defunct shipyard near Nice. High T nodded. He removed a silvered, steel briefcase from under the cart and handed it to H. "Here's your arsenal."

"Standard phase case?" H asked. High T nodded.

"We added a one-way hyperwave transmitter. Once the case is open and activated, we will hear everything going on and can move when it sounds best for us to do so."

"Perfect."

High T's expression was stern. "I'm thrilled you're happy. Now, why haven't I heard a word from you in almost a week?"

"I've been in… deep cover."

High T chuckled. "I'm sure you have. I saw the surveillance photos of her. What are you doing, H?"

"T." H sat on the edge of the couch. "I want to quit MiB after we shut Stavros down."

"I see. For this woman?"

"Yes." H couldn't read his old partner's expression. "What do you think? Am I crazy to be thinking about this?"

"If love doesn't make you a little crazy, it's not really love," High T said. "What does your instinct tell you, really tell you? Sift through the fog of all those feelings, and listen to your gut."

H was quiet for a moment.

"She's… unpredictable, maybe even a little unstable," he said. "But when we're together, it's like some secret code is passing between us. A connection. I don't feel like a ghost in the world with her. I just don't know, T."

"I think maybe you do." High T placed a hand on H's shoulder. "Whatever you decide, I'm in your corner, son. You've done your bit for Queen and planet." He checked his watch. "Now get your head back in the game."

He left the cart but picked up the small capsule-jammer as he walked to the door. "I have strike, intervention, and clean-up teams ready to go. We'll be watching if you need any help. Good hunting, H, and good luck."

* * *

The stretch limo picked him up in front of the hotel. Inside were Whistler and Skeeze. Luca was, thankfully, absent.

"No trick cufflinks tonight?" Skeeze asked.

H showed him his sleeves. "No cufflinks at all." He patted the side of the case. "Phase case—works on a similar principle to the cufflinks—but it has a stable dimensional portal at the case's opening. The whole cargo is in here."

"Good," Whistler said. "The sooner we wrap this up, the sooner everyone gets paid."

Soon they arrived at a decrepit shipyard, a graveyard of unfinished ship hulls, mountains of rusted industrial steel, collapsing factories, and skeletal cranes. Their destination was a dilapidated freighter squatting in the black waters, the deck patrolled by guards armed with assault rifles and exotic alien weapons. The limo parked in front of a gangplank that had been extended from the freighter's deck down to the dock.

Skeeze led H up the gangplank, toward an open hatch and to a narrow set of stairs that took them below decks. As they descended into the ship's hold, H saw weapons of every possible kind, from millions of different worlds. Massive interplanetary and exosolar missile systems, hover tanks, and huge robotic battle suits, crates of alien rifles, and torpedoes marked with the warning symbol for deadly biological weapons. He recognized a few engineering components that made him suspect that the ship was also spaceworthy. The sight of a poorly disguised hyperdrive engine as they passed an open door on the way down confirmed it.

They reached the floor of the ship's hold, a maze of crated weapons, and stopped when they came to a set of steps leading up to a metal catwalk. A cadre of armed mercenaries stood at the base of the stairs, eyeing H with trained suspicion. Above them on the catwalk, he could see Luca towering next to a shadowy humanoid form H figured for Stavros.

"It's a pleasure to finally meet the Merchant of Death in person." H's voice echoed in the vast hold. "Big fan."

H handed the phase case to Skeeze, who set it on the floor and opened it. A warm, white light spilled out of the case, and Skeeze peered into the dimensional portal. He looked up smiling. "It's all there, boss."

"I hope to quickly have payment in hand and be off the Love Boat," H said to the shadowy, unmoving figure. Whistler came forward, pushing past H.

"Boss, I'm the one who made this deal happen. I'd like that commission you and I discussed, now."

"Of course," a voice came from the obscured figure. It wasn't a man's voice. "I hope you don't mind getting paid in diamonds." There was a blue flash of energy from the direction of the figure's hand. It hit Whistler, and he screamed and writhed. H watched, horrified, as the arms dealer's body twisted and contorted. His flesh was stripped away and his exposed bones began to crack and crystallize.

Whistler's screams ended seconds before the remains of his body—his skeleton, which was now pure diamond—clattered to the floor of the hold. "That's your payment for bringing a cop to my doorstep," the figure said, descending the stairs, still cradling the alien weapon. Luca was right behind her. She stepped into an island of light. It was Riza, her eyes bright and cruel. "Hi, baby!" She waved at H as she reached the floor and stood among the glittering remains of her dead lieutenant.

She kicked Whistler's diamond skull over to H's feet. "Pretty cool, huh?" She slapped the alien rifle. "It's one of my favorites. Diamonds are a girl's best friend, right?"

"So, I guess you were waiting a few more dates before telling me anything about all this?" Guns pointed at him from every conceivable direction.

"Don't even." There was anger in her eyes. "I found your neuralyzer in your room. When were you going to come clean and tell me you were MiB?"

H began to say that he almost had, several times, but instead he said, "So, you run Daddy's business for him these days, right? You are Nirous Stavros's daughter, aren't you?"

"I am. Come on, let's do the whole villain scene. I'll give you the tour." She snapped her fingers and the mercenaries herded H along to follow Riza and Luca, her shadow. They moved about the hold, past military munitions and arms and exotic experimental weapons created in defiance of every treaty H had ever heard of.

"This place is like a Costco of death," H said.

"This is my inheritance." She spread her arms wide. "A lifetime of death and destruction gathered together by Daddy, by General Nirous Stavros." She paused, and her whole demeanor changed instantly. "Oh! You have to see *them*!" Riza almost squealed. The aisle was full of cages holding tiny, adorable aliens from countless worlds, packed in among the horrific weapons. "My babies!" Riza shouted, tapping on the cages as the tiny creatures acknowledged her presence with song, chirps, and trills.

"I've collected them my whole life. Daddy would bring one back to me from every world he traveled to. Even my dear Luca came to me as a tiny little creature, so ugly he was adorable! You can see he kind of grew out of the whole adorable thing, but still, he loves me. I rescued him when your nasty Men in Black were hunting him down. I saved him, gave him a home."

Luca stared at the small cages and the tiny animals.

"Is that how it was, mate?" H asked the giant bodyguard. Luca said nothing.

"*They* love me."

"They're your prisoners. If you love something, set it free."

Riza's face hardened as she turned from her adorable charges. "And if it doesn't come back, hunt it down and kill it." She led him to another aisle.

"All this is the end result of a career as a merchant of death. My father encountered every kind of weapon, every kind of war in his career—"

"It wasn't a career," H interrupted, "it was a crime."

Riza turned. Her smile grew tighter; the glaze of craziness that H had seen in her eyes a few times over the past week reappeared.

"Some unenlightened oafs thought as much," she

said. "They chased us off Tribrachia, called him a despot and a tyrant. They simply didn't understand the primary underlying principle that the universe runs on: war."

"War is an abomination," H said.

"Wrong!" Riza made a noise like a quiz-show buzzer. "Life is war. From the viruses, microbes, and mutated cells that try to kill you from within, to the animals that fight and kill one another for resources, for dominance. It's all war, and everybody, *everybody* is looking for an edge."

Riza paused in her wandering to stop at a coffin-like pod that was propped up between several pallets of crates and containers. "Take this little one-of-a-kind beauty." She tapped the door of the pod. "A naturally occurring bioweapon. Its name is Bakklus. It's a sentient, extra-dimensional organism that can only interact with our reality through a viral medium. It infects people to say hi, and it's a nasty little bug, too—98.9 percent communicability within seconds of airborne contact.

"Once it's in you, it telepathically bonds with you. It can control your body and read your thoughts. Very handy for infiltration and pacifying populations... if you can afford it. After about three days, your immune system fights Bakklus off, but three days is long enough to invade a world, or put down a resistance, without a shot fired.

"Dad managed to get his hands on Patient Zero and put him stasis." She wiped away some of the condensation and slush on the door of the pod, and H could see a humanoid alien slumbering within. "He has sold off crippled strains of the original to clients over the years. Bakklus went along with it, because if the original strain in Patient Zero doesn't get a chance to go free and telepathically bond with another host, the whole organism will become extinct in our space-time. It's a brilliant setup, I have to say."

"It's slavery," H said, "and extortion, and genocide."

Riza shook her head as she cupped H's cheek. "It's business, darling. The rest is the parlance of politicians."

"That sounds like your father's words drilled into an innocent child. You didn't want this life; he did." H searched for the Riza he loved, but behind her eyes, he saw only the ruthless businesswoman, the Merchant of Death.

"I told you my father began to make mistakes, to grow feeble. He was endangering our market share." She held up the weapon she had used on Whistler. "I told you this was one of my faves. I used it on Daddy. I kept his skull. It sits on my desk. It's sparkly, it's a badass paperweight, and it's a great motivational tool for the workforce.

"This is my business, my life, now," Riza said. "I do have daddy issues, to be sure, but he didn't raise a fool."

"So why hide behind his name?" H asked. He had spotted something up ahead, and an idea was building in his mind.

"Dad's name and reputation are useful to keep the gnats off of me. Gnats like MiB, like you. Which I guess brings us to the close of our little tour… and of your life."

H needed to buy time and a dozen feet. He turned to Riza and approached her. Her men and Luca all moved to intervene, but Riza stopped them with a gesture. H walked past her a few feet and then turned back to her. "I have to compliment you on your acting skills. I really believed you when we were together, believed that was the *real* you."

"Wow. Coming from someone trained to lie for a living, that's high praise," she said.

H took the opportunity to make his way a few more steps backward. Riza was close now.

"I never lied about how you made me feel." H didn't hide the pain in his eyes. For a moment, Riza's ice queen act disappeared, and H saw how much this was hurting her too. He hated what had to come next, but this was his only chance.

In a single movement, H shoved Riza backward, hard. He didn't like pushing a woman, but he had to get her in the clear to keep her safe. H jumped, grabbing the edge of a group of large crates that were stacked precariously on the massive shelves. The crates came crashing down, starting an avalanche of boxes, pallets, and collapsing shelving. H launched himself off the shelf on the opposite side of the avalanche from Riza and her men.

Luca lifted Riza to her feet. If H hadn't shoved her backward, she would be dead now.

"Find him, all of you!" H heard her shout. "Bring him to me!" She didn't sound very grateful.

The mercenaries moved through the ship's hold, searching. Several groups of Riza's men moved past H without seeing him. H had considered cracking open one of the cases of weapons all around him, but he was pretty sure he'd be found out before he could activate anything. And some of them could vaporize the whole coastline. He knew of only one weapon in the hold that he could activate quickly and quietly in the time he had. Now, he just hoped it would cooperate.

He backtracked as quietly as he could to the aisle with the medical stasis pod. H looked about to make sure it was all clear as he switched off the stasis generator and opened the pod's door. He smiled at the occupant as they came around. "Morning, mate. I have a proposition for you…"

It was almost too easy for them to find H, crashing about in the stacks of weapons. He was struggling to put together a gun from a wooden crate he had broken into when Luca found him.

"It had to be you," H said, and charged the massive Tarantian, smashing him in the face with the steel barrel of the weapon he was trying to assemble. The barrel bent with the impact, but Luca didn't even blink.

Luca's fist shot out, and H narrowly ducked under it, driving a staccato pattern of punches into Luca's stomach. It was like punching a mountain. Luca backhanded H and sent the agent airborne for a good twenty feet. H slid to a stop near the edge of the corridor.

He climbed to his feet to run but found a dozen of Riza's mercenaries behind him, weapons trained on him. He looked back in the direction of Luca in time to see the bodyguard's boulder-like fist headed straight for his face.

H saw a strobe of light and then darkness. The last thing he heard was Luca's voice saying, "That's for breaking her heart, MiB scum."

* * *

Luca dragged the semi-aware H back to the stair landing. H groaned as Luca pulled him to his feet.

"Well, now that hide and seek is over," Riza said, "gentlemen, prepare to earn your pay."

The mercenaries raised their weapons, ready to incinerate H.

"There's no way that I can convince you to walk away from all this?" H said. "I was prepared to do that for you; I truly was. The underlying principle of the universe isn't war, Riza. It's love."

"I wish you were right." Her voice was softer now. "But we both have our duties and our destinies." She kissed H sweetly, deeply, then stepped away from him. The mercenaries prepared to fire. "Any last words?"

"Yeah," H said. "Bakklus, mate, now would be a good time."

"Fire!" Riza shouted. Nothing happened. The mercenaries all stood as still as statues, their fingers frozen on their triggers, panic behind their eyes. Riza tried to bring up her own gun, but her body refused to obey.

Be still, a voice in her head said. *Don't struggle.* Luca seemed unaffected by whatever this was. He looked around and saw H smiling as one of the mercenaries handed his rifle over to the agent willingly. H powered up the rifle to maximum and aimed it at Luca.

"Don't try it. You're not that tough." Klaxons went off all over the ship, and there was the distant sound of gunfire from the deck, far above. "And that would be MiB, right on time."

"The sentient virus." Riza was still trying to move. "Bakklus. You... let it infect you?"

"I did. I told it I'd free it, if it helped me shut you down, and it agreed."

"It was stupid to trust you," Riza spat. "You're a liar."

"It read my mind," H said. "It knew I was telling it the truth."

The sounds of battle above grew closer. H saw the fear on Riza's face, even though she was trying to hide it.

"I knew you were MiB from the start," Riza said. "I knew you were here to bust me, to wreck everything. I could have killed you dozens of times over the last week."

"Why didn't you?" H asked, stepping closer to her but keeping Luca covered.

"You know why."

"I thought I did." He could see the pain in her eyes.

"I know you think this is me saying anything to get out of this, but I really do care about you, and I know you care about me, too. Go on, ask your viral buddy, ask him to read my mind."

H thought to the strain of Bakklus in his body, and it spoke to the strain in Riza's. Then, it said in H's mind, *Yeah, she's got it bad for you. She's homicidal and scary crazy, bro, but she's got it bad for you.*

H regarded Riza. "You were going to gun me down?"

Riza nodded. The gunfire above became sporadic. H heard MiB agents ordering mercenaries to drop their weapons.

"And I would have cried for you every single night for the rest of my life. You have feelings for me, and you're busting me. I'd say that makes us even."

Black-suited MiB agents were moving quickly through the upper levels of the freighter.

"Bakklus," H said. "Let Riza go, please."

What? Are you serious, H? Bakklus asked. *I can see your mind, of course you're serious. She's got some evil thoughts rattling up in there with the hearts, and the unicorns, and the space puppies, man.*

"I know," H said, "and if she tries to act on them, you shut her down, as long as you are in there." H turned to Riza and plucked the alien weapon out of her hands. She was able to move again. "I'm confiscating your inventory and letting you off with a warning this time." H used his best stern-cop voice. "But next time…" Riza stepped closer. Their eyes kissed and held for as long as they could.

"Next time." Riza smiled. "You know there will be a next time, right?"

"Counting on it."

"It's a date, then." She brushed his cheek with her third hand. The sounds of the approaching MiB team were almost on top of them.

"Get her out of here," H told Luca.

The massive Tarantian scooped his charge up and leapt into the darkness of the crowded hold, lost to the scrutiny of the light.

The night air was a relief to H after his time below decks. He leaned against the rail and watched the MiB forces mop up from the raid. Support agents carried wave after wave of weapons to waiting secure transports. Riza's mercenaries, passive under Bakklus's direction, waited in a line to be processed and incarcerated. H spied Skeeze hastily trying to cut a deal with one of the senior agents as he was led away, still under the influence of Bakklus.

He tried to cut a deal with me, too, Bakklus chuckled. *Oh, don't be so alarmed, H. What could he possibly offer me? I've got everything I want now I'm free.*

"A good bust." High T joined H on the deck. The two old friends turned away from the circus and watched the black water of the sea lap at the pier's posts and the freighter's hull. "I see great things in you, H. I have since the night we met. MiB needs agents like you. Who knows, one day you might even save the world."

"I'm not going anywhere," H said. "This is my duty, my destiny. I was stupid to think I could be anything else."

"You weren't stupid. You were human. That's a very important requirement to do this job day in, day out." They were both silent for a while and then High T said, "Still, it's a shame Riza Stavros got away." There was a hint of a smile on his old partner's face. He smiled back, but his heart felt bruised.

"Don't worry, sir," H said. "I won't make that mistake again."

High T patted his friend on the back. "Of course you won't." The wry smile was still on his face as he walked away. "You'll make brand new ones."

ACKNOWLEDGMENTS

Thank you to Sam Matthews, my editor with Titan Books, and all the other terrific folks at Titan and Sony. To my agent, Lucienne Diver of the Knight Agency. To Greg Cox, an amazing writer, a stellar editor, and a great person. And to Susan Lystlund and Sandra Wheeler for invaluable editorial assistance in the writing of this book.

ABOUT THE AUTHOR

R. S. Belcher is an award-winning newspaper and magazine editor and reporter. Rod has been a private investigator, DJ, and comic book store owner, and has degrees in criminal law, psychology, and justice and risk administration from Virginia Commonwealth University. His many acclaimed novels include *The Six-Gun Tarot*, *Shotgun Arcana* (a Kirkus Reviews Top Pick), *Nightwise*, and *Brotherhood of the Wheel* (Locus Awards finalist).